Christine Krieg Photography

Alison Anderson has lived in Switzerland, Greece, France, and Croatia, and is now based in Northern California. She is a recent NEA grant recipient for literary translation. Her novel *Hidden Latitudes,* which was based on a sailing trip on a thirty-foot ketch, was a *San Francisco Chronicle* Best Book of the Year.

also by alison anderson

Hidden Latitudes

picador

a thomas dunne book

st. martin's press

new york

alison anderson

darwin's

~~~~~~

wink

a novel of nature and love

www.picadorusa.com

Picador® is a U.S. registered trademark and is used by St. Martin's Press under license from Pan Books Limited.

For information on Picador Reading Group Guides, as well as ordering, please contact Picador.
Phone: 646-307-5626
Fax: 212-253-9627
E-mail: readinggroupguides@picadorusa.com

Library of Congress Cataloging-in-Publication Data

Anderson, Alison.
    Darwin's wink : a novel of nature and love / Alison Anderson.
        p. cm.
    ISBN 0-312-33200-9
    EAN 978-0-312-33200-6
    1. Naturalists—Fiction. 2. Endangered species—Fiction. 3. Loss
(Psychology)—Fiction. 4. Rare birds—Fiction. 5. Mauritius—Fiction.
I. Title.

PS3551.N354O37 2004
813'.54—dc22   2004017763

First published in the United States by St. Martin's Press

First Picador Edition: November 2005

10 9 8 7 6 5 4 3 2 1

for my family

Ki lalang ki zamé ti manti?
Lalang zanimo.

Which language never lies?
The language of animals.

—TRADITIONAL MAURITIAN SIRANDANE, OR RIDDLE

When we reflect on this struggle,
we may console ourselves with the full belief,
that the war of nature is not incessant,
that no fear is felt, that death is generally prompt,
and that the vigorous, the healthy, and the happy survive and multiply.

—CHARLES DARWIN, *ON THE ORIGIN OF SPECIES*

evolution

At dusk the woman stands at the edge of the island to watch the birds in flight above the lagoon. Hers is not a usual, distant, appreciative watching; she has a trained eye, and she looks for signs in the birds' flight, for the slow, imperceptible markers of evolution.

She is in a place where evolution can be witnessed in a bird's lifetime, not far from the island of Mauritius in the Indian Ocean. Two generations of Dutch and Portuguese explorers transformed an uninhabited fifteenth-century paradise into a laboratory for naturalists for centuries to come. There were the plant and animal species they brought: tamarind, eucalyptus, banyan, casuarina and flame trees, sugarcane; cats, dogs, mongooses, rats, asses, monkeys. Humans. There were the species they destroyed or endangered: entire forests, the habitat for hundreds of small wild creatures. Their most famous victim: the dodo bird, *Raphus cucullatus*.

The woman's name is Fran, a sturdy, practical name, like the woman herself. She has been studying the evolution of birds all her life. She is a trained naturalist, a behavioral ecologist, efficient and unsentimental. She accepts the inevitability of death but refuses the inevitability of extinction. She is closer to fifty than to forty, an unpopular age, although for her, age is a man-made convenience, a sort of Linnaean classification system used to facilitate assumptions. She sees aging in more Darwinian terms, and her own age troubles her only for its childlessness; the years have given her a wise and youthful strength. She is sun-hardened, life-hardened, life-ripened, with short graying hair and sharp blue eyes that can spot a kestrel a mile away. She is a woman with an instinct for the coming hurricane and a loneliness like a bastion, impregnable.

Now she turns, and the young man is there. Ah, you've finished unpacking, she calls. A friendly statement, formal nonetheless; she does not know what to say to this stranger in her domain.

His name is Christian; he looks older than his thirty-some years.

He is unmarried, perhaps childless, sunburnt, burnt-out, life-shattered, a gentle lad with brown eyes behind wire frames, a small neat mustache, and a shock of dark hair, a shock of dark experience. Christian is Swiss. He used to be a delegate for the International Committee of the Red Cross, and he had tried to save humans. He had been trained to believe in the inevitability of war, but his experience left him with a deep scar of failure: as if he were witnessing his own extinction. A survivor from a land of refugees, he has been driven to the island to survive himself, to seek protection behind this woman's knowing fortress—although he does not know this yet. He believes he is seeking refuge among the birds, to work with Fran on Egret Island.

Egret Island lies half a mile off the coast of Mauritius: a hatchling of coral reef, separated from its mother island by a lagoon swept daily by the trade winds of the Indian Ocean. Egret has been designated a nature reserve by the Mauritian government; Fran is the field worker charged by an independent foundation with returning the island to its prehuman condition. She will replace the exotic with the endemic; she will restore birds and small reptiles to their natural habitat. And she will try to save the mourner-bird from extinction.

There are no egrets on Egret Island. After the Portuguese and the Dutch came the French and the British, and the egrets, too, vanished.

The first night, Christian cannot sleep. He lies in the cocoon of mosquito netting until he can no longer stand the woven closeness of gauze, night air pressing upon him as if holding all the darkness of his waking dreams. He gets up from the low bed, pushes away the gauze veil, takes a flashlight from the bedside table, and lights his way to the veranda.

The moon is low, a sliver of light above the thickness of trees. Stars salt-sprinkled on a sea of night. He listens to the nocturnal sounds—cicadas, geckos chirping—and wonders how he found his way to this place. Wonders what trick of perception has replaced the known and familiar with a strangeness, as if he were drunk on his own escape from pain.

In the dark he lights a cigarette, seeking comfort in the familiarity of gesture. But finds none; coughs uneasily, fearful of waking Fran. He thinks he will try to stop smoking, that it belongs to that other life he must forget; that familiarity is also continuity, and will bring the waking dream. The sounds that in his memory keep him from sleep, the visions.

There was a woman, there was a child, and there was his own weakness. His inability to save them. Visions too, that he cannot resist, of the past, and of what might have been.

He holds his head in his hands, too full. The night sky spins around him, a centripetal force bearing memories to a center, to a core of helplessness.

~~~

It would be the last time.

They had been up all night long helping the medics: a nearby village had been shelled and the local hospital had run out of beds. Christian had filled the Jeep with the unused mattresses from one of the shelters: back and forth from Jeep to hospital he carried the unwieldy mattresses, bumping blindly into hurrying medical staff or equipment left scattered in the long corridors where pain echoed dully, as if to say, We've heard it all before. For three years we've been hearing it, and we don't know anymore if it will ever stop.

At dawn Nermina found him on the low wall outside the hospital, sitting with his hands loose and empty, missing a cigarette. There were dark circles under her eyes and a frown line between her eyebrows that he had not noticed before. Now she took his hand in hers and said, Let's go for a walk, there's a path that leads down to the river. We can sit there and watch the sunrise.

Is it safe?

She laughed. Since when do we worry about safety!

Things have changed, you know what I mean.

She looked down, put her palms on her belly. As safe as I am, she said. I believe it is safe to walk to the river, yes. There are no snipers, no mines, no bears or wolves or snakes.

Her face was open and laughing now, the frown had disappeared. Her warm brown eyes held him, the faint upward turn of the corner of her mouth encouraged him. He tried to shake off the woolly, drugged sleeplessness, and rose to follow her.

The path led along the side of the hospital compound, then out into a wild undeveloped oversight of Nature: tall, lush summer grasses, almost yellow in the early light, the last wildflowers bending modestly to a slight breeze. Nermina paused now and then, leaning over to pick a spray of blue forget-me-nots, yellow buttercups, white daisies. She had removed the elastic from her long brown hair, which swung before her as she moved. Christian watched her and his heart filled. She belongs here, he thought, it is her country, she belongs here in this pale tender light, among the grasses and flowers and in the sudden freedom of my gaze to love her unconditionally.

At the river they paused, looked for a spot to sit. Others had been there before them, and Christian regretted the bright field. Here there were plastic bottles and broken glass and old newspapers, even bullet casings, all scattered with the carelessness of the very mortal. But the river flowed clean and bright on that morning, hiding its secrets, indifferently offering them a smooth mirror of tranquillity in which they could find a restful image of themselves.

They did not sit, in the end; Christian held her, kissed her, told her what he had been thinking when she found him outside the hospital.

We must leave, he said. I want us to leave Bosnia, quit the Red Cross.

She laughed nervously. Leave? And go where?

I want to resign. I want you to come to Switzerland with me.

He did not tell her the dread he had been feeling for the last few days: a sudden eruption like a rash, a fever, that woke him with a start and held him in a grip of insomnia, that drove him to work until he thought he would drop. Like now. But while he could still change things, he must try.

Christian, she said, I can't, you know why—

You must, Nermina, this is something more important than the past, than either of us—

And what do you think the other Bosnian women do? You think they don't manage somehow?

She turned and gestured violently toward the hospital.

He closed his palms around her face, kissed her again. Felt how powerless he was against her will, against the war that had brought them together but still divided them. He felt her warm, round shoulders, her full hips, her breasts; he could lose himself, for now, in her kisses, in her response.

There was a tree by a river in western Bosnia where they had made love for the last time. Their fragile skin against its rough bark; briefly, it had seemed to offer a kind of shelter: a woven canopy of early light and new green leaves. There was a dappled veil of sun and shadow against their skin, and the light would blind them in a sudden flash, then be subdued again by a gentle movement—whether it was their own, or that of the leaves in the breeze, or even of the sun, was not important.

~~~

The warden's house is small, and Fran awakes, hearing the muffled sounds of Christian's insomnia. The batteries of her flashlight are low, so she lies in the dark listening to the whispers of night-living creatures. Her birds sleep, but she imagines she can hear a chorus of contented breathing, light as air, beaks tucked under wings. Or the scurry of small reptiles, or the ponderous scratching of the tortoises. Her tortoises. Her realm, her defenseless children. Those she cares for. Hard dusty shell or soft fragile feather, no space in between for the warmth of skin, no, that is gone, that was Satish and he is gone and there can be no thinking of him, that's all done with. She turns her thoughts to the bird, to the urgency of its survival. It does not know that its barrenness is more than a mere lack of children, it does not know that all of its kind will become mere fossil memory, very soon, unless she, Fran, can save it. She fears she is working against terrible odds: even if she can overcome the obstacles Nature leaves in her way, how can she predict, or fight against those that man is deliberately and stealthily placing before her?

The broken eggshells, the injured birds, the disappearances.

But she refuses to be worn down or discouraged; that is what they want, after all. Her role is to affirm life.

My bird, thinks Fran, drifting toward sleep. Both noble and flamboyant, gorgeous plumage of deep blue, verging on teal, with a rich crimson crown and breast. It has long tail feathers, flecked with white. A bird prized by kings, called *l'oiseau Isle de France* when it was a regular exhibit of the menagerie at Versailles, where it languished and died of *mal du pays*.

The Mauritians say that it is good luck to see the bird, because rarity gives it added grace, and magical powers. Fran does not credit superstitions; if anything, she resents them. The local name of the bird is *oiseau-languit* because of its long, yearning, homesick cry; in English, the mourner-bird.

Often in the pink softness of early morning, before heat, before work, Fran goes to listen to the waking call of the mourner-birds. There is a particular tree where they gather, an old, tall *bois de fer*. She takes a worn cushion with her, and places it on the hard coral ground beneath the tree, then sits Indian style, her head bent, her eyes dreaming.

Sometimes it is the male who begins, sometimes the female; usually it is the pair she calls Mimi and Rodolfo. In such a small, isolated place, you reduce the grandeur of your opera to scale, but for Fran art and Nature are not comparable. She accepts that Nature has taken the place of art in her life, and does not think that is a bad thing.

She waits, then the call comes. Mimi. Soft at first, a gentle, repeated clucking, then more urgent, an open-throated call, full of avian longing. Mournful, lonely, not unlike the cry of a seagull on a bleak coast; somehow out of keeping with the warmth and softness of this island.

Then Rodolfo's answer, neither reassuring nor scolding, not an alluring mating call but some other ritual reply to an obscure atavistic necessity: a series of short croaking sounds, as if to say, Yes, I am here, and then a soaring response which echoes the same mournfulness, with brief inflections Fran has found peculiar to the male, just a few notes, a poignant trill before the call soars again, impossibly forlorn. Visitors to the island have remarked upon this unusual melancholy; Fran smiles and shrugs, does not tell them that even with time the sadness does not diminish for the listener; one never grows used to it.

But for all that, Fran loves to hear the call, the island music which is her reward. We are here, the birds are saying. As if in thanks, though birds have no such notions. Fran is the one who is thankful.

She closes her eyes, leans her head back against the trunk of the *bois de fer.* It is warm; there is a gentle breeze. The song will be repeated perhaps three, four times, no more. Then again at dusk. During daylight hours the birds cluck, chatter, tweet, but do not sing. Their song brackets the darkness, in honor of the sun's passage. The world most beautiful, close to night.

A sweetness of warmth and light rouses Christian from dreamless sleep. He never dreams anymore; his dreams are waking, hallucinatory visions he is never sure he has lived.

Fran has made coffee, and he lies for a moment luxuriating in its aroma. And in the anticipation of the warm day, and of a new beginning. He luxuriates too in the certainty of a right decision. Smiles at the memory of the chain of events which brought him here, after the months of restlessness, *désœuvrement,* the frequent phone calls to Sarajevo, his parents' worried, silent gazes. The days he spent walking along the lake: its pewtered bowl was filled with a depth of mountains—still not deep enough to drown in. Then one day he ran into Thierry, a former colleague with whom he had been in Afghanistan, a young man bearded and balding and pushing a stroller, where a small dark child lay sleeping. They had sat by the lake comparing lives, since Kabul; his friend had found a new life in starting a family; no, his wife was not Indian but Mauritian, she was a biologist, at the university in Lausanne, she'd just been offered an interesting job back in Mauritius by a former professor, an eccentric Irishman who ran a conservation program, they needed an assistant with a scientific background . . . Thierry had paused, looked at Christian, gauging his sadness and apathy, then continued, My wife's turned it down, it wouldn't really be practical with Séverine here—he nodded at the sleeping child, pausing to smile—it's on a little island off the coast of Mauritius itself, Ananda says it's a lovely place, if you're on your own, I suppose . . .

If only he could have traded places with Thierry. If only he could, now, have been married to a dark-haired woman, strolling a sleeping child along the lakeside; he would gladly have traded his anguish and envy for that simple joy. But there could be no trade, only a substitution of a kind; thus, now he is here on the lovely little island in Ananda's place—wifeless, childless, less envious but no less anguished.

Now Fran is calling him, firmly, with that relentless American enthusiasm for work, as if to say, Let's go! Your new life has begun!

Twenty-five hectares of tropical vegetation, the island is a short green poem of a place. Upon his arrival, Fran had offered to give him the tour. They dropped his luggage—two battered duffel bags—on the veranda of the warden's house. Former officers' residence, said Fran; the Brits used the island as a military base during the Second World War. But don't expect the Raj, Fran went on; it's very basic. Solar panels for some electricity, but we use mainly oil lamps, gas for cooking, jerry jugs of water from the mainland and whatever rain we can catch in the cistern. No television, no phone, mobile or otherwise; no computers, no e-mail, no fax machines, no dishwasher, no washing machine, no microwave—do you think you can survive?

Christian had raised an eyebrow and a corner of his mouth, and nodded. He wanted to say he had lived without water, electricity, or heat in the middle of a Balkan winter, but he did not wish to spoil her obvious pleasure in tropical deprivation. He looked at the low white building with its tin roof and outhouse: the long veranda with its worn wicker chairs suggested some legacy of colonial ease, offered a promise of moments of indolence over sundowners, with lazy conversations into darkness and mosquito-time.

As if reading his mind, Fran had said suddenly, No, you're tired, you've had a long flight. We'll do the tour tomorrow.

Now trees and plants wait path-side as if for an introduction; Fran points them out, *bois de rat, bois d'ébène, bois de bœuf, bois de chandelle.* The plants have a history which she relates in detail but hurriedly, as if out of habit; some are nearly extinct, others have been reintroduced from the mainland. All are rare, protected species.

She shows him a precious orchid, *Oeoniella aphrodite;* some tourists will linger behind, she warns, to steal them, you have to watch out. She points out three old giant tortoises and says, They're not from here, no, the original tortoises died out centuries ago, these are immigrants, pets, we're not sure where they're from, probably the Seychelles or Rodrigues. They could tell us, if they could speak: they're older than the human memory of their origin.

The tortoises nudge their dinner of papaya, move toward Fran and Christian with that deliberate slowness as if tuned to a different time, a different gravity.

Bois de fer, says Fran, as the name indicates, ironwood. It was used to build icebreakers, you can see where it got its name. This tree is the only one of seventeen remaining endemic trees in Mauritius to bear fruit. Very very difficult to get it to germinate—so you can imagine we were worried. A local botanist agreed to take some seeds to Kew Gardens on a recent trip, but then he forgot the seeds in the bottom of his luggage in a plastic bag so they just sat there and fermented the whole time he was in England, and then by the time he got back to Mauritius the berries had sprouted in his suitcase!

Fran's face a sudden, luminous smile; germination of her rare generosity, sharing that which she loves best. Around her eyes a crinkling of humor. Can you imagine! she exclaims; Christian nods gravely. Fran knows from his CV that he studied botany, years ago at the university; he learned respect for science, for method. Has life taught him, then, the role of the stochastic factor, the random determinant, which subverts all method, all reason?

Rarity, concludes Fran. Take the dodo; already unique to a small island, already rare compared to any mainland or archipelago species. There is a threshold, a point of no return where extinction is concerned. Cross that threshold and even if you have a few breeding individuals alive, it's too late. So the threshold for a rare species is even lower. That is why our work on Egret—on all of Mauritius—is so important. And the smaller the island, the greater the likelihood of extinction. Ninety percent of the 171 extinctions of species of bird since 1600 have occurred on islands.

The bird blinks down on Fran and Christian, as if in wise agreement. It moves a step or two sideways along its perch in the tree, ruffling its brilliant feathers as if to catch color in sunlight.

Now. Only twenty percent of the world's bird species live on islands.

Christian stares back at the bird, concentrating, fighting sudden clumsiness and cultural jet lag. The earth exhales its stored warmth.

That means, if my math is correct, that the chances of extinction for a given bird are fifty percent greater on an island, and even greater still on a small island.

Why? asks Christian, trying to show interest. The bird seems again to nod approval.

Interspecific competition . . . smaller habitat . . . rarity, greater impact of human interference, pollution, predators, disruption of the food chain . . . a number of factors.

She pauses, runs her fingers through her light hair. Her skin is the color of speckled toast, just right.

In the case of Rodolfo here, man is mostly to blame. Two centuries ago the Franco-Mauritians started to clear the mainland for sugarcane plantations and destroyed much of the habitat; then in more recent times what was left was sprayed with DDT against malaria, particularly over in Moka and Bambous . . .

How many of these birds are left? asks Christian.

That we know of, perhaps a dozen. We have four here on Egret. The two pairs. The others are in the wild up in the Black River area, near where Sean, the program director, lives.

Only four?

The bird ruffles, shifts, settles again, seems to look benevolently upon Fran. She turns her face to the bird, ignoring Christian's question, and coos, Yes, Rodolfo *caro mio,* where's your lady? When you gonna make some little ones for Mama Fran, eh? When's that nest gonna have some little babies for me?

She breaks off, looks sheepishly at Christian. He has been watching the bird, his face impassive; now he looks at her, a slight smile breaking his rigidity. Her eyes glow; the love of her work lends her a certain beauty. She is lucky indeed: that she can see the rewards of her work before her.

They're very faithful, these birds, continues Fran thoughtfully. They generally mate for life. Very attentive males, too; they get food for the female when she's nesting, and take over the nesting themselves for part of the day. Once the females begin to lay, if need be I can start to incubate them, see if there's a better chance of producing hatchlings . . . It would be ideal here. On the mainland they have all sorts of problems with monkeys and mongooses stealing the eggs.

No monkeys here?

Fran looks shocked by Christian's question, forgets that he is a newcomer and a novice. Monkeys and mongooses are exotic, she explains, and they're pests. We've gotten rid of the rats on Egret, thank God, and the shrews, and there have never been any mammals larger than that. When you have a regular, thriving population, she continues, the occasional breeding failure—could be genetic, habitat-related, theft of eggs by monkeys, whatever—the occasional failure doesn't matter. The species survives. But with so few individuals . . .

She does not tell him the rest, the other factors which may be destroying her work. She does not tell him about the birds she found with their necks broken, rare genetic codes gelled in the still blood of frail carcasses. She does not tell Christian that if he is here it is not because she needs him, but because she is afraid.

Minimum viable population, writes Fran in her field notebook, then stops.

She works with figures, reports to Sean, to the people at the foundation, analyzes the data, plans strategies for encouraging survival. We must encourage survival, says Sean, drawing his thick brush eyebrows together. And what if it were not that simple, she thinks, looking up. And what if the numbers refuse to cooperate, because Nature is not order but chaos, and numbers don't add up in chaos? What if Sean is speaking an optimism of cooperative numbers, of applied science, and refuses to admit the human madness that is killing off the birds, despite my efforts?

Two pairs left, she writes. Two pairs, and no offspring . . . except the time last year when I found two eggs crushed. Crushed not by a mere fall but by an instrument—a hand?

And Satish is gone. Satish who hatched three babies, and I haven't produced a single fledgling since then. I do not have his gift; he was a natural. He knew the ways of birds; he loved them in a way they understood, without data and numbers, and he was saving them. They would have survived. They would have risen above the threshold of a minimum viable population. I love them too, but with him gone, can I succeed?

In the beginning he was so polite. Satish believed that to compensate for his lack of education he must be polite, that politeness was the poor man's only possible introduction to a better world. *Yes, Miss Fran, no, Miss Fran. Absolutely grand, Miss Fran.* Fran teasing, saying, You'll be calling me Memsahib next; and Satish reacting, embarrassed, chastened. My name is Fran, and yours is Satish, and let's call each other like that.

After that he seemed to settle in, and within days Fran realized that he had a real gift. He knew the local names of all the plants, knew the history of reptiles and fish and birds and small mammals. But mere knowledge was not his gift, no: he seemed to know instinctively, rather than intellectually, the life cycles of the creatures and plants, knew how to feed them, how to care for them, how to place his nurturing so that every species would prosper. Fran even had difficulty persuading him to clear the island of exotic plants and animals.

She watched in awe, supervising in name only, as Satish restored several species of endangered plants and strengthened the resurgent populations of pink pigeons, kestrels, and Mauritian fodies. She watched in awe as he operated on injured birds on the kitchen table, the ease and grace with which his long fingers executed delicate procedures. Satish had what she could never have, a living instinct; she was already generations removed from the earth, and could only learn, and apply.

If Mauritius had not been free of humans until the Portuguese came, Fran would have said that Satish was a native, an endemic species. He felt his way through the tangle of the island as if he had always lived there—no sixth-generation Tamil immigrant from India, orphaned, impoverished, uneducated, doomed.

He told her he used to play on Egret as a boy, long before the conservation program began, when it was still a wild place open to truant schoolboys and wood-poaching locals. They would ferry over from Mahébourg on a borrowed pirogue, skimming their freedom across the turquoise plate of the lagoon. And while his friends played pirate or Brits and Japs or cowboys and Indians, more and more often Satish would slip away to explore the trees and small animals which scurried among the thick growth. Nature's wealth to balance the poverty of a toyless childhood in a tin-roofed *case*.

But when he was twelve his parents were killed in a bus crash and he was sent to live with an uncle in Curepipe—far from the island, far even, for a small boy, from the sea, which they visited only on holidays or special occasions, and only when there was a bit of money for the bus fare.

He showed up one day, shortly after Fran first came to Egret, frightening her with his quiet suddenness, standing there asking in words which tumbled over each other like eager puppies whether she would need assistance with her work, and it wasn't right for a woman to live there alone, and he could cook and shop and deal with the locals, and repair outboard engines, and tell her the names of all the plants, and she needn't pay him much, just room and board and some pocket money, and he didn't drink, and she would not regret it.

But she does regret it, though not in the way Satish imagined back then; she does regret it, yes; oh yes.

This Swiss fellow: a new species, writes Fran later, in her journal. *His sort is rare unto extinction: soulful, self-effacing, just something I can sense rather than actually know, apart from his curriculum vitae, his humanitarian history.*

Yesterday evening, she writes, *in the Land Rover from the airport: he was silent as he looked from the window at the women walking, saris the color of the sky, bundles of cane poised on their heads, wrists glinting gold in the sunlight, et cetera, et cetera . . . So he was watching sari ladies, villages, schoolgirls passing on the road, all blue cloth and dark faces and white smiles, and he shook his head in disbelief, didn't speak. Have you been to this part of the world before? I asked. A long time ago, to Madagascar, he said, with his slight French accent. Then he asked abruptly, You say there are Hindus, Muslims, Creole Africans, Chinese, and white Europeans living here—and they all get along?*

Knowing where he's been all I could do was shrug and say, There are invisible barriers; there is government censorship to protect ethnic diversity and harmony, but there is also a great deal of tolerance and there are a lot of laws to promote that tolerance. Problems are mostly economic and social, not ethnic.

He only nodded. Perhaps his entire frame of reference is based upon his experience; he can't imagine where he is yet. I suppose he is surprised by peace, by schoolchildren and sari ladies walking undisturbed along the road. He must be thinking, How can this be the same world?

Good spaghetti, says Christian, nodding.

Fran shrugs. It's my usual recipe. It was my husband's favorite dish.

You were married?

For a time. For a long time.

She wonders why she said that, why she mentioned her husband so automatically, as if he were naturally connected to spaghetti. And now her thoughts follow that same frequent path. How it all began at a dinner party, which had a bitter irony for Fran, because she hated dinner parties, hated the networking, the posing, the subtle one-upping. Peter's department chair had invited colleagues and spouses and the more brilliant or favored of his students. Fran was seated next to a visiting professor from Germany; Peter was next to a student, a young woman from the Slavic languages department who was attending classes in Russian history. This was relevant:

there are times when everything is relevant, when nothing happens by chance, as if everything had been planned for years, merely waiting to fall into place.

Her name was Irene, but she had everyone call her Irina because it was more exotic, and she darkened her eyes with liner and gave herself a mysterious pseudo-Russian (pre-Revolution, naturally) air, even used an ivory cigarette holder, and everyone thought she was charming (in the way women under thirty can do almost anything and still be considered charming) except for Fran, who wondered if she was the only one there with clear vision.

These are the simple events which bring about the destruction of what has taken years to build. Fran later understood that one ought never to think of love as being solid, tangibly indestructible. Even of having its own essence. The only substantive proof of love is the child, and then, not for everyone, and not always. Fran had wanted a child, but it had not happened, and by the time Irina slithered along in her black cocktail dress, it was already late, and Peter was concerned about his lack of progeny.

He now had two little boys, Nicholas and Alexander. You sound like a Romanov dynasty, said Fran, the last time she saw him, at the commencement ceremony at UC Berkeley, just before she left for Mauritius. Perhaps he had found a suitably dry reply, Not bitter by any chance? and Fran would have answered, Call it bitter if you like, I'm just trying to be funny.

Words did not matter; no amount of words could change the way things went. Blunt arrows against emotion: there were times, among the birds, when Fran wondered why man had invented language, when song was often more true.

How, wonders Christian, do you learn the ways of a place that is given not to progress but to a return to primeval innocence? How do

you learn to work for—and live with—a woman who is both tyrannical and tender in her devotion to the wilderness? How do you do that
when you have seen all innocence and tenderness crushed by a wild
and drunken tyranny?

Christian is like a man shipwrecked and charmed, Ulysses to Fran's
Circe. She bosses him, from the dawn of the first day, telling him firmly
what he must and must not do. She has pinned a meticulous schedule of
feedings and cleanings and note takings and trap checking on the wall of
the kitchen, she dictates lists of chores, of shopping, of weekly trips to
Mahébourg or monthly trips to Port Louis or Black River.

You will love it here, she concluded with a strange smile, looking
away at the same time in the direction of the trees where her birds
will settle briefly, temptingly, each visit an affirmation of her divine
mission on Egret Island.

Is she God, wonders Christian, or is she Darwin's Nemesis?

Christian begins to understand that the island is not a place one can
casually love or ignore but a thing of study, a living laboratory. When
Sean from Black River originally took over the project, he learns, vol-
unteers were recruited to rid the island of invasive nonnative acacia
trees, or rats, or shrews, and beneath the tangled legacy of colonization
they found both venerable trees and fragile saplings, all rare, all endangered. Christian learns their names, learns to distinguish the young *bois
de rat* by its sharp red leaves, learns to tell the cooing of the common
barred ground dove from that of the pink pigeon. Pigeons are airborne
rats, he has often thought, but these pink pigeons (*Columba mayeri*)
please his sense of irony. Imagine, he will say to Fran, the Piazza del
Duomo in Milan covered in cooing pink birds: is it the grayness or the
commonness of the usual variety we begrudge? When you see a pink
pigeon you imagine life differently, you imagine possibility.

Fran looks at him, raises her eyebrows, and says, That's what this
place is about, possibility.

He doesn't drink, she writes, *and he's so quiet. So so quiet. At night he disappears into his room with a book, and his unspoken thoughts seem to hang on the night air, clustered on the veranda like small midges of sadness.*

Fran is wrong when she thinks that Christian does not drink. In Mahébourg he found a Chinese merchant who recommended a potent blend of cane liquor, and he has learned to cough, to scrape a chair as he pours out two, three shot glasses in succession. He learned to drink back there, first because the Serbs would not negotiate with him otherwise; then out of fear, out of necessity. Here the fear is gone, except before sleep.

Then Nermina is there, as surely as if she were visiting him, sitting at the side of his bed. She shakes her head, smiles. You have nothing to reproach yourself with, *dušo moje,* she says. It was war.

No, no, he protests, and knows she cannot hear him; it was my fault. Mine alone.

She vanishes and leaves him in the small room to lie awake and watch geckos. There are two of them, one on either side of the room, at the top of the wall. First he imagines that they are having a race, but they are too hesitant, so he then imagines that they are lovers trying to find each other across the huge void which separates them. This idea holds him, even when the alcohol nudges him toward sleep, and he starts awake again, looking anxiously to each side for the motionless little streak of brown. Exotic geckos, sniffed Fran the first day, from India. I wish I knew a way to get rid of them; we have our own green geckos we need to encourage.

Imperceptibly, Romeo has nudged forward, close now to the rafters where they will meet, but Juliet has not moved. Christian swallows the last of the cane liquor. He closes his eyes. When he opens them again, Juliet gecko has disappeared into the rafters.

Christian walks to the landing. Washed silk, he thinks, looking out across the lagoon. Two or three pirogues move slowly against the morning breeze. In the distance dark volcanic shapes, steeper than mountains, pierce the clouds. Light moves across cane fields, carrying cloud, forming changing intensities of green. He is not indifferent to what he sees: he knows that this beauty will be a screen of light across memory and darkness, given the time for his memory to adjust.

Fran has given him the day off and the keys to the Land Rover. Go kill a few macaques over in the Black River Gorges, she urges.

Fran, he has learned, hates the monkeys even more than she hates the brown geckos: because they are not native to Mauritius, and because they steal birds' eggs and charm tourists, whom she hates nearly as much as the monkeys. Tourists are just a different species of monkey, she says. How silly they look hanging from their camera straps—straps like liana in the jungle—taking photos of their fellow monkeys, you'll see them up there on the road by the waterfalls, polluting with their cars and litter and noise—

Fran, asks Christian, is there anything other than the birds that you do like, any other species? He asks this gently, with no trace of irony, like a mother asking a fractious child what else it might like for dinner. And still she is caught off guard by his question and looks at him severely, yet openly, and answers quickly, Yes, I like composers. Of classical music.

But they're mostly all dead, says Christian.

Exactly.

Then she laughs, throws her head back, and he thinks she has a fine laugh, and he chuckles too, a welcome feeling spreading like a warmth.

Christian stops in Mahébourg to buy film, a tourist guide, and a road map, and feels a sudden childish impulse toward disobedience and extravagance. He has been on Egret for nearly three weeks and has seen little of mainland Mauritius other than a rain-obscured succession of small one-story concrete or tin-roofed houses and brilliantly colored Hindu temples on the way to Port Louis. Fran was driving, and he spent much of the time clinging to the seat, trying not to call out in warning, amazed at his own fear, as if the fearlessness with which he had driven in Bosnia were of no use here on narrow roads cluttered with buses and cars and motorcycles and trucks, all speeding blindly past equally blind and suicidal pedestrians.

Now the Land Rover feels solid and safe but too big for the road, and Christian has little experience of driving on the left. He drives slowly therefore, lets his mind wander with the landscape, pulls over now and then to take a photo or consult the map.

He enters a wild territory of deep forest and steep ravines, primeval Mauritius. Gray monkeys sit waiting for him in the middle of the road, then scamper off. He pulls over at the signs for the waterfall, parks the Land Rover.

He stands for a long time at the edge of the gorge, his hand on the railing between himself and the cliff, as if he is on the deck of a dusty ship sailing through forest. Tropic birds circle, brilliant white against the green. In the distance long ribbons of water streak light and movement down the opposite cliff face, raising a steam of power which now and then catches the cloud-borne sunlight. Beads of rainbow form briefly and dissolve.

~~~

It was her favorite place, Nermina had said. The lakes and waterfalls of Plitvice. Before the war, she said, they went there often, regularly, for the day, it was not far from Bihać, and you could swim there and take a picnic, there were boats which crossed the lakes or you could walk, and the waterfalls seemed to grow in size and beauty as you walked, brides' veils against the rocks and trees, perhaps that is why they celebrated weddings there.

Christian looks at the waterfalls before him but sees Nermina's waterfalls, her lakes, the lakes in her voice, imagines the cool water against his skin, imagines her skin cool and damp against his; an imagined cascade raising memories of touch.

~~~

The light moves through the cane fields like a ripple of wind, changing vibrations of color, pale tender green. Christian drives slowly, observing.

In the middle of the fields, scattered like monuments to a prehistoric deity, are flat-topped pyramids of black stone. He wonders, for some time, what martial purpose these towers might have served: windowless, doorless watchtowers of history.

On an island in Dalmatia there are fields with stone mounds, neat clusters of limestone growing among the fragrant lavender. Christian learned that the stones were placed there over the centuries by the islanders who had to clear the land in order to plant the lavender, or the vine.

But here the stones are torn out to plant the cane, have been torn from the soil by generations of indentured laborers and their descendants. Mauritians say that the stones grow.

He tries to imagine the wilderness that preceded the cane plantations. The kingdoms deep within the forests; the bounty of silence, stones growing.

An open-air restaurant spills down a hillside, shaded by palm trees and draped with bougainvillea. Christian stops the Land Rover in the parking lot and walks down a flight of steps to the entrance. A dark-skinned girl greets him with a menu and a smile, takes him to a table. He orders a beer and a curry dish.

The other tables are occupied by tourists, mostly French and Swiss. Christian listens idly to a neighboring conversation, lengthy complaints about prices, about service, about the frequent rains, about the local drivers. Christian might agree about the drivers, but weariness comes over him as he listens, a sluggishness accompanying the first swallows of beer.

The tourists' voices are giving him a headache; he turns briefly to look at the speakers. A lovely woman, pale and feminine, her equally handsome companion, dark thick curls; they wear a glaze of well-being, as if they had somehow received finishing touches in the banks and boutiques of Manhattan or Monte Carlo. And still they complain; as if even their gloss could not guarantee that their expectations of the good life would be met.

The lovely woman catches Christian's eye, narrows her gaze. He looks away, calls for the bill.

As he leaves the restaurant he pauses by the hostess. *C'était bon, M'sieu?* She offers him the brightness of her smile, and on impulse he tells her he will be working in Mauritius and will need a local guide from time to time, does she know anyone who might be free to show him around? And her eyes are dark pools of warmth, her smile surprised and flattered. She writes her name on the restaurant's business card. Asmita. Christian nods, gives her his hand, says his name. *Merci, Asmita,* he says, carries the light of her smile away with him for a few moments, and is glad of his boldness.

Asmita watches the tall young man climb the steps back to the parking lot. She thinks he is handsome; his quiet manner is appealing. Her sisters tell her she dreams too much; now she folds her arms across her chest and sinks into the favorite dream: the romance with a European. Until Prakash the headwaiter looks at her with that unforgiving leer of his that is a double accusation: she is slacking off; she is looking not at him but at another man.

On exploring Mahébourg that evening Christian comes across Les Dents du Midi, named for a mountain range in his native country. It is a restaurant which features Swiss cheese dishes, inappropriate to the Mauritian heat: it would be an act of defiance to eat *fondue au fromage* in such weather. He strikes up a conversation with the proprietor, Bertrand, a man his father's age; Bertrand explains that he left Switzerland twenty years earlier in pursuit of something more— a real world, with a capacity for wildness and anarchy. For unqualified joy. He is jovial and sour by turns, red-faced from drink and the heat. As Christian sits on the terrace drinking white wine and sampling the well-traveled cheese, he observes Bertrand arguing with his Mauritian wife and yelling at his teenage children, who wait lazily on tables and, no doubt, dream of nightlife in Geneva or Zurich. Christian listens to Bertrand's sighing complaints and asides, and he sympathizes but thinks a man could do worse.

Then Bertrand says, It will be good for Fran to have some company out there. That was a bad business, with the fellow who was there before you. Poor Satish.

He shakes his head. Christian looks at him questioningly, expecting an explanation, but Bertrand looks away and starts to hum quietly to himself. Then he stands up and moves off into the kitchen, leaving Christian to wonder what this bad business might mean: was the fellow fired? A bad worker? Or was there some sort of sexual misunderstanding?

Christian stops in the bar of a hotel near Mahébourg. He sits at the bar and orders a beer, looks out toward the misshapen forms of night, thinks about his long day, all that he has seen, the brief moment of Asmita's smile.

A young black man, handsome and neat in khaki trousers and a white polo shirt, walks over to Christian and says something in Creole. Christian asks him matter-of-factly to repeat what he has said in French; *mo pas connais Créole,* he adds hopefully, and the young man giggles, then asks in French if he can join him for a chat.

Christian gestures to the barstool next to him, and the young man sits at an angle to the room so he can see who is there. Gives Christian his hand, *Moi, c'est Jean-Baptiste.* Christian returns the introduction, then immediately regrets it, for this gives Jean-Baptiste license for curiosity, and a string of wearying questions—Where are you from? Haven't I seen you with the woman from Egret? What are you doing there? Maybe she is your mother?—and another fit of giggles.

Christian drinks his beer, answers tersely, carefully. But in his mind's eye sees not the smooth smiling black face before him, so boyish and congenial, but the strong jaw, the thick hair, the sharp blue eyes of Colonel Vlatković: they too often met in such a way, over a drink. But Vlatković carried an assault rifle, and his smile rarely dissolved into laughter, only threats.

Now Jean-Baptiste is smiling, waving his long fingers in the air, bringing Christian back. You'd better be careful, you know, you hear about the last fellow who lived over there with the American woman?

No, what happened? says Christian lightly.

He died. And I had just seen him, you know. I was the last one to see him alive.

Jean-Baptiste pauses for effect, his eyes wide and shining, and Christian for the first time in months applies both training and experience: he has been an innocent in Fran's company, but now it comes back, the extreme calmness, the refusal to enter into a game, the preoccupation solely with the welfare of others.

But now there are no others, and Christian understands that it is he himself who must be shielded from harm. Unless this is merely a joke, an adolescent attempt at humor at someone else's expense, but

Christian cannot be sure. So he asks: What do you want me to do with that information?

Jean-Baptiste shrugs, waves his arms, contorts his face mock-doubtfully. He died, he repeats, and nobody knows why he died, they say it was an accident but you don't ever know, do you, so you want to be careful out there.

Christian nods slowly, swings one crossed leg as he watches Jean-Baptiste's eyes grow larger, then smaller again, as he tries and fails to impress. Finally Christian puts out his hand, takes Jean-Baptiste's smooth long fingers into his own, squeezes. Thanks for the advice. Stands up and drops a few rupee notes on the table for the beer, and walks slowly out of the hotel.

Probably I should have done that differently. Probably I was meant to buy him a drink, find out what he really wanted. Maybe he didn't even want anything, maybe he just likes foreigners and wanted to be friendly.

I'm too used to words at face value, to threats and ultimatums. Which hide other things too.

He turns back and waves to Jean-Baptiste. The young man flashes a bright smile, returns the wave.

The mourner-bird looks up at Fran from where it lies, its little bead eye tremulous with fear, or hope, or mere animal confusion. Her hands tremble—or is it the bird's trembling—as she feels through feather for fractured bone. On the shelf the single gas lamp casts shadows amid a cold white light; cicadas penetrate the mosquito screens with their frictional chorus. From time to time the bird flaps briefly, defying its injuries; Fran coos gently, hoping it will not hear the hesitancy in her voice.

She found it just before dusk, oceanside, where it lay at the foot of an ebony tree, a small inert parcel of red and blue. Fran cried out, as if there might be someone to hear, as if the natural reaction to distress is to call out for others even in the wilderness. Christian was gone for the day, for the evening, and she was alone on Egret without the dinghy; she had only the VHF radio linking her to Sean in Black River fifty miles away. So her cry met silence, and resounded within her rising fears— who are these unknown visitors, nightly assassins of sleep and birds?

Mimi injured, writes Fran in the field notebook. *Set splints where I could, right wing broken in two places. Fed as well as can be expected, so I am hopeful.*

What she does not write: and what if it was not an accident.

She makes supper in the small kitchen. A pleasing sizzle of oil, then she adds an onion, a few pieces of green pepper; their skin crinkles and softens in the heat. Eggs poured creamy yellow over the vegetables, gently stirred.

How many times has she made these gestures? Yet in her ascetic solitude the moment she sits down to eat is a sudden release. She is more aware of it in Christian's absence: he has cooked for her, similar omelets or simple pasta dishes, but to have someone else cooking changes the nature of a meal, changes its very taste. Eating alone reinforces the familiar, makes one concentrate on the taste and texture of the food itself in the absence of human exchange.

I am flavoring my solitude, thinks Fran.

From time to time Fran goes to a restaurant on the mainland: in Mahébourg, or along the coast. With luck, Sean or another field worker might join her, but most often, in defiance of her solitude, she walks in and asks for a table for one. The waiter quietly removes the other place setting. The long stretch of waiting for her meal: sometimes she reads a newspaper, or takes notes in her notebook, but often the light is too dim. Mere romantic candlelight, meant for others, for quiet lovers on honeymoons, or aged couples silent and bored; or even large boisterous families of tourists or local Franco-Mauritians who create their own glare. She is ignored; her skin seems to shrink on her limbs, giving her a nervous twitch. Yet she enjoys the restaurant, needs to have someone else cooking for her now and again, spoiling her; needs to show her face to the world, even if this particular world does not see her in the dim candlelight. On occasion she strikes up a conversation with someone—the proprietor of the restaurant, or a solitary airline pilot (family men, all) between two flights, or an oddball voyager like herself.

She never went to restaurants with Satish: he refused. Now she is glad, for the private time they saved for each other.

When she first came to the island, the white Anglo community tried to invite her to teas, to cocktail parties. She quickly tired of their talk of material things, of their polite indifference to her work. They tired of her strangeness, and stopped inviting her.

Once, too, in the early weeks, she had been approached by an older man who was on his own. He had seen her sitting on the veranda of an elegant restaurant in the countryside, slowly absorbing her drink at the gentle close of the day; he had ordered a bottle of champagne, and they had talked for a while.

Soft-spoken, with a trace of a French accent; he was a local man, he told her, from an old Franco-Mauritian family. He talked about the history of Mauritius, the early French colonists who fled the Revolution, and while Fran was not altogether ungrateful to learn more about the island, after some minutes she wished she were alone again.

It was not that he was uninteresting, or arrogant, or that he said or did anything that would alarm her. It was the odd mixture of smug self-confidence and a piteous neediness to be heard which made her ill at ease. The man, who never introduced himself, was impeccably groomed, wearing expensive clothes and a gold signet ring. But he wore these external signs of wealth awkwardly, twitching his shoulders as if the fine soft cloth irritated him, rubbing the fingers of one hand along the other, as if to make sure the ring were still there. His hair was smooth and gray and thinning, his skin pale and dry as if he never saw the sun. And there was the way he talked over and around her, as if he sought to encircle and capture her with his words, as if escape were unthinkable, and the more she tried to be kind, to smile and nod and prepare for a polite retreat, the more he seemed to leer, squinting his pale blue eyes at her, suddenly smiling to reveal curiously bad teeth filled with gold, which reminded her of a gypsy's smile.

Fran was not good at detecting a man's sexual interest in her; but this man made her uncomfortably conscious of his negative sexuality; she tried to dismiss it as her own fear, but could not pinpoint what disturbed her.

Or was it his curiosity? He seemed to know who she was, after she had briefly confirmed that she was indeed working in Mauritius. Or on Egret Island, to be exact. And he knew a great deal about her island. Initially she was heartened, thinking he might become a friend, or an ally, if never a lover, and that he might visit her there, but his quiet probing, his eager, insistent gaze, his smoothness, gradually induced a corresponding resistance in her which she had no inclination to question or overcome: she trusted her instincts. She declined his offer of dinner.

I've hurt him, she thought at the time, he seems offended; but is it not my right to refuse?

Later she would think she had been too hasty—discouraged not so much by the man himself as by her own domineering solitude. She was so used to it after all; it was so easy. Hadn't she misjudged him, committed the sin of rejecting him for his unprepossessing looks and his gypsy teeth? In those early weeks she sometimes hoped she would be given a second chance and meet the man again; he did seem interested in her, he had offered to show her around; perhaps he would improve on acquaintance.

Then Satish came, and she thought no more of it.

Meals together with Christian have been mostly silent and hurried. Brief commentaries about the day's work, or the work to come. Christian suits her in his respect for privacy. She does not fear, or care, that it might be indifference. She gives nothing away, no remarks of the type beginning When I . . . or Have you ever? Only birds, plants, the odd impersonal detail about Mauritius itself.

I would rather be alone, thinks Fran, but I cannot be, for the sake of the island. He startles me when he enters the room, or calls out a question. And if he does not speak, he looks into me through his small wire glasses; his eyes seem to say, I will look into you and read what I find.

And what would he find, that is so terrible? What do I keep from myself? Is it my own body—never perfect, now aging, a sag here and there, wrinkles, dark places, still a childhood shame, pride only in the sunburnt gold of my skin? Or is it something more terrible—the person I have become?

Am I not going slowly mad in isolation and in my will to play God—to rule, to determine life, unseen by others?

But it has not always been like this, thinks Fran.

She is sitting on the battered wicker sofa on the veranda, a finger weaving, curling its way through a hole in her T-shirt. Mosquitoes alight on her arms, and she chases them, slapping herself.

They were a couple, Peter and Fran. He was a tall, good-looking man, a history professor at Berkeley, respected and even idolized by his students. She was the brilliant associate professor of behavioral ecology. But what they lived separately at the university was different in nature from what they shared in their married life—the simplicity of an intellectual harmony which needed no books or research to lead them to conversation, to a communication which they took or mistook for love.

She pictures them as they were some years ago, sitting in a restaurant high above the Bay. They must have been eating some clever, delicious meal, drinking some Napa wine, and this always seemed to add depth and meaning to everything: their conversation, their reasons for being together, their love.

If other, later images come, willy-nilly, to the veranda on Egret Island, Fran chases them, slapping herself. She will not be bitten by memories of intimacy.

Christian finds Fran asleep on the veranda, curled up on the wicker sofa. It has begun to rain, soft drops drawing down a freshness over the night. He shakes her gently by the shoulder. Her skin is cool and taut. Fran, Fran, he murmurs, it's starting to rain, and she mumbles something in response, sits up abruptly, like a child caught out, confused. I didn't hear you, she says huskily, almost a question, or a reproach. What's the time?

It must be late. Eleven or so.

God. I didn't hear you.

He steps back and she stands, moves past him into the house, lights the lamp. Christian waits on the veranda, uncertain. He hears her brushing her teeth, intimate sounds he thinks he should not be hearing in this isolated place, for her sake.

He listens to the rain on the tin roof. Steady drops, pinging, comforting because he is sheltered. A maternal sound, irrationally referring to a space of womblike darkness and warmth. He has always liked the sound of rain heard from a place of shelter.

He died, says Fran the next morning, in answer to Christian's question. *What happened to the fellow who was here before me?* She looks at Christian with big eyes, and he thinks he has never before noticed how big her eyes are.

He died, she says again, and looks down. He drowned. A stupid accident.

Christian returns from an inspection tour of the island and finds Fran hunched over the kitchen table, in tears. She has always carried herself with strength and poise, and even now looks at him angrily, but does not tell him to leave. Her anger, he realizes, is not just against her tears: the bird has died. It lies before her on the kitchen table, small heap of bright color, all the ruffle gone from its feathers, its eyes staring at Fran in rigid puzzlement.

I'm sorry, Fran, he says, I'm so sorry. You did everything you could.

(He used to say these words, too often. We did, are doing, will do everything we can. An anthem.)

He hands her a paper towel from the drawer, watches as she blows her nose; she does not look at him. Then she says, This wasn't an accident, you know. It didn't need to happen.

What do you mean?

It's as if someone killed her, deliberately took her and crushed her. Someone caught her and tried to break her neck but failed, so she lived these two days.

Christian is reluctant to imagine or accept malice in this peaceful place, so he says, Are you sure?

Fran blows her nose, continues, Because they—who they are, I don't know——have also crushed her eggs, or stolen them. As if——

But why would anyone deliberately do that? It's only a bird——

Only a bird! Now when Fran looks at him her eyes are dry and angry. Only a very rare bird, she says, and we can't get them back, ever. I've got one female left, and Sean has a few up at Black River but they're in the wild and he hasn't got the time or the resources, and it's desperate, so there's just me, and one female bird left, and you say only a bird!

She stands, picks up the dead bird and the keys to the Land Rover, and hurries past Christian down the path.

By dusk Fran has not returned and Christian is alone on the island. She radios him briefly at the appointed time from Black River, where she is conferring with Sean. Her voice is normal, polite, asking him to check something, asking if there is anything they need from Mahébourg, and she tells him that she will be back the next day.

He sits for a long time on the veranda with his packet of cigarettes and the bottle of cane liquor, enjoying the solitude and the openness with which he can drink and let his cane-colored emotions loose upon the warm air.

Images crowd in and there are some he chases away, with a gesture, a sip of his drink, a deliberate shift in his thoughts. Others, more welcome, linger; still others he calls on for understanding, wondering if there are ways to give clarity to their blurred contours.

In the distance, on the mainland, they are burning the cane, deep orange wraiths moving across the fields, trailing veils of smoke in the wind. Only cane, he thinks, chasing other fires from his mind, villages burning. Klenovac, Bravsko, Vrtoće.

As a child he would stand before the village bonfire every first of August, the national holiday, and as he grew taller with each passing year, the fire seemed smaller, and taught him disappointment.

But now his vision has been changed, so changed; he can no longer see fire as celebration or agricultural practice, can see it only as a weapon.

For Christian it is as if the rare mourner-bird has lost its rarity—it is true, he does think it is "only a bird," and this is because human death, in his experience, has not been rare enough. How can he explain to someone like Fran that this shift in vision does not mean he does not care, but that he has used up a lifetime's supply of gestures, that the words he needs to show compassion are now dry shells, because he has learned their inefficacy?

Christian smokes, and swallows his cane liquor, and looks up at the night stars. *Et puis merde,* he mutters, Fran will get to know me, she's human, she'll understand, sooner or later, when I can talk about it, when I can trust her.

He suddenly recalls the girl from the restaurant, Asmita; he could call Asmita. Would her smile expand to include him, would he be able to lose himself in the strangeness of her skin? There would be no memory there; perhaps she could open the future to him.

So how's the new fella working out?

Sean looks at Fran from under his beetling eyebrows, lifts a mug of lukewarm coffee to his mouth as he waits for her reply.

He's all right, I suppose, says Fran, frowning because she does not know quite what to say, so goes on to explain the frown: He's quiet, does the work, does it pretty well now, he was a bit clumsy in the beginning but he's learned . . . I mean of course he has this Swiss pride in his work, you don't have to push him like the locals.

(I never had to push Satish.)

But?

Fran smiles. Sean often reads her mind. How did you know there was a but?

With you, Fran darlin', there's always a but.

Well, you know he worked in Bosnia during the war there, and he resigned toward the end . . . I don't know, it's as if he's absent— absent from here, absent from himself . . . as if he's left himself there. He's been here a month and I don't know any more about him than when he arrived. Except that he likes spaghetti.

She pauses, then continues, And there's something else: he just doesn't get it, metaphysically that is, just doesn't get what we're trying to do on the island. That's what's strange. He doesn't seem to care whether the place is full of monkeys or whether we get rid of the remaining acacia and now with what's happened to the mourner-bird . . . he just doesn't get it.

Sean looks down into his coffee mug, scratches his ear. I suppose it'd be what you call relative, now, he says thoughtfully. Egret's hardly a war zone, now, is it?

But it is! exclaims Fran. We are fighting—literally—for the survival of these species. Fighting against people and pollution and misuse and—

She breaks off. She is not ready to speak to Sean of what may be just nerves, or her overactive imagination. In any case she sees he is hardly

ready to listen when he replies, Ah, but there's a wee difference between your Mimi-birdie here and whole villages disappearing, love.

Fran looks with exasperation at Sean, then says, I don't mean to
belittle what happened in Bosnia, but this is a fight, too, I have a whole
species disappearing. We're here, they're why we're here, they're
what matter at the moment. That's *our* job, our war.

Sean pauses, taps the end of his spoon against the table. He loves to
see her like this, her eyes flashing; loves the way in which despite all
that has happened she has kept cynicism at bay. He knows that the day
he's had enough, the day he retires, she'll take over the whole program and probably bring the dodo back to life.

Look, love, he says finally, it'll be a personal, private thing. The
lad's seen things you're not meant to see, not ever. They'll be trou-
bling his mind . . . There's your difference, here, now. This little
fella in the box . . . even in death he's a pretty sight.

She, says Fran shortly.

Give the lad time. If he's doing the work . . .

I'm just so afraid he'll screw up. I'm afraid he'll do something
wrong and just shrug it off. What to him might seem an innocent
enough mistake could have huge consequences.

Stop your worrying. You'll only communicate it to him and make
things worse.

But Fran cannot stop worrying, and that afternoon when she returns to Egret she decides to take on more of the critical work—the
birds, the tortoises, a few of the plants—and leave the everyday dog's
work to Christian.

Thus he finds himself building a small aviary behind the warden's
house. It's the only way, Fran said tersely on her return from Black
River. I've got to keep the last pair in captivity at least until they
breed. I hate to do it but I think I have no choice.

The birds come willingly to Fran. They sit like falcons on her wrist, feed from her hand, settle their feathers against her skin. Ecologically naïve, she thinks; they are not afraid. That is how Mimi was caught. Slowly she places them, the female and her male, one after the other, in the new aviary. She tries not to liken its enclosed space to that of a prison, a coffin. They can see the sky, they can see the place they have known. She murmurs to them that if they are good randy birds and lay lots of eggs and make lots of chicks they will move again into their blue sky, above their treetops. It's for your own protection, she murmurs. Because you are too precious, and you don't know your own price.

Christian stands outside the aviary and looks in. He thinks he has built a fine prison, and sees a certain irony therein.

It was Hasan who said to him, You think because we are in prison and not massacred that we are still alive. Go, take this card I've filled out and tell the world I'm only in prison, I'm still alive. And what if they are keeping me here just to make the world believe that they are complying with international law?

Hasan was a small man, deep lines of farm labor in a still-young face, deep blue eyes, a square head. He lowered his voice and looked right into Christian's eyes and said, I spit on your law. They are killing us all the same. There will be none of us left in this town, in this valley, you will see.

Three years later all of Hasan's people were gone from the valley, driven, chased, exiled, convoyed, killed. Hasan had been released in an exchange of prisoners, and the last Christian had heard was that he was somewhere in Sweden.

Days of cool rain and low sky, water seeking roots, soaking earth, shaping captivity. Christian and Fran hardly leave the warden's house, seem to wander through days of dampness, leaks in the roof and in any sense of purpose. The birds huddle in the aviary, neither well nor ill; it is still early; there are no eggs.

Christian reads, Fran broods. She has nothing to read, and Christian's books—mostly thrillers and classics—are in French, which she speaks poorly. She writes extensively in her field notebook, as if trying to work out a mathematical problem. Christian, through the open door of his room, can just see her in the kitchen, and thinks there is a certain sadness to the set of her back, neck, and head as she bends over the table, writing.

My life, writes Fran, *seems stalled. Nothing evolves; nothing changes. But I know I'm waiting for something; I tell myself it's the birds. It is so important for Butterfly to breed: the idea that she could be barren horrifies me. When the season begins, will she reproduce? Sean has promised me that if she breeds he'll devote the time and money to capturing the birds in the wild so we can breed them all and maximize our chances. But I must succeed with B . . .*

And if I fail with her . . . It's become a personal thing: I cannot allow myself to fail. All I want from her is the odd egg, the eventual hatchling. She's a young bird, there is time still, but for me—what will remain of me if I cannot leave the fruit of my work to the island? This godlike endeavor . . .

At times I wonder if it would be better if I had Christian's quiet indifference after all. Of course he doesn't have a career at stake, he gave that up, fell from a great height, seems to be struggling with recovery. Keeps it all inside; yet I wish he would talk, would tell me what it was like there—the war, his work, how people managed. But it's as if by silencing his experience he can deny it; as if speech were proof of other lives.

I, too, silence what came before. What would happen if we were to share our hidden selves? Could we survive such intimacy? Do I want anyone to know what happened——who I became, who I was——or is it merely an unburdening I want, relief from the mirror of events?

But he does know some of the story, inevitably: who Satish was, why he was here, how he died. He drowned. A stupid accident.

Tell me about Switzerland, says Fran finally, to break the cycle of rain and separateness.

What do you want to know? asks Christian.

They are sitting together on the wicker sofa on the veranda, watching the rain, the moods of clouds, water reflecting sky.

All I know, says Fran, is mountains, cuckoo clocks, Heidi, chocolate, banks, and Swatches. There must be more; tell me the rest.

Christian lifts a corner of his mouth. You might not want to know the rest, he suggests.

But you, for example . . . working in a war zone, dangerous work, then here . . . what can possibly prepare you for such a life when you grow up in such a peaceful, affluent place, where nothing ever happens . . .

Christian lets out a laugh then says, It's because nothing ever happens, because the mentality is so enclosed that you go crazy, you need to get out . . . since we don't belong to the rest of the world and we're surrounded by big powerful neighbors, we have to seem harmless, agree to everything, remain neutral, offer to look after other people's money for them so they won't harm us . . . it's survival tactics, maybe. We're too small and the mountains can't keep our enemies out anymore. So we look after their money and sell them luxury watches, and they agree to leave us alone. Or seem to, at any rate.

Don't you ever miss it?

Again Christian laughs. You basically have two extremes with the Swiss. Some of them are quietly, fiercely nationalistic, xenophobic, and they love their country and defend it with rigid laws and conservative behavior. Then there are young people who leave, like me—we're emotional asylum seekers or whatever, voluntary exiles, but we need to live somewhere else, as far away as possible, in radically different places where things happen, where there's life. So you find us here, or in the States or Australia or Brazil. Big sky countries, with faraway horizons.

So you don't miss it.

He shakes his head, reaches for his cigarettes. I miss the cheese, he says finally and laughs, looking at Fran over the top of his glasses.

But there are times when he truly does miss Switzerland—the extreme domesticity of the landscape where he grew up, a promise of order in a chaotic world. Vines planted in strict straight rows, not one plant taller or thicker than the others; the village houses sleeping in a benign sunlight, their backs to the road, their shutters open onto a square or a courtyard, window boxes of geraniums splashing color into the daylight. Christian misses his country whenever a darkness settles inside him, a darkness more oppressive than any shadow cast by a mountain. He missed Switzerland when he was among the fields and mountains and rivers of Bosnia, because their green-gray Alpine beauty was both so familiar and heartachingly sad: as if the decor of his own childhood had been desecrated, redrawn beyond recognition.

But now that desecration is inside him, still, as he tries to joke with Fran (yes, he can almost taste the salt buttery tang of the Gruyère on his tongue), tries to be a different person, one who will be friendly and cheerful and sociable. But he finds himself struggling against his own words, flesh pulling against a scar.

This is the first time, thinks Fran, that he has spoken so openly. Even if it is to criticize, it tells me something about him.

So she asks him other questions, hopeful that they too will cause him to open up: Where did he grow up (small town on Lake Geneva), go to university (Geneva), does he still have family there (yes, all his family); but his responses confirm both the trouble-free nature of his Swiss life and the total lack of interest he has in the place.

Finally she says, Do you think you'll ever go back? and Christian shrugs and says thoughtfully, again with a touch of irony, To retire, for sure. It's safe and quiet and full of old people already.

And all this time, he is too reticent to ask Fran anything about herself.

The clouds lift, the rain stops. Floods of sunshine dry the earth with a steamy rush. Fran returns to work, Christian goes to the mainland.

From Mahébourg he calls Asmita. She is free after four; if he can pick her up at the restaurant she will take him to a lovely place on the south shore where there is no reef and the sea is wild; or would he prefer the botanical gardens at Pamplemousses? (It might still be rather damp, she says primly.) I think I'll take wild over damp, says Christian, and as he replaces the receiver he feels a forgotten boyish surge of happiness.

As soon as he sees her again, lithe and lovely, waiting under a coco palm in the car park, Christian knows the young woman is a gift. And a gift full of irony, he learns, as they drive bouncing southward: like many Mauritians, Asmita knows Switzerland. When she speaks of her visits to her uncle in Sion, or her summer spent training in a hotel school near Montreux, a trace of Swiss singsong harmonizes with the Mauritian lilt of her French. Christian finds it touching, and strangely moving. He sees the road ahead, twisting and narrow, but hears her voice. It enters him, and when she laughs, her laughter spreads, concentric ripples of delight and anticipation.

She guides him along winding roads through villages, past cane fields, then out again along the coast. He will not recall the names of the places or their sequence, but rather an impression of an exotic beauty due more to Asmita's presence than to any scenery: beyond the bougainvillea and cup of gold, the villages are shabby, *cases* made of cardboard and tin and concrete clustered among the filaos and palm trees, with their football pitches and one-roomed stores, their bicycles and stray dogs, and the green jewel of the lagoon never very far away. But then, as if suggesting an ironic return to another reality, Asmita directs him through a village, where they stop and leave the car behind; after a short walk they come to a cliff above a blue-gray ocean, a northern seascape. Asmita leans into the wind, her long braid whipped by a vicious wind, her face uplifted, her eyes almost closed.

I like it here, she says finally. There's no reef, it's the ocean, it's cold and full of danger. It's different. Some say that Gris-Gris means black magic.

Christian smiles. He would have found the place quite ordinary himself, were it not for her presence, her own subtle sorcery.

The restaurant is small and simple. Christian feels himself opening like a child in the presence of a favorite adult: safe, admired. Asmita talks volumes, pages turned by laughter; Christian sits back with his wineglass and listens, sips, nods, echoes her laughter. She has a big family, spread around the world and across the island, and her stories are many.

But then the question comes, as Christian feared it would, more a request than a question: I've told you all about my aunties, now what about yours? And Christian opens his hands in apology, laughs hesitantly. I haven't got a single auntie, I'm afraid. Asmita wags her head at him in reproach, until Christian accepts that he must give her some of his story at least. So he comes forth slowly, like a lizard from its hiding place into the sun. And the more he speaks, the more Asmita's serene, listening gaze encourages him. To her he can speak; she is not an employer like Fran, who might someday use his confession against him. His instability, his human frailty. Also Asmita is, despite her time in Switzerland, far from Europe—traditionally, historically far, and this gives him a freedom in his unburdening. But he will not tell her everything, only the essentials, only the things she might want to know, that might interest or amuse her. Only the things that he himself can let go of without unraveling the weave of sacred recollection.

Christian describes himself for Asmita: the quiet boy, single child of strict Calvinist parents (father a railway official, mother a housewife, both elementary school textbook figures of model, devoted parents); then the restless teenager, given to dreams of running away on a sailboat (to find the ends of the earth, he muses; perhaps that's why I'm here). The idealistic student who spent his summers in Central America studying tropical plants and experimental Marxism. Then the young graduate, whom Christian paints most fondly, in warm, bold colors, glowing with his humanitarian hopefulness, for he is still untried, and strong, and confident. Or naïve, he adds, and sees himself outside the imposing building of the ICRC on the Avenue de la Paix, the chance to change everything still before him, the road not taken, the sweet girlfriend who wanted marriage, the worried parents, the years of study— For what? said his mother, to deliver aid packets to heathens?

They trained him, sent him to the Middle East, to Iraq, to Afghanistan, wherever his skills as a neutral and impartial caregiver, hopegiver, could be used. He visited prisons, coordinated relief operations, negotiated with local warlords, mullahs, generals. Breaking through front lines to deliver medical personnel and supplies, he learned the fearlessness of adrenaline-masked fear.

It was a difficult job, he says to Asmita, but worthwhile. She is nodding, showing her concern and understanding (now that it is all behind him, now that the concern is for him, and her, alone).

But I could do it, he continues. I believed in it. I believed that I could still help people; that their conflicts were inevitable and perhaps for some of them even just, but anyway they were not my conflicts, and I was still an outsider, and most of the time, I was protected by an ancient code of honor.

There is a photo of him which appeared in a brochure: Christian as the benevolent outsider at the prison in Kabul amid the dark turban-framed faces, and he seems almost ridiculously bright and boyish with his official badge and his neat short (then) hair and mustache; he looks helpful, and the warriors look fierce, but he is there to protect them, care for them.

But now his words slow, and the self-portrait begins to blur, as if painted by an unsteady hand, with muddied paints, and the mud is the snow-slush road from Split, over the mountains, and already the memories melt together like emulsion burned by flames, and the flames are the villages burning. Christian takes a breath and looks up at Asmita and her face is unbelievably smooth and fine to him, and gives him some courage to go on.

He tells her how something changed in Bosnia. It was no longer only their conflict . . . it was no longer a strange place. He tells her how he used to go to Yugoslavia with his parents when he was a child, and now he was recognizing things the way you do when you have a long memory of them. An instinctive recognition . . . faces, the sound of the language, the landscape—everything was European, familiar. He did the work but could no longer find the distance in himself, and it was incredibly difficult, they were constantly under attack, the chief of the delegation was killed by sniper fire in Sarajevo. The ICRC actually left for five weeks, it was so bad, but then they sent them back in, and even then he thought of resigning. There was so much dread in his heart, and anger, and complete helplessness, and he realized that what was happening was that he was becoming one of them.

He pauses, and Asmita asks him to explain.

He sits for a long time, says nothing. In the distance there is a thunder of surf, the irritated squeal of a car horn. Asmita is no longer smiling.

Do I tell her, he asks himself; do I tell her the whole story, the easy explanation, the truth in fact, that when you love someone you can love her people; all their personal music resonates within you in a same chord and your emotions harmonize—only such words suggest well-being, and there was no well-being, her people were tearing each other apart in unspeakable ways; no, I cannot tell her this. I would have to explain what happened, expose my guilt, and loss. But there is something I can show her, and maybe it can be left at that. Maybe it will be enough.

Christian takes a sip of his wine and continues.

I was in a village near the front line in the spring of 1994. There was a cease-fire, and then the fighting began again, as if people had just had time to come up for breath before they were pushed under to drown. It was a Serb-held village, and the Serbs began driving out the last Muslim families.

I went to find the local commander, to protest. I found him in a house where the family had just been forced to leave, and he was standing there while a couple of his soldiers went through the family's belongings, looking for jewelry or electronics or even food.

They'd scattered a box of photos in a corner on the floor, and I knelt down there and looked through the photos and I felt too sick in my heart to say anything to those men. There were photos of children and teenagers and mothers and grandparents and local football teams . . . such ordinary photos, people standing in gardens or in the snow or on the beach, and I thought to myself that these people were gone now, and some of them might be dead, and the only record of their exis-tence, the only testimony, was these photos which the soldiers would soon destroy, and anyway they were meaningless now because no one who loved them would ever see these photos again. And you could re-peat this scene a million times, all over Bosnia.

Christian pauses, reaches into his pocket and pulls out his wallet, gestures to the waiter standing nearby. Asmita begins to say something when Christian takes a photograph from the wallet and hands it to her.

It is a little girl, perhaps seven or eight years old, blue-eyed, her frizzy blond hair held in braids. She is smiling, and in her smile there is a gap where she has lost her baby teeth. Asmita turns the photograph over, and on the back she reads, *Jasminka, Juli 1984.*

What do you think? asks Christian. Is she alive and well somewhere? I had to save her memory—and is it even her memory, since I never knew her? You'll tell me that in any case the little girl in this photo doesn't exist anymore, that she is or would be twenty-odd years old now.

Christian watches Asmita as she studies the photograph. She seems puzzled. Perhaps she does not understand: that we shed our different selves as we move through life. But it is the right to remember and honor those different selves which was chased from those villages, thinks Christian. The right to a history, to a continuity.

And the soldiers? asks Asmita. Were you able to stop them?

Christian waves his hand, reaches for the photograph. I protested, but it did no good. It was too late, anyway. The people had fled, or been taken away. They made me leave; they burned the house.

Christian looks down, pulls notes from his wallet, and hands them to the waiter. Then he looks over at Asmita, whose face is troubled, almost frowning, and says, Shall we go? He forces a smile, stands by her as she reaches for her bag, guides her gently by the elbow from the restaurant into the cool evening air.

You must try to forget, says Asmita gently.

Perhaps. People say that. Maybe it works for them. I can't forget, I don't want to forget. I just don't want to talk about it, that's all. I've said too much already.

Asmita is silent for some minutes, perhaps aware that this is something too large for her to understand, and that whatever she says will be wrong. To speak of other things seems wrong; to stay silent seems wrong. Finally she turns to him and says brightly, Thank you for a very nice evening.

Fran is enjoying Christian's absence. As the sun sets she patrols the island, singing, calling out to the birds, talking to the tortoises, swimming naked off a secluded shelf of rock in the lagoon.

In the house she puts a cassette of *La Bohème* into the old boom box, reheats some curry, pours a large glass of South African wine. She drinks moderately in front of Christian; his quiet presence inspires restraint and modesty. But now she sips and hums and sits on the veranda among the cicadas and stars as they click and twinkle in time.

It was hard, after Peter left, to be alone. To come home to the dark house on Shasta Road and turn the key, opening the door onto vacancy. In the beginning, she had been violent with herself, fueling her self-hatred, her sense of failure, eating too much, drinking too much, driving too fast, forcing herself into the company of people for whom she did not much care but who would distract her and prove to her she was not alone. It would be months, perhaps years, before she understood that her solitary self didn't need to be an enemy, that the enemy was the self who dressed and laughed and talked and wore makeup for others, for some social, collective conceit of what a Berkeley professor of behavioral ecology, divorced and approaching middle age, must be. That she could take her solitude and use it, might find in it a selfless, patient friend.

But Satish changed all that, again. Because with solitude she had been flying on drafts of spirit, pure intellect; because he reminded her of her wings.

The beam of headlights from the Land Rover traps a beast's eyes in fascination, two coals glowing in darkness. Christian slows the vehicle, waits for the animal to move. It is a monkey, curled in an insolent sitting pose on the tarmac; Christian finally stops the Land Rover. The monkey does not move. Hey! Get out of the way! he calls. It's rather stubborn, says Asmita. Christian blows the horn and the monkey slinks off into the dark cluster of trees, looking back at the vehicle with its shining eyes. Christian laughs, turns to Asmita; she giggles, nervously, eagerly, and Christian reaches up to her cheek with his hand, ever so briefly grazes her skin with the back of his fingers, then places his hand firmly on the gear stick, as the vehicle accelerates.

He does not know why he did that, for some minutes he chats with her, tells her a little bit about Fran and her hatred of monkeys. But he is thinking of Asmita's skin, the small patch of warmth he stole as his fingers passed.

He kisses her good night. Being Swiss and reserved and gentlemanly, he doses the kiss with just the right amount of interest and restraint; being a man he wants much more and fights his own self-control. How much of his desire belongs to him, to his emotions; how much to an intellectual or rational longing for solace, distraction, or company; and how much to that purely genetic instinct implanted to assure the survival of the species? Christian himself, having a melancholy Central European strain in his blood, would say it was solace he sought. Asmita has been raised on Indian films and is a true romantic young lady; she is not disinterested, she returns his kiss demurely in hopes of a future: more kisses, flowers, wedding marches, children, a respectable life with holidays in the Alps.

But if Fran, who is sitting now somewhat drunk on the veranda under the stars, were consulted, she would laugh and shout, Darwin! One hundred percent, nothing else!

Darwin, one hundred percent.

Before Peter, there had been a number of other men, students in high school, undergraduates, lanky thick boys with self-absorbed conversation and eager expansive bodies. She had indulged their bodies and tolerated their conversation, in the name of something she would call not love but hopefulness: the search for an ideal, the skewed and lonely belief that if she gave her body, showed her goodness, the love would follow. That was why we "fell" in love, wasn't it? With Peter indeed she finally found it; a collusion of ideals and pleasure that lasted for nearly fifteen years, its longevity propelled more by a lack of time together than by some romantic fuel. As if there were an allotted amount of love to any relationship; as if when that amount was used up, the ability to see the person opposite you as somehow different and special now failed, and you saw only an ordinary, emptied stranger and in Peter's case, a traitor.

But after her divorce Fran saw men differently: they were all expendable, animal, conveyors of sperm. Perhaps the loss of the romantic ideal was due to Peter's betrayal, but she liked to think it was her own maturity, her hard-won wisdom. There were not many men in her life—again, there was so little time, and she wagered more than ever on her career. But the sex, when it came, had changed, was more spontaneous and marvelously uncluttered with recriminations or explanations.

Nothing lasted: the men were either married colleagues or students fearful of discovery. And while Fran told herself such brevity was preferable, even desirable, she was powerless against the loneliness which grew like weed in the untended garden of her longings. If anything, loneliness was nurtured by those brief, tantalizing lapses of pleasure.

Mauritius came as an escape, a way out; Mauritius (who in Berkeley had ever *heard* of Mauritius?) was a way to confront loneliness, on a single front not mined with memories or familiarity.

She dozes on the old sofa on the veranda, her hands curled girlishly under her chin, her legs tucked up under the sarong she sometimes wears. There is a glaze of night upon her, a dew-blessedness of dream. Christian rouses her gently. He shakes her shoulder, warm beneath his palm. She smiles, as if she has been dreaming of lovers.

Christian is clearing underbrush, weeding on a large scale with a machete in the cool of early morning. Sleep was short and full of sweet tension, as if Asmita were there with him; now he thinks of her, idly, happily, a goddess of petty labors, helping him past tedium and effort. He sweats, wipes his brow with the back of his hand, allows fresh images of the young woman to grow large in his imagination.

And here is Fran, running down the path, skipping lightly past his piles of acacia branch, calling his name; her face is flushed, excited; her fingers curl around an imaginary space and she exclaims, An egg, we've got an egg!

And is she nesting?

Yes! At last! I can scarcely believe it.

Fran's face is a smooth globe of triumph and contentment. Christian holds his machete awkwardly, as if it should not be in his hands, as if the right thing to do would be to hug her, or dance around, but he merely says, Congratulations, Fran, that's wonderful, and he can hear her breathlessness on the morning air.

But that evening she comes to him and her expression is tense: will he keep watch over the aviary until two in the morning, when she will take over?

What's this about, Fran? The birds are protected, and they're in a cage.

She shakes her head and says softly, I'm afraid, Christian, after what happened with Mimi; I'm afraid . . . this egg is just too precious.

But who's to know there's an egg? Who apart from Sean even knows there's an aviary? I don't see—

Please. If you won't do it, I'll stay up all night.

No, no, it's all right. I'll do it.

Christian watches stars swinging overhead, wishes he knew how to find the Southern Cross. But when he asked Fran she said shortly, I haven't had time for stars. I'm a bird person, not an astronomer. And he finds it strange that for all her love of Nature she does not include stars. Next trip to Port Louis, he thinks, I'll get a planet finder.

But Fran knows very well where the Southern Cross marks its path in the sky.

Satish sitting next to her by the landing, pointing out stars, teaching her names and constellations, even in Creole when he did not know the English, telling her tales of childhood—the ancient Creole woman they called Matante, who would call out the names of the stars when her drunken husband did not come home at night, and she had learned them from a mad Jesuit, back in the dawn of time; or as a boy with his schoolmates drifting in a pirogue on the lagoon, lying on their backs and imagining the pirogue was a spaceship. Fran liked to think she could see the stars reflected in the lagoon, but it was only a wash of moonlight and the distant twinkle of Mahébourg.

But in her palm she could feel the tingling of stars where Satish's fingers rested gently, connecting her to the universe.

The island is full of shuffling, rustling, sniffling, clicking sounds, enhanced by night. And the constant thrumming rush of surf against coral, the island breathing. Like the resonance of altitude in the Alps: how you could hear everything, so clearly.

Christian listens to memories of sound. Silence of the mountains, distant clatter of gunfire; voices muffled by fear. He knows too much about enemies, knows their subtleties and simplifications: Colonel Vlatković, the bottle of brandy between them, passing a glass to Christian, hospitable, agreeing to all Christian's recommendations with emphatic nods of his head; his hard lipless smile, the handsome face, one might say, a good face for an enemy, and briefly Christian imagines Vlatković crashing through the underbrush of Egret Island with his AK-47 over his shoulder, and returning to his stronghold carrying Fran's fragile egg in his heavy hands, a trophy, a victory, a symbol. One egg on the black market could fetch ten deutsche mark; a rare tropical egg would be filthy lucre . . .

In the space between waking and sleep he treads a shifting, nebulous territory of improbable imaginings, often stranger than the dreams offered up by deep sleep; the dreams he does not have.

Fat lot of good you are, whispers Fran, shaking him awake.

He mutters an apology, gets up from the canvas chair. In moonlight Fran's expression is fierce, her eyes unusually pale. Come and get me if you're tired, he offers gently, but she pushes past him to the chair, plops down rigid in the seat. Sleep well, she mutters; Christian heads back to the warden's house, following the yellow beam of his flashlight as small nocturnal reptiles scurry out of his way.

In the morning Christian is again clearing acacia branches, preparing to fell the tree. Another memory of trees: looking out of the frost window of the delegation office, across a square, a young woman clumsily swinging an ax at a naked young oak tree as her small daughter watches, bundled in a ski outfit. He could hear her grunts as the ax hit the tree, but she was not strong enough, and finally she gave up, took hold of her small daughter's mittened hand, the ax and a few branches in her other hand. She will go home and burn books, or furniture, he thought: this is my failure, that I could not keep them warm, though that is what I was sent here to do.

Mother and daughter passed the window, breathclouds like ghostly reproaches on the blue air.

Christian looks out at the lagoon. A pirogue is slowly circling, not far from Egret Island. Two men. He cannot see their faces. Fishermen, no doubt: but something in the slow circling, no gestures of fishing activity, suggests they are observing the island. Christian walks down to water's edge, the ax in his hand. The pirogue turns again, slowly, then accelerates, cuts across the blue water toward Mahébourg.

Fran is buoyant, joyful. Her female has produced another egg. She sends Christian to Mahébourg to buy champagne.

Thus one evening in a rosy light Fran and Christian stand outside the aviary with raised plastic cups, toasting the plaintive twitter of two hatchlings. Christian has never seen Fran like this, raising her fist to the sky, letting out a war whoop that almost shocks his placidity. He wishes he could share her sense of triumph but knows his only contribution has been to build the aviary and keep watch over the captive birds.

Yet perhaps his watch-keeping has been vital: several times he has seen the pirogue circling in the lagoon, and once he thought he heard a sound of voices somewhere near the island, but could not tell whether it came from land or water.

On the trip to Mahébourg, Christian called Asmita, explained that he could not get away from the island, that his presence was indispensable while the bird was nesting. Asmita's voice held a pouting, almost pleading regret. She wanted to see him, she said, they had had such a good time together. Christian, as he put the phone down, having made no promises, realized he could do little else than drive Asmita around, take her out for dinner: she lived at home, and Fran so rarely left Egret Island. Perhaps it was better this way: he did not know the local custom, how free a girl like Asmita might be.

But now as he looks into Fran's radiant gaze, he thinks this might mean that soon the birds will be set free, and he will be released from his guard dog function.

These birds, explains Fran, are philopatric—home-loving. They don't migrate, they don't like to move away from their known habitat, and that's part of the reason there has been such a decline in population. They won't disperse; they'll stay within a few square kilometers. It's extraordinary when you think of it—everyone supposes birds should be able to cope anywhere, no? Freedom of flight and all that? Migration over thousands of miles? No. Not all of them. These birds set their own limits, fix their own boundaries. Even migratory birds go to the same places year after year, and get disoriented if the habitat changes or disappears. These birds are not comfortable elsewhere— why should they move? But over the last century they've been literally evicted—starved—from their homes.

What irony, then, that we have to imprison them temporarily in order to restore them to the place they belong.

If only, writes Fran, *Satish could have been here to see these little puffballs of air. To hear that peeping grasp on life: like a reward for all our efforts, not just mine.*

Christian stood there with me, and he was pleased, I know he was, gave me one of his rare grins, but he was pleased for my sake, or for the birds' sake, it was nothing to do with him, and today he's taken the day off, gone to Mahébourg.

And when he goes away like that, and I'm alone on the island, it's as if I'm waiting for Satish to return, as if he is the one who's only gone for the day, and into this space of thought left empty he comes, I can hear his footsteps on the veranda, light as a cat's, but I know he's there, the memories are all there, nothing's changed.

How do I, the behavioral ecologist, explain the instinctual reaction I have to his remembered presence?

This quickening——and he is only a figment?

What chemistry is this; how does the brain play God, creating flesh where there is none?

With Asmita, Christian is visiting the gardens of Pamplemousses. Tall, elegant palm trees form long avenues of shade. Christian points out flowers and plants he has not seen since his years as a student botanist: lotus blossoms and giant water lilies. Asmita smiles, but seems bored. Lovers come here, she says, casually. Then looks at him, gives him an almost cynical smile.

Yet once or twice he catches her looking at him with a strange possessive hopefulness. They are harassed by thin, eager young men who offer to guide them to the statue of *Paul et Virginie,* or to the tortoise with the shell-chipped-by-very-bad-stone-throwing-tourist, or the sex palm (an appropriate wink). Finally, exasperated, a thin mustache of perspiration on her upper lip, Asmita turns her head to one side and says, It's really quite warm, let's go for a drive.

In the Land Rover she relaxes, flinging her hands, relating anecdotes from work, while Christian concentrates on the road, laughing as he changes gear, frustrated that he cannot look at her. He sees cars and motorcycles, schoolgirls in their uniforms, women walking carrying children or bundles, but he is absorbed by the lilt in Asmita's voice, her rhythmic outbursts of laughter. They have no destination, and Christian navigates by poetry——a wave of Asmita's hand, To the left,

To the right. Towns on the map compose a poem: Ruisseau Rose, Nouvelle Découverte, Espérance, L'Avenir. Names, thinks Christian, which reflect the bright hopefulness of migration: Pink Stream, New Discovery, Hopefulness, Future. Mauritius itself, he thinks, a pure product of colonization and immigration. Do you know, he asks Asmita, where your family was from? Asmita replies vaguely, Southern India somewhere, but you know I am Mauritian, and I really get annoyed whenever I go abroad and someone thinks I'm Indian or Pakistani you know, my family has been here for more than a hundred years—how can I be Indian! Mr. Gandhi and all that. I would have been British if we hadn't obtained our independence!

Christian muses to himself that if Fran applied ethnology as she does ecology, she would include Asmita as an exotic imported species.

You know, he begins, on Egret we're trying to put everything back to the way it was in 1511 . . . Imagine if you were to try to do that with the whole world, for the sake of purity, authenticity . . .

Some people have tried, says Asmita glumly.

Yes, you're right, of course, I should know, of all people . . . but it's as if there were two laws of migration, one for humans and one for wildlife, and the fact that humans migrate for survival is considered normal, though less and less desirable to those who are surviving well enough . . . whereas animals migrate much less often, usually inexplicably, to us, but also for survival. And all the animal immigration on this island at any rate has been caused by man. The only natural migration, from Mauritius, has been extinction.

Don't start with that bloody dodo bird! There's a fellow who comes to the restaurant selling these hideous stuffed dodos and he goes around chirping in five languages, Famous dodo, *fameux dodo, oiseau disparu*! Such a cult for something which doesn't bloody exist, it's ridiculous. Or maybe people should be happy it's extinct so they can sell souvenirs.

But, Asmita, there is a bird which is going extinct before my very eyes, and it can't migrate, it won't migrate. It is totally dependent on us for survival.

So? It never would have started going extinct if it weren't for people in the first place. Personally I think it's a bloody waste of time and money—someone wants to turn your island into some Indian Ocean Galápagos, and all you'll get is bloody tourists tramping all over the place. Wait and see. Tourists are just cheap package colonists if you ask me. They are looking for their delusions of lost grandeur—their privileges. And anyway my family weren't colonists, they were practically slaves, brought here by the Brits. Where does that fit in with your migration theory?

But they came here to survive, no? Because they hoped for a better life?

Asmita sighs. What's wrong with that?

Nothing. It does fit in. Hope is just a human instinct, an emotion linked to survival, driving survival.

Asmita laughs. You're such an intellectual. You can't explain these things with words—they just happen.

It has begun to rain, a cloudburst of tropical intensity. Christian pulls over to the side of the road where a dirt track leads off into a thickness of neat, tender green bushes: a tea plantation. He stops the engine, and in the sudden silence of pounding rain and motionlessness they are muted by each other's presence, bereft of words. Things just happen. Hopefulness. Christian leans over to Asmita, reaches for her shoulders, feels the warmth of her skin like a sudden shock, her lips with his own a deeper shock, unquantifiable. He reaches for the long whip of her braid, removes its ribbon, releases the thick weave of hair with his fingers. Beneath this cascade of silk she seems insubstantial, delicate. With her delicacy she has power: to attract, to resist. She kisses him back, ever so lightly and tentatively, but guides his hands away, confines them with a whisper, Please, no. Christian restrains his desire, looks at her questioningly. She shakes her head, smiles, kisses him again, fleetingly, places her palms against his chest.

Christian had not known he would feel desire again so easily. Asmita, with her modesty and chastity, will fuel that desire. He has no experience of an older form of courtship, shaped by traditions of purity and restraint. Asmita can bewitch him with the simplicity of a kiss, fill him with the anticipation of all her secret charms, unknown to both of them.

Fran does not know about Asmita. She likes Christian's seriousness and reserve, thinks that perhaps he is *different,* although she of all people should know that there is no such thing. Women burned by the scorched-earth withdrawal from a relationship often shun sex, the other sex. Men rarely do: it's about biological accomplishment. That much Fran knows, empirically, objectively.

How then has she reached this notion of *different,* a label to be stuck to Christian's heart like the red-and-white badge he used to wear?

Because she needs to believe he is different. Because if she knew that at that moment Christian was sitting in the Land Rover engaged in the frustrated seduction of a lovely young woman, she might only congratulate the young woman for her modesty, while losing respect for him; she would judge him, she would no longer trust him.

But Fran does not know, and she is lying peacefully in the hammock Christian has strung next to the aviary, under an umbrella, listening to sounds of chirping in the rain. Leaves sway heavily, slick with wet, *bois de rat, bois de chandelle.*

Time passes, linear trajectories of pirogues on a closed lagoon. The coral earth grows warm in the sun. In her notebook Fran chronicles the nestlings' progress. Like a mother hen she defends them, an invisible shotgun at her side. She sees less of Christian, hardly leaves the aviary except to eat and sleep, briefly, between two stars. Christian continues to clear the degraded area of acacia trees, to keep watch at the aviary, to fetch supplies, and when time, or Fran, allows, to tryst with Asmita in the Land Rover on a forest-sheltered dirt track.

Do you like me? asks Asmita.

Of course I do.

How much do you like me?

If you would only let me, I would show you.

Asmita looks away. Then murmurs, You know I can't. You know it's against my religion. And my parents—

Christian caresses her cheek. And what would it take to make it acceptable?

Asmita does not answer, shakes her head, then reaches for him in a childlike embrace. Holds him, then says quietly, You know that there are still arranged marriages in Mauritius. And those women might never know what it is to love. Of course it's changing, we are a modern country, but before I am married, I want to be sure. Before it is too late.

Christian laughs gently and says, I don't think you'll ever need to worry about an arranged marriage.

Fran lifts the hatch to the aviary and reaches in. The birds look down at her, bright-eyed and puzzled. She puts her finger near the beak of one of the fledglings; he pecks at her, then bites gently, a nibble in curiosity. She laughs softly. Time to give you a name, she murmurs, and ring you and your brother. The bird makes a swooping, nodding motion with its head, and she laughs again. Then she strokes him gently on the neck. A human gesture of affection. These soft feathers in the place of skin or fur: do birds perceive touch? Is it pleasurable, or indifferent, this extraspecific gesture?

She spends the morning by the aviary, cleaning the cages and nesting boxes, tidying, checking that there are no holes or weaknesses in her frail fortress. She examines the birds, one after another, for weight change or abnormalities; they are all healthy, robust. She takes notes, humming to herself, and replies when one of the birds tweets or clucks at her. This is her unchanging routine, her stability. It fills her and satisfies her, and at the same time it has a gentle touch, like a fingertip upon feather.

Stars change position on a circle of sky. Fran is ready to release the birds from the aviary. For the occasion she has invited Sean to come down from Black River. Christian ferries to Mahébourg for champagne and fresh fish for the barbecue.

He leaves Chen Li's grocery with a bag full of bottles, canned goods, and a bag of ice, and heads for the market.

The market is a heady blend of smells and colors, voices calling, a rich offer of both freshness and decay. Strawberries from Zimbabwe; potatoes and greens from South Africa. Tiny fragrant bananas and pineapple from Mauritius. Fresh fish in wooden crates steaming the breath of the lagoon onto the close air. It is hard to obey a list, hard to confine oneself to choices, when the heat and color and smells, the exuberance of living things all cry out, Here, now! How can you choose? He looks at the faces of the vendors, brown and black, young and old, mostly men but the occasional older, round Creole woman; they smile and laugh and call to each other, abruptly changing their patter if they sense a sale. Christian looks not at the produce but at their smiles, as if they might help him choose, and they sense his weakness: ultimately it is the most beguiling and persuasive vendors who win his trade, and when he leaves the market he has a bagful of things he does not need.

The streets are crowded, if for no other reason than that they are small and narrow, and there are often no sidewalks, so when the young man touches Christian's arm he thinks merely that it is in apology, or crowding. Then he touches again, and Christian turns and recognizes Jean-Baptiste.

You still here? exclaims the young man. Christian gestures to his heavy sack, As you can see.

Oh! A party, I see. Celebration?

Sort of.

It is hot, and Christian can feel a rivulet of sweat cooling, tickling his back. Jean-Baptiste looks crisp in a white T-shirt with the small logo of a restaurant. Politely, in hopes of being able to move on, Christian asks him if he works in a restaurant.

Yes—he beams—I dance the *séga,* for tourists; you should come and see me. Then he seems to pause for effect and says, How is your friend from the restaurant?

Which friend?

Oooh—(a suggestive cooing, a knowing look) that *zoli mam'selle* from the restaurant near Chamarel.

Christian's heart sinks; he has wanted to keep his relation with Asmita as discreet as possible—avoiding Mahébourg or Curepipe; now it looks as if even the local lads know his activities. He says nothing but knows his sober face is answer enough; Jean-Baptiste continues, But we never see your *patronne* here anymore. Does she know you have a friend?

Christian feels a kind of helpless anger rising; he has no ready, smooth answers. He begins to move past Jean-Baptiste and says, I'll come to see you dance the séga when I get a chance. I'll bring the *patronne,* okay?

Good idea, mate! She'll like that.

At the jetty where he has left the dinghy, Christian meets Sean for the first time. Battered Panama hat to keep the sun off his bald pate; intense blue gaze under those bushy eyebrows; Irish speech which Christian sometimes finds difficult to understand. But there is a sympathy, perhaps a male thing: where thus far Christian has found relations with Fran strained and quiet, with Sean he feels an immediate ease. There is too a kind of soul-warming hospitality he has often found in Europeans who are not of the Protestant faith; a mysterious quality which makes him feel instantly more at home on the planet.

Sean shouts queries at him over the roar of the outboard—how does he like the island, how is the work, how is Fran doing. To all these questions Christian's answers are both vague and diplomatic, yet true: Fine. So he is surprised when Sean says, Well I'm glad to hear that, she was in a bad way for a while there. His surprise must show, because Sean then says, Not that you could ever really see it— she's a strong lass, is Fran.

The lagoon slides beneath the flat bottom of the dinghy, turquoise, cool. How much thought have I ever really given her? wonders Christian with surprise: would I even realize if there were anything wrong? He sees Fran in his mind's eye: a sturdy, unfeminine woman, yet boyish in a pleasing, disarming way. If he has not thought about her, has not thought about her personal life, it is because his ability to consider people in the light of the personal and the emotional was greatly diminished by his time in Bosnia, where the personal became urgently impersonal—an aid recipient, a numbered prisoner, a wounded patient, a victim, a statistic—and the emotional became unbearable. And Fran has shown herself to be neither a victim nor emotional— except when the bird died. And then, was she mourning the loss of the bird, or weeping frustration at the loss of her work?

She was in a bad way for a while there.

Disingenuously, not to seem too curious, Christian asks, You mean when the bird died?

Sean snorts. Not the bloody bird. No, I mean when Satish died. She thought the world of him. He was a born naturalist, a great help to her.

Sean pauses, looks toward the approaching island, then continues: It can't always be easy for you, coming along after him. Well, you wouldn't even be here . . . Still, Fran's a reasonable person . . . But if you ever have any difficulties—she can be blind in her love of the beasts—let me know and I'll see what I can do; I mean, technically you work for her, but I'm head of the program, d'you see what I mean?

Christian nods. Lowers the throttle, sends the dinghy into a smooth curving scythe to approach the landing. He cuts the engine, reaches for the mooring post, makes fast. Strains of opera filter through the trees to the men as they jump out. Sean looks at Christian and raises his brows: a party?

Fran is waiting for them on the veranda. She is wearing a sheen of excitement, an inner delight at the company and the celebration. She is also wearing a dress, short and tailored and simple in a coarse russet-colored linen; Sean turns to Christian, winks and nods approval. The veranda has been swept, old books and papers tidied away; plates, glasses, and candles wait on the low table. Christian pulls the bottles of champagne from the bag. Sean goes to kiss Fran on the cheek, a brief hug. Fran takes the champagne glasses, nods to them to follow, leads the way to the aviary. Flap and rustle of wings: the adult male sits expectantly, gazes at them; the young birds fly from branch to branch; the female hops in place. Sean and Fran exchange views, opinions, advice. Christian watches and feels himself recede, become remote, as if they are speaking a language he cannot understand, not merely technical but structured by passion. Passionate despite its dry catalog of the birds' functions and habits; passionate like the talk of young mothers comparing infants' feedings and bowel movements.

Now Fran is handing him an empty glass; Sean removes the foil from the neck of the champagne bottle. Fran stands by the closed hatch of the aviary, and as the cork pops from the bottle she lifts the hatch and they all cheer. The birds stare and blink, puzzled, in no hurry to leave. Fran fixes the hatch in its open position and walks over to Sean with her glass outstretched, smiling.

It's a sweet feeling, a small triumph. God knows there haven't been many, thinks Fran; and even now this is just hope, a gesture toward evolution, against extinction. Nothing is sure. One by one the birds leave the aviary, light flutter of wings, splash of color against the purpling light.

Splendid, aren't they, says Sean.

There is a catch in her throat, which she acknowledges and suppresses with irritation, to say, loudly and brightly, More champagne! We can sleep now, can't we?

She tilts her glass against Christian's, nodding significantly; he responds with a gentle smile. Sean looks from one to the other, raising his eyebrows; the ambiguity of her words lifts on a flush of champagne, dizzying, and she adds quickly, No more night watches.

No more bottles in the middle of the night, says Christian, and Sean mutters, Isn't that the truth of it.

But Sean's quizzical gaze was enough to penetrate Fran's hermetic world, enough to remind her of her own species and her own unnatural isolation. She looks at Christian, at Sean, at Christian again: they are men, for Chrissake, she thinks, but she won't be joining them in splendid flight. And they are looking at her, and talking to her, and saying all manner of funny things, and she is answering and pretending to be part of this conversation, and as they are walking back to the warden's house Fran feels her mind taking off, lifting splendid in flight above the coral earth, the *bois de rat* and the *bois d'ébène,* the aviary, the tin roof of the warden's house, lifting splendid in flight above her own linen-clad champagne-buoyant body, her mind in flight, looking down

on herself and on the two laughing men as from a great blue bird's-
eye distance.

Thus Fran's body continues alone on the island, drinking champagne, eating wonderful grilled dorado and *poisson sacré-chien,* laughing
outrageously, talking fascinating nonsense with Sean, with Christian,
fascinating because of the sense of lightness and release, nonsense because it will all be forgotten in the morning. And when Sean produces a
cassette of old Fred Astaire dance music, her body becomes Ginger
Rogers, whirling, stepping, swooping along the veranda in Sean's arms,
then swinging freely with one arm from the pillar of the veranda; this
body lighter than she ever thought possible without the weight of her
mind. Sean attempts a run up the wall of the house, stumbles backward; Your mind, she cries, let go of your mind, don't think about what
you're doing and you'll dance upside down! She pulls Christian up from
the sofa, berates him for being too quiet: does he prefer the tango? No,
he answers, confused; I've just never seen you like this.

Oh, come on, it's the champagne, I'll be a bitch again in the morning. Won't I, Sean?

Won't what?

Be a bitch.

That you will.

Fran nods. It's all nonsense anyway, she thinks, all words rising
bubble-empty on the buggy night. Suddenly tired, they will part, heading for their separate beds, Sean for the sofa on the veranda. The absence of their own voices, their laughter, will be oppressive to them,
heavier than sleep; they will wonder where they have gone, and why.

Christian wakes early in the gray-blue light. His head is throbbing, an
inverse champagne buzz. From the window he sees Sean sitting on the
edge of the veranda and calls to him softly, mouthing the word *coffee.*

They sit companionably, holding their mugs and their hangovers in mutual understanding. They speak in low, gravelly voices thick with sleep and a longing for cigarettes.

I've been out here nearly twenty years, Sean is saying. I've seen a lot of changes, not all of them for the better.

What about Fran? How long has she been out here?

Sean is surprised. You mean you don't know?

She didn't tell me.

And you didn't ask? He shakes his head. Five-odd years would it be now? Give or take. We had a local fella doing the island before that but he didn't work out.

You mean Satish?

Noooo, just a gardener sort of fella, he's up at Pamplemousses now. No, Satish was working out brilliantly—like I said yesterday, you'd not be here if the poor devil hadn't drowned.

What happened?

Ah, who knows. He just disappeared one day, never showed up after a trip over to Mahébourg; first they found the empty dinghy still chugging around the lagoon, then a few days later they found the body.

Didn't he know how to swim?

Aye he did, that's the strangeness of it, but he might have tired, depending on where he fell off; and they found a lot of alcohol in his blood. That was strange too, because Fran told him never to drink like that, and he respected her. But he'd fallen in with a fella from one of the hotels, a séga dancer, and Satish couldn't take the drink.

I've met a séga dancer . . . tell me more about it, is it worth going?

The national dance. A sort of Mauritian samba or what have you. Lots of the hotels organize séga nights for the tourists. You'll have to go along one evening and see it, it's good fun. Lovely women.

Christian wants to ask more about Fran and Satish but feels that Sean has deliberately changed the subject. So he is surprised when Sean says, He was the world to her, aye, but she was the sun and moon and all the stars to him, mother he never had, that sort of thing.

He pauses, then continues, I nearly lost her then. She just wanted to pack up and go back to California. Said she couldn't do it without him. So you see these two wee birds are an emotional victory for her too. She can move on now. Stop her grieving.

Christian nods, is silent.

Sean reaches into his pocket for his pack of cigarettes, holds it out to Christian. He shakes his head. No thanks, I've quit.

What, just now?

Yeah, just now.

You're daft.

There is a silence, then Christian asks, You're not married?

Aye, I'm married all right, kids 'n' all. Wife's back in Britain, it suits her better, doesn't it, comes out here for the holidays, I fix them up in a nice hotel . . .

You don't miss the children? Twenty years?

Well, they came out here at first but my wife couldn't stick it. Lasted three years. Too hot, too foreign . . . she's English, she missed the Christmas stuff, her family . . . The boys missed their mates, and Mary wanted to work . . . To be honest, I think she has another fella, has done all these years, but I help to pay the mortgage, don't I now. I live cheap enough out here, and the pay's decent . . .

Sean laughs, a hearty, cynical snort, then speaks more quietly. And yourself? Shouldn't you be getting hitched?

I was going to, says Christian very softly. We were going to, but she disappeared, in the war.

Oh, I'm sorry, lad. That's terrible. Terrible.

Then he adds, thoughtfully, Does Fran know that?

Christian shakes his head. I—you're the first person I've told. Here, that is.

Sean sighs, shakes his head. No good keeping it a secret, man, it'll eat you up. Talk to Fran. You've been through the same thing. You need to talk. She'll understand.

Christian nods, gives a half smile, pulls on his mustache as if he might find some strength there. Because he knows he won't talk, can't talk, not to Fran, or even, really, to Sean; can't talk and he'll need all his strength to live with the silence.

Christian's mother was the type of tidy, pragmatic Calvinist who threw out his clothes and toys as soon as they were worn or damaged beyond repair (his mother, patiently darning). Photographs were considered narcissistic and expensive: there are few. Mementos were clutter. Heirlooms, nonexistent: Christian's grandparents had been poor, at a time when there was still such a thing as poor, working-class Swiss. Christian himself has slept on four continents in hostels and campsites, traveling light. His photograph of Jasminka is his most treasured possession.

Fran, however, is a different story. Like most Americans, she had built a huge monument to herself in the form of her house on Shasta Road, full of photographs, mementos, heirlooms, antiques, old vinyl records, dusty hardback books, and her dried wedding bouquet. She had a baby grand piano; she could hardly play, but if nothing else it reminded her of the moment of triumph when Mrs. Rosenberg said she could play in the school recital at the end of the year. A short piece by Schumann that she would never forget, a piece she would play on evenings when the fog came in on her loneliness.

But when she left for Mauritius she sold everything that others could use, donated her books to the library, sent her photographs (Hawaii, the river-rafting holidays, camping in Alaska) and heirlooms (a grandfather clock, some old silver pieces, a nineteenth-century landscape painting, darkened and gashed by time) to an old college friend back east. Now on Egret Island she keeps nothing, only her notebooks and, like Christian, one photograph.

Fran's photograph is not of a stranger but of a young man. One brown face like thousands, one face in a thousand, smiling to her with that perverse ability of photographs to defy time, to defy mortality.

But neither Fran nor Christian knows that they are both one-photograph-keepers. Sean knows, and has hinted at it, but it will be some time before Fran and Christian discover that they share a way of moving through the world.

Christian pauses in what he is doing, removes his glasses, wipes them on a corner of T-shirt. He finds himself doing this whenever he wants a cigarette. And then, because cleaning glasses is a reflective, soothing, circular, rubbing motion, he finds himself thinking of Asmita. And wondering when he can next go over to Mahébourg and drive up to the restaurant to meet her.

Fran, however, now that her fledglings have grown and have returned to Egret's wilderness, turns her attention to more mundane things. The bill from the local service station in Mahébourg, for example. A marked increase in petrol consumption.

I don't mind, she says to Christian, if you drive around, but I'll have to take it out of your pay.

Christian, despite his brilliantly polished glasses, feels his gaze blurring, an inability to focus. Fran is looking at him over the half-glasses she uses for reading, and her eyes are accusingly clear. And she flashes him a half smile, bemused, until she begins to laugh outright. Come on, she says, how many times can you visit the sands at Chamarel? What's her name?

Asmita, says Christian, caught off guard. And he wonders, as he registers Fran's shrug, if this will make things harder between them; remembers Sean's words of advice. But he cannot bring himself to talk about Nermina, especially now, when Fran might view his time with Asmita as a betrayal; when he himself feels he is betraying something.

So he rushes headlong into his desire to see Asmita. Waves good-bye to Fran, calls out again, Sure you don't need anything?

Christian has filled the tank, and already he imagines her skin, the small, tempting tastes she gives him, salty-sweet. The sky above the road, beyond the cane fields and the casuarina trees, is a brooding gray, rain-making. He recalls her skin, but then suddenly he thinks of Nermina, how precious little they had of each other's skin: coat-covered, cold, unwashed. But it did not matter, then; it was enough to be together, alive, able to talk and look into each other's eyes for reassurance when all the rest was falling apart.

He needs, in the loss of his humanitarian idealism, to believe that somewhere there is more; the proverbial reason for living. If he loved Nermina it was because she had no fear, and in the space created by that absence of fear she was able to embrace others. If he loved Nermina it was because she saw beauty everywhere, even when it was most violated. Because she herself could scatter seeds of beauty: courage, dignity, the small, noble gesture. Or so he had to believe. To keep on going, for her sake, as she kept on going for her people's sake.

~~~

In the darkness, bursts of light day-bright against the window, singeing the doorframes. And the pounding of the big guns, ear-shattering, masking moments of silence with a loud ringing echo in the ears.

There were sandbags against the windows, and from time to time the rush-sound of sand leaking grew strangely loud against the ringing silence. They lay on the floor of the office, holding hands, holding fear, knowing they would wait all night for sleep, if then; they might be needed. Nermina was shivering—with cold, with fear; the harder he tried to hold her, to protect her, the more she shivered. He did not know, yet, that she was shivering with love.

They told each other childhood stories. That is when Nermina told Christian about her trips to Plitvice with its lakes and waterfalls, and how they would play in the waterfalls, childhood-bright, running from one cascade to another along the lakes, in the heat, and how she lost the others and was found by an elderly couple who fed her pork crackling cakes and taught her card tricks and took her back to the campsite flushed and fattened with stories of Tito's partisans.

And Christian told Nermina about trips to the mountains when there was so much snow they couldn't leave the chalet for days, and he would go to the little dairy with his sled and buy fresh milk still warm from the cow and waste spoonfuls of it just to watch the craters it would melt in the snow.

Then in the midst of the telling a different sound struggled against the ringing: faint, then louder, then faint again, a sad, desolate sound, from the street. Christian peered through a chink in the door, and in the light of a fire stood a small boy, crying for his mother, his father, anyone who would take him from this terror printing itself on his memory of childhood. It's a kid, said Christian, what the fuck—

Nermina was already gone, already running past him, through the door, like a mad messenger into the darkness, silhouetted against the fire; Christian never had time to stop her and she was out there, swifter and braver than he was, than all of them were, grabbing the boy, running again not to safety but to a lesser danger, the danger where Christian waited, loving her more than ever, against all odds.

Asmita is wearing a short, tight, coral-colored linen dress that turns her skin a deeper brown, lustrous. Christian feels his lust like an appetite, insatiable. I could eat you, he murmurs as she climbs into the Land Rover. Mango-woman, he murmurs, kissing her neck, shifting gear.

He has a girlfriend, writes Fran. *All this time he's had a girlfriend, and I suspected nothing.*

Am I surprised? No. Male behavior pattern. Disappointed? Yes. I thought he was different. Even if I know the way a male—of any species—is supposed to behave, I always hope the male of the human species will use those specific faculties which make him human *to change the more animal sides of his nature. Or that experience will teach sensitivity, restraint, et cetera, et cetera. I make exceptions to my own rules, though, don't I, in the case of human beings; I had years of practice, with Peter. Because I wanted so badly to believe.*

But why this disappointment? Why do I even care? Is it because he sleeps in what was Satish's bed? Because Satish really was different?

Fran remembers how it began. How from her telling him he began telling her, teaching her, showing her.

There were little scraps of things that she might take for weeds or windfall, cracking dried brown or mottled green or pods or seeds or wooden stones, and he would lay them out on the kitchen table and call her over, *Guette ça,* he'd begin, in Creole because he was excited, and almost forgetting himself, then in English he'd explain that this little wooden stone was a seed from the tambalacoque, and some people believed that it had once been spread all over the island, all over Mauritius, thanks to the dodo bird, who would swallow it and churn the thick husk with its powerful gizzard before releasing the actual seed to the soil . . . And other small treasures, and whence they came, and where they might go.

There were voyages of discovery, to the other side of Egret Island, to show her where a seed had found a niche, shooting a young sapling toward the sun. Or by the lagoon, where a crab was scooting widdershins along its coral homeland. And city-bred, TV-fed Fran was never bored, never tired of Satish's discovery journeys, because the warmth in his voice and words was like the warmth of the sun, nurturing and vital, and she could feel the transformation within her like a physical well-being, like pale skin turning brown.

They shared life on the island, in the warden's house, companionably, naturally. As if they had always known one another. They knew the limits of discretion and privacy; they knew too when to interrupt was not to disturb but to share. Sharing became a giving game, each one eager to outgive the other, to be the first to do a chore, make a meal, bring a surprise.

Then one day Fran was doing laundry and musing. What lovers do, mused Fran. The mundane—here I am washing Satish's shorts—is made into a sort of sacred ritual.

She lifted Satish's shorts from the red plastic basin. Thick dark khaki, pocket-heavy, dripping soap bubbles, slippery stiff wet cloth. Fran's hands wrinkled and rough from the soap. A small stain on the left leg she had been scrubbing, lovingly.

Too late, she tried to retreat from the word, to go back to her mundane scrubbing, tried to empty the word of meaning. The power of an adverb to change scrubbing to ritual, innocence to realization. *Lovingly.*

At first, she panicked. So she scrubbed harder, trying to make the stain of the word disappear. Then she thought, Accept it, love's an illusion, you'll know as soon as you see him, when this feeling will vanish.

So she went to look for him, and found him sitting by the lagoon with a fishing line, and his dark eyes turned to her in greeting. She looked at him for a moment, said nothing, and knew. Despite all her learning, all her experience and cynicism, life could still offer wonder.

Satish looked at her, still waiting, and his expression grew troubled, puzzled. Fran did something she had never done in her life: she allowed an impulse to formulate, and she obeyed the impulse. She knelt next to Satish, and kissed him.

Satish returned her kiss, shyly at first, then more eagerly, laughing, teasing, *Fran, what are you doing—*

Be quiet, hush, hush, she said, and took his face in her hands, his cheeks remarkably cool, firm and soft at once, and his laughter stopped, he gave in to her gestures, to silence, briefly forgetting, until Fran suddenly held him away from her, firmly, shaking her head and muttering, I'm sorry, I've lost my mind, forgive me.

She stood up and ran back into the shelter of trees, her cheeks burning, her lips sweetly bruised; ran back to what she thought she knew, thought was safe and familiar. The image of Satish was there, his astonishment, delight, sadness, a kind of wondering reproach in his dark eyes, his lips slightly parted as if seeking to retain the kiss and the surprise.

She ran into the warden's house and threw herself on her bed, curled in upon herself to contain the throbbing and the madness, but knew even as she did this that she was deepening the wound, swelling the love. Knew she should be walking through the island to see what needed to be done—check on the orchids, feed the tortoises—all simple, safe, practical things, but she also knew Satish had surely done all that already, and it seemed like a greater madness to her mind (orchids? tortoises?), inflamed as it was with his image.

She lay on her bed until dusk, wondering what to do next. I am deranged, she thought. I am nearly twice his age. I am his employer. I am from a different world—I need the barriers, I need to keep things as they are. How can I continue to work with him if I allow a male-female relationship to come between us? We will compete, we will disagree, we will use professional responsibilities as weapons in our personal struggle.

But each time the thought subsided, each time her reason re-treated, his face was there, his cheeks in her palms, his lips just there, just there waiting, curious, offered. Hardly a memory, after all, too brief, too recent, for that. Almost a dream, a fantasy, yes, said Fran to herself finally, it didn't happen, I imagined it, I lust after him, perhaps that's all right, perhaps that's normal. I don't love him, I can't love him.

She stood, walked out to the veranda. The sheen of the lagoon was changing with nightfall, the green of turquoise draining away as the yel-low sun disappeared, leaving a clear, silver brilliance. Fran stretched, felt weakened yet triumphant: she was still stronger than her nature. Tempted, perhaps, but ultimately sensible. There would be no more lapses. She was a professional, reasonable woman.

Satish did not have supper with her that evening. She heard the sound of the outboard just as she sat down to her plate of spaghetti; she pushed away her disappointment. Then pushed away her plate: she was not hungry. She went to bed early, and in the morning he was there, making tea, and she was herself again, cheerful, firm, and distant.

But of course the kiss changed everything, the way kisses do. Some kisses, at least. For some a kiss was the threshold to the creation of a new member of the species. For Fran, this time, it was a physical ges-ture which would come to symbolize a whole belief system, a faith which could change her life.

Asmita leans with her head against Christian's shoulder. She stares off into the trees, her fingers rub against the veins on the back of his hand. His head is thrown back against the headrest; his eyes are closed.

What are you thinking? says Asmita softly, dreamily: perhaps the sweetness of her voice will gain her entry into his thoughts.

Nothing much, says Christian, without opening his eyes.

It is true that Christian is not thinking about much. Rather, he is letting images enter at random to flicker against the screen of his mind, like an old silent film, poignant and full of contrasting planes of light and shadow. Faces, poplar trees on a hillside. Then a woman's skin, her deep brown eyes, a wretched memory of parting.

You know what I'm thinking? says Asmita in response to his vagueness—as if thinking for both of them—I'm thinking how lucky I am to have met you.

Christian responds, now, by squeezing her fingers. (But Asmita too is hiding things, her thoughts mysterious even to herself. Her certainty, her faith that somehow her strength will bring its rewards; she is lucky to be so serene, and still innocent.)

Fran knows about us, says Christian suddenly. And people in Mahébourg know.

Asmita sits up, looks at him. What people?

This fellow I met in a café—he seems to follow me around; his name is Jean-Baptiste, a séga dancer, do you know him?

Asmita frowns. Why would I know him?

Mauritius is a small place. I thought you might.

Asmita stares out the window, brooding. I thought no one knew. My parents must not find out. No one must know. Why did you tell Fran?

I didn't. She asked. Because of the petrol. She's my boss. Do you mind?

Asmita says nothing, but it is clear from her frown that she does mind. Finally she says, She's a strange woman, your boss. Really strange. If you could hear what people say about her . . . Is it true?

Is what true? What do they say?

That she seduces young men and makes them eat the birds' eggs?

Christian begins to laugh, holds for a moment an image of himself pinned against the wicker sofa, Fran leaning over him with a spoonful of runny yolk and a wicked gleam in her eyes. Poor unsuspecting Fran.

Not true at all, he says. She's a good woman. She cares about her work.

Asmita giggles and says, Then that's strange, don't you think?

What's strange about it?

Asmita moves closer to Christian, smiles. I think a woman should care about other people, not birds.

You really believe that? You think that because she cares about birds she doesn't care about people? She can't do both?

Does she care about you?

He laughs and says, If you put it like that, I doubt it. Then he pulls her closer to him, says jauntily, And do you care about me?

Of course I do, you know I do.

Later he drives her home, to Curepipe, where she lives with her sisters and parents in a modest house with a small courtyard garden dominated by coconut palms. Christian has never met Asmita's family, has always assumed he never will, because meeting the family would imply a commitment to marriage. They always kiss good-bye well before reaching the town, and he usually drops her off at the corner; now Asmita touches his hand, furtively. Then she opens the door to the Land Rover, slips out, lets her fingers slide over his hand again, slowly. Her eyes full of warmth, insistent. Christian watches her go, watches the source of his well-being turn and walk down the hot street in twilight: mango dress, her long legs moving with an inborn grace, a tropical grace, languorous, unhurried.

Briefly, it is as if his whole future is walking away on those legs, with that rhythmical gait, down that little palm-guarded street. As if he feels there is nothing else he wants in the world more than to watch this woman walking, this woman calling all the evening sun to light her way, golden sorceress. He does not move, leaves his hand loosely on the gear stick, listens to random sounds: dogs barking, a distant throb of motorcycle, children calling. And then another sound rises on the air, haunting, like a lament: the muezzin's call to evening prayer from a nearby mosque. Christian's hand tightens against the gear stick. This is the first time in many months, the first time in Mauritius, that he has heard the muezzin's call. He leans forward, his head against the steering wheel, the rush of his past pounding not with distinct images but as a vast emotion let loose in his brain, Afghanistan, Iraq, but more lately, more resoundingly, a deep concentration of his despair, Bosnia.

His hands tighten around the steering wheel: the Land Rover is moving, speeding backward in time, back through a blur of faces, Nermina, Vlatković, Dubravka, whir of cities, Mostar, Jajce, Bihać, plundered towns, minarets leaning shell-split over the sun-charred bones of nameless villages.

Allahu Akbar, God is great. Christian invests the foreign words, the foreign faith, with a meaning the Prophet never intended. Music evokes. Memory calls to prayer. Christian shivers until the street goes quiet again, lifeless.

California. The road to Sonoma: hills like the flesh of a newborn puppy. There are times when Fran grows homesick, when she wearies of tropical heat, cyclones, amiable chaos. Times when she longs to flee to the familiar, to flee from the loneliness. But in flight you always leave something behind; you create a new homesickness. Fran thinks she fled from California to annul her marriage and advance her career, but loneliness drove her. To flee Mauritius would be to exchange one ascetic's cell for another. For those who are seeking refuge from their own lives the only true reckoning is within, and Fran, with her degrees, her years, her experience, knows this.

Hills like the flesh of a newborn puppy, golden brown in summer, soft as fur. In Mauritius the hills are either gentle (round curves of tea plantations) or rugged and sharp, les Trois Mamelles, la Montagne du Rempart, fantastical shapes luring sailors and adventurers. Egret Island is flat, so Fran must look to the mainland for contour, to its steep mountains, purple-black against the afternoon sun.

Fran grew up in New England and went to California to study. It was a place of possibility, free of restraint and rigidity and snobbishness. It was the edge of the known world, hence, the beginning of another. Was it the ocean-borne fog which brought intimations of elsewhere— vapors of the mysterious East—and inspired thinkers, philosophers, scientists, Nobel laureates; poets, gurus, tarot readers, and crystal gazers? There was room for all of them. They gathered on chilly summer evenings on hillsides overlooking the Bay, sipping Chardonnay, smoking joints; they had questions, and sometimes answers. Fran, increasingly, had questions. She flew into the fog to travel halfway around the world for her answers; but she has found no answers, only more questions. Must she go back to California?

But the birds are here, and they need her. Her work is not finished. Her loneliness, since Satish's death, has grown tropical and lush, the loneliness of enforced solitude. In Berkeley her solitude was, at times, a choice, a form of mourning for her past. Now, perhaps, she could have friends again there, move beyond the bitterness and voluntary asceticism. But she is here, and the birds need her.

Christian does not need her. As long as he too was alone, she was comforted in her solitude. Less alone, as it were; another monk in the monastery. But now he has companionship, and pleasure. Mauritius is a small overcrowded place, Egret even smaller; there is no room for others, and Fran despises promiscuity.

She thinks of the middle-aged Franco-Mauritian man she met that time, early on, what now seems so long ago; she wonders if he is still here. But immediately rejects the idea; it was only to please some societal conformity within her, some vestige of what once seemed a logical dream.

Thus there are moments when she misses the wrinkled hills of California, the vastness of America, when she is filled with a desert-wish.

Satish used to ask her about California. Did they have *oiseau-kondé* and *poisson-capitaine* in California? Did Hollywood make as many films as Bombay? Were there lagoons in California, and macaques on the roads (skunks, said Fran); were there tropic birds and kestrels and mynah birds? Did they have four religions, and four races, like Mauritius? Did the markets sell a hundred kinds of tea, like the famous vendor at the covered market in Port Louis?

To Satish, Mauritius was a universe; it was all he needed. Still, she said to him, I'll take you to California someday. It's beautiful, you'd like it there.

But even as she said it, and Satish was shaking his head, uncertain, she knew her offer was based on a sincere yet misplaced generosity: she wanted to be able to give to him, but what her country had to offer, for all its beauty and grandeur, was not something Satish either needed or wanted. California was strong, vital, brutal—it could crush souls. Vast as it was, 34 million people competed there for space and survival, for success. The simplicity of mere existence was absent; respectable poverty, saved by dignity, was absent. Satish would sense this, and question it; would feel beholden to Fran for everything. Already, once when she was trying to explain the competitive difficulties of an academic career, he shook his head and said, I think that maybe someone let loose a lot of mongooses in that university of yours.

And you think it's not like that here? Probably worse, it's so small. Besides, competition is part of human nature, just as for animals.

Then he said something which astonished her, something sad and misguided and prophetic all at the same time. If human beings stayed where they belonged, he said, and didn't go running around trying to be better than what they are, than what Nature made them, maybe they'd get along better. Maybe they'd survive better. There'd be room for everyone.

And you, Satish? Just being here, aren't you trying to make your life better?

He shook his head. No, this is my place. This is where I belong. If other people see things differently and think I'm trying to be better than what I am, then that's their problem.

Fran, remembering this conversation, thinks how well Satish knew himself, but also how naïve he had been. He could not see the dangers around him, could not see that his very gifts might be a source of envy to others. That there were others who resented his position, saw it not as a return to the place he belonged but as an effort to step up, to find a niche in the prosperous, capitalist West as represented by Fran and the foundation which supported her. In simpler terms, even on a wage modest by American standards, Satish was making more money than most young Mauritians of his background could ever dream of.

Perhaps those envious people knew something about why and how he died.

What is ambition? wonders Fran. Will I be a department chair some-day, when I publish the findings of my experimentation and research here? And Christian—will he regain a sense of ambition once the wounds have healed over? Is ambition the striving for more than mere survival? Animals have no ambition—where did ours come from? Or is it part of survival, our means of hoarding, protection against a bad win-ter, a hurricane, an act of God?

Fran patrols the island at dusk, sentry duty. She is like a country doctor, making calls, checking on the health of patients. All are well, quietly prospering and growing. First her eyes scan earthward for ev-idence of new growth; then her gaze lifts, looking for the birds. A kestrel circles against an evening sky darkening with storm. The pi-geons preen and confer in the branches of the *bois d'ébène*. She visits the tortoises, who acknowledge her presence grudgingly, like old, in-firm gentlemen resenting the youth of their nurse. Fran talks to them, tells them her day, slices open their papaya dinner with her Swiss Army knife.

She is walking back to the warden's house. It is almost dark. She can hear an outboard in the distance; perhaps it is Christian. She will be glad of his company tonight. Again she resents that he has found di-version and fulfillment elsewhere; there will be less room for her in his life. These are the secret, self-centered thoughts which Fran al-lows herself in the safety of her mind as she walks home. Absorbed, she almost misses the crushed pieces of shell by the path.

A few scattered pieces: she recognizes the kestrel's eggshell. There is a nesting box not far from there. She examines the shell: there is a trace of the egg itself, as if a meal had been interrupted. Predators, thinks Fran. Therefore, the scampering sound indicates she just missed the beast. But there are no beasts on the island, they have seen to that, carefully and thoroughly, eradicating shrews, rats, mice. No small mammals of any description, in accordance with the island's original, prehuman ecology. A mammal must have been planted, therefore: captured on Mauritius and brought over at night, let loose to rampage amid Egret's fragile bounty.

Fran swears, beats her fist against her thigh. Nature, she thinks for the millionth time, has its own set of rules: that I can deal with. For all its arbitrary cruelty it has a certain logic. Chaos has its own reason. But if this is human meddling—it's utterly unfair, and I'm their intended victim. So why can't they just leave my work alone, and go after me if they have to?

Fran is frowning at Christian, at his extreme calmness, his lack of anger.

And? she says finally. And?

He feels uncomfortable under her angry gaze, as if he were somehow responsible. As if he hadn't done his job properly; as if by virtue of being a man he was inherently guilty.

A trap, she barks finally. You've got to get one from Sean, he'll have spares. We need to set a few traps. It might be a mongoose, even a monkey. First thing, okay?

Sure, answers Christian. I'll take care of it.

Fran lies awake listening to darkness, listening for sounds of scurry, pillage, predation. On the screen of her insomnia she sees battalions of mongooses, regiments of macaques; she sees dark-skinned generals in their regalia, anonymous behind their dark glasses, commanding their forces. And herself all alone, armed only with ideas and knowledge, with none of the cunning or ruthlessness of a mongoose, or of a man with an agenda.

She could go to the police. She could say someone has been trespassing with a mongoose. But they would laugh at her, tell her the island is not private property. Broken eggs? Oh, someone wants an omelet, or a *rougaille dizef.* A tasty specialty, have you tried it?

She knows their jovial indifference. Remembers the policemen who questioned her after Satish's death: their staring courtesy, their cheerfulness, their gently mocking insensitivity.

She'd give anything for a California park ranger, who would nod and take notes and make calls on his two-way radio and say "ma'am" to her; she'd give anything for someone who might believe her and take her seriously.

Campaigns in California, protect the spotted owl, the redwood tree: a long tradition of respect and seriousness. Is it a first-world luxury, wonders Fran, the natural result of our ill-gotten wealth, our surfeit, that we can turn our attention back to birds and animals and plants? Mauritius is not doing badly, in fact it is doing very well in some ways, but it takes a long time for mentalities to change, regardless of the economy. People's priorities: *farata* on the table.

Then who has the time, the luxury, to be planting predators on my island? And why?

Circle, circle, Fran's thoughts, like the childless kestrel, restless and seeking, afraid to land, afraid of truth. Circle, circle, her restlessness, her struggle against resurgent emotion. Keep it in. Don't think about Satish, about why he died. An accident. He drowned. *Did he fall, or was he pushed?* Hands pushing, hands crushing bone and feather. Hands holding sleek fur bodies of mongooses.

Whose hands?

Sleep, Fran, sleep, stop this whirling of thoughts and fears. You need sleep, for cunning. Your only ammunition.

Christian, too, is sleepless, listening to the same nightnoises, wondering not what they represent but where, in this curious detour in his life, they are taking him. As if the island were a vessel—Dutch brigantine, Portuguese man-of-war commanded by an irascible captain, at the mercy of moods and emotion in place of wind and current.

Asmita, port of call, safe harbor, anchorage against a storm? He seeks refuge in the lee of her chaste kisses and their promise. But is it love? Is love not certainty, in the eye of the hurricane, not of safety or survival but of immortality?

Christian enjoys the drive to Black River. He has been there a few times before, with Fran, but Sean was always absent—at the university in Port Louis, or in the dense wilderness where his birds lived, or out on his boat, fishing. Christian does not expect to find Sean at home even now, but he is relieved to be on the road, to be away from Fran's outbursts of paranoia.

He is not sure what to believe. The eggshell was there, evidence; she showed it to him at first light, so eager was she to push him into action. And although her arguments are sound, and although he believes they will indeed find a mongoose or another small predator on the island, he is loath to believe it is part of a plot.

Fuck, he thinks, addressing Fran, I lived for four years with a constant enemy whom I could see and hear and even smell; I came here to get away from that fear. Now you're going to have me believe I'm threatened by a silent, odorless, invisible enemy who plants mongooses in the place of land mines? It's ridiculous.

Christian drives fast, shaving the edge of the road, the edge of the forest. He has grown used to the Mauritian style of driving now, has learned its inner logic of fatalism and pleasure. His anger shifts gears, impels him into a sense of release and relief. If Sean doesn't keep him, there might be time to visit Asmita at the restaurant.

The sky is dark, threatening rain. The forest moves, vibrates with wilderness. It oozes a rich humus of smells: black volcanic soil, rank decomposition, fragrant young growth. In silence it would ring with choral chatterings and whirrings, clickings and murmurings of wind and creatures. Cries, shrieks even now pierce the engine noise and the rubber-tread swish of the tires on the road. Christian pounds his palm against the steering wheel, full of an abundance of hormonal longings and adrenaline which rush through him, stirring uneasy memories. That gut anticipation when he would head off in the Jeep looking for Vlatković or his lackeys, never knowing if they would respect his immunity, his impartiality. They had respected little else. Why now this edginess, when he has been so lethargic, phlegmatic, since arriving on Egret? Did he grow so used to danger that now he needs its dark impulse to feel he is alive?

Around a bend, and in the road ahead sits a macaque. Christian has time only to register its scruffy gray coat, its long fingers playing with a tuft of fur or some other monkey-treasure. He does not hesitate, stays on course, clips the monkey with the right wing of the Land Rover. The vehicle records a thud; the macaque flies squealing, injured, in an arc. Christian does not stop but shouts, I got one for you Fran! checks the rearview mirror, sees the monkey lying in the road, too badly injured to move. Perhaps dead.

I hope it's dead, thinks Christian, contritely, a second later; I've got nothing to finish it off with. Bloody creatures. Then thinks, there was a time he would never have done such a thing. There was a time when he was a mild and sweet man, anguished by the suffering of all creatures.

The macaque is trembling to the rhythm of its internal bleeding. In a few hours a Franco-Mauritian farmer will drive by in his Peugeot, pull over, and take a rifle from the trunk. He will look down at the macaque, hesitating, scratch his head, then fire point-blank into the animal's chest. Waste of a bullet, he will think, walking back to the Peugeot.

~~~

Once, Christian and Nermina were in the Jeep, driving slowly through a desolate countryside of icy roads, naked trees, and gape-eyed houses. Snow drifts bloodstained: a peasant woman lay in the road. More bundle than woman: layers of cloth against cold; under her arm, a dead goose. The woman had stepped on a land mine; a blood-soaked rag of flesh and stocking where her calf and foot had been.

She was alive, breathlessly muttering, cold crystals of imprecation on the air. They lifted her as best they could, half-carried, half-dragged her back to the Jeep. Nermina's thick, deep voice, murmuring comfort in her language; the woman's cold blue eyes, pain-blue eyes staring hard at them. Her body, shaking violently. What's she saying? asked Christian. She's fucking Radovan Karadžić's mother and his grandmother too. Wait—and she says she fucks all Serbs including her own father and mother for giving birth to her in such a country, may they rest in peace, and says if she survives she'll convert to Islam.

Nermina looked up at Christian then, a sad smile crossing her face, as if to say, You see why I love my people?

Sean waves to Christian: he is sitting in his small, cluttered yard in front of the colonial bungalow that is home, laboratory, and guesthouse for visiting naturalists. Next to him is a low table with a bottle of whiskey and some glasses, and sitting on Sean's knee is a lithe Creole woman half his age.

Eh! La Suisse! Meet Miss Mauritius runner-up of 1995. Where were you in 1995?

Christian smiles, does not answer.

Marie-Chantal, meet Christian, shouts Sean, and Christian realizes that Sean is quite drunk, with the unquestioning happiness of inebriation. So much for mongooses, he thinks.

Marie-Chantal has a lovely face beneath a crown of plaited, coiled braids. She smiles at Christian, and with a sixth sense of male hubris he suspects she fancies him over Sean—weather-beaten, balding, bushy-eyebrowed Sean, on the verge of being embarrassingly drunk.

Marie-Chantal's my new assistant, gloats Sean.

Really?

I help him with the birds, says Marie-Chantal smoothly. Have a whiskey.

Yes, man, have a whiskey, shouts Sean.

But Christian declines, looks restlessly around him: the peeling paint of the lovely old bungalow; the tamarind tree, the row of coconut palms leading down to the lagoon. Above the ocean the sky is clear, fringed with combed and carded cloud; behind them, inland, a dark grumble of patient storm. The light seems poured from the sun through a clogged filter of cumulonimbus.

Got any traps? Christian asks at last.

Wha' for?

Fran's found a kestrel's eggshell . . . she thinks a mongoose must have eaten it.

Oh, shite. Sean pushes Marie-Chantal from his knee, his hands

briefly gripping her hips through her thin sundress. He walks unsteadily toward a shed where there are piles of empty cages and traps
still wafting the personal pong of their former tenants. Christian rubs
his nose, looks down. Marie-Chantal has followed them; while Sean
rummages through the cages Christian turns to her and asks, Is it true
you were Miss Mauritius runner-up?

What rubbish, she murmurs. Well, yes, I participated . . . I hoped
if I won I could get some money, to travel. I'm a student, you see, and
it's not so easy here. If you have no money.

What are you studying?

She nods toward Sean. Animal conservation. Then she giggles and
adds, He's our hero.

That explains it, thinks Christian. Muse to the poet, mentor to the
disciple.

Found it! shouts Sean, Shite, looks like I forgot to remove the ver-
min, well, you've got yourself a skeleton, pity that won't scare the
buggers away instead of the trap. Nuisance to clean . . .

Christian looks at Marie-Chantal. She is laughing, mirth barely
contained behind her hand. So much for heroism, thinks Christian.
He smiles and shakes his head.

As they stand there the clouds break open, unfurl a sheet of cool,
vaporous rain, effluent with charged ions. Marie-Chantal moves into
the downpour, laughing, spreading her arms, lifting her face to receive the rain. Sean moves to stand beside Christian, holding the trap,
watching the young woman. Aye, she's gorgeous, he says softly,
sobered. Then, It's not what you think, man. She's sweet to me and
all, but we just cuddle. Avuncular, right? That's all.

Christian looks at him. Sadness settles over Sean's features as he
says, More's the pity.

Christian stops at the restaurant on his return trip from Black
River. Asmita sees the Land Rover from the entrance on the terrace

and walks quickly up the steps and across the tarmac to greet Christian before he gets out of the vehicle. The air steams as the rain dries in a now fierce sunlight. Christian leans his head against the window frame, watching her approach. She skirts puddles, eyes looking now down at the ground, now quickly at Christian; puddle-skirting Asmita in a long silk skirt; graceful, image-crafting Asmita weaving her way toward the man waiting in the vehicle.

They'll see you, he warns mockingly.

I don't care.

Can you get off?

No. A big party just arrived for a late lunch. Monsieur Razel from Floréal. You know Monsieur Razel?

Christian shakes his head.

Her eyes glow, her gaze deepens, her voice lowers. The richest man on the island. Notoriously powerful and corrupt.

What does he do for his power and corruption?

Asmita leans closer. Everything, legal and illegal: hotels, restaurants—but he doesn't own this place, yet—a bank in Port Louis, travel agencies, a shipping line, and they say, arms, prostitutes, and drugs.

The thoroughly modern man, says Christian. Well-rounded.

Like God, no?

Christian nods. He is not thinking about Razel; he is gazing at Asmita, touching her fingertips curled over the edge of the door. Connecting, making current, capturing ions of storm residue in the damp, charged air. He could kiss her, close the circuit, circle the sensation, but she has pulled back, looks in irritation in the direction of the restaurant.

I have to go, they'll be looking for me.

Watch out for Monsieur Razel, says Christian regretfully.

She squeezes his hand, but does not bend down for a kiss. Waves, tilts her head in greeting, turns to puddle-navigate, lightly, skipping-skimming over the damp ground.

Christian leans back, watches her go, then closes his eyes. Blackness, and a reverberation of light. A woman skipping-skimming, shimmering, storm-charged.

The man Razel sits back in his chair, ignoring the conversation around him. These people annoy him; they are employees, not friends. It could be said he has no friends—such is the price he has paid for power. His long, sallow face, the jowls of age, his unsmiling eyes: he knows, has known since youth, that his looks are unappealing, perhaps even repellent, and that he has never learned the social charms which might have caused people to overcome their first impression. His wife left him years ago, and lives somewhere on Réunion with the money from the divorce, and he has never remarried—though no doubt one of the local girls might have him for his money.

Take that one, in the coral dress, smooth, feline: she smiles at him and he sees no recoil, no repulsion. She has manners, or she is different: considerate. He can usually sense the ones who are after his money: they are the very ones who recoil in spite of themselves. They think, instantly, I will have to sleep with *that* in order to have my shopping trips to Jo'burg or Paris.

In the end he owns them, the girls who recoil. They work in his hotels; some stay chaste, in offices or kitchens, but some of them are there to sleep, discreetly and professionally, with guests who are always better-looking than he is, but never as rich. From time to time he exacts his tribute; from time to time he sends for one of them, tries to believe that if her eyes are closed it is because she is enjoying what he is doing to her, for no other reason. Although it has been months, now, since the last one. He has not been feeling well, has not wanted his malaise to become known. So lately, even if these girls are actually doing their job, Razel has begun to think of himself as a charity: with the money the girls earn in his hotels they buy their elegant clothes and jewels, some go on to open a tourist business in Grand

Baie or Port Louis, one of them even went to university. Because, once, in a moment like this, he fancied her; because too it was never mutual, and the money was never enough.

His eyes stray from the lovely girl to his executive director, Yves de Froberville. All the looks but none of the power. Razel had seen to that early on; after all, it was one of the de Froberville family's Hindu workers who had organized the strike, back in the 1940s— the strike which had led to the destruction of his family, of everything that had mattered to him until then. Razel had been an adolescent at the time, an only son; he had grown up quickly after that. Had scuppered all his adolescent dreams—travel, love, poetry, a Bohemian life in Paris—in order to find retribution. Now it could be said that de Froberville belongs to him, and not only financially. There are few limits to what he will do for Razel—whether out of fear or some sort of servile respect for authority Razel has never been sure.

Now he looks at de Froberville and knows he has only to raise an eyebrow and glance from him to the girl in the coral dress to have her in his office the next day and, if things go well, sooner or later in his bed. For he would not force her, no, he has his pride, and on some levels, he is still what those wretched *Anglais* would call a gentleman.

We're having tourists, says Fran.

What, for dinner?

She laughs. Grilled, or on skewers?

On a spit, says Christian viciously, and they both laugh.

They are placing the trap with its bait of hen's egg among the trees some way from the house.

No, says Fran, I've had a visit from the mayor of Mahébourg and two of the tour operators, and I've agreed to allow one group of no more than ten, once a week.

Until now tourists have been few and random—the odd individual swimming over from the hotel across the lagoon, or those with rented boats and enough pushiness to ignore the Private No Trespassing sign, or people Fran has met on her rare trips to the mainland, or invited visitors—specialists, other naturalists or ecologists. Mainstream tourism has not been encouraged. Christian recalls Fran's remarks about the tourists stealing orchids.

It will be, says Fran, a major disturbance and a minor source of income. But I could not refuse; it's a public relations thing. They wanted three times a week and larger groups; this is already a decent compromise.

When do we get the first group?

Next Tuesday. It will be on Tuesdays, for now.

Tuesdays, thinks Christian. Asmita's day off.

Will you need me? he asks, feeling adolescent, evasive.

Fran looks at him, astonished. Of course.

Right.

Irrationally, he thinks of quitting. He lies in bed, gecko-staring in lamplight, and considers his options. He thinks, in the end, he does not like being told what to do, having to answer to someone else. In Bosnia he answered to faraway Geneva, but he was his own master. Wherever he worked: answering only to those who were in need, whose well-being depended on him, and to a set of principles he agreed with, for so long. And to his own conscience—until he could no longer agree with those principles of impartiality, of neutrality.

Fran is not in need. She does not, he supposes, feel that her well-being depends on him. Certainly a group of overfed, spoiled tourists does not need him. And perhaps the wildlife of Egret Island does need his protection—but he cannot see things that way: what is he getting in return? All the job satisfaction is for Fran. Christian is tired—morally, emotionally depleted. Not from Egret, from before; but now the only thing which moves him, which restores him to life, is the time he spends with Asmita.

So he thinks of quitting. Unless of course Asmita could change her day off. But that is all academic: it is the feeling of enclosure, the feeling of being trapped on the island, by Fran or by circumstances (it makes no difference), which has become overwhelming. He has been here for nearly six months.

He thinks of the mongoose, wherever it is, if indeed it is a mongoose. Feels a certain pity for it, a pity he did not feel for the macaque. The macaque chose to sit in the road: ignorance, or supreme indifference? But the mongoose, very soon, will be tricked, unable to escape.

In the morning he finds the small beast in the trap. A snarling, slippery creature, suggesting guile and nastiness, snapping sharp and dangerous little rodent's teeth. Christian picks up the trap, holds it gingerly at one end until he is certain the screaming mongoose cannot reach his fingers, then walks clumsily with the trap to the water's edge. He pushes the trap into the water, holds it firmly submerged for some minutes, until he is sure the little beast has drowned.

What's this? shouts Fran.

Christian looks up slowly from the bowl of muesli in his lap.

It's a dead mongoose.

But it's soaking wet!

So? It's a dead, soaking wet mongoose.

(Lying, very dead, on a sodden old newspaper, on a corner of the kitchen table.)

Asmita, on her day off, deprived of Christian's presence, takes the bus to the hotel complex Grand Sud. She takes a business card from her bag, hands it to the receptionist, and after some minutes spent waiting in a plush wicker-framed armchair she is asked to follow the receptionist out through the courtyard and into a small elegant thatched bungalow.

The bungalow is dark, the curtains are drawn, as for a siesta. Faint strains of classical music enhance the impression of repose. Asmita could be nervous but isn't; after all, it was his suggestion. She merely followed a whim; nothing formal between them. Now Monsieur Razel, long pale face in the darkened room, gestures to her to sit down. A tray of refreshments is brought. Asmita sits with her hands folded across her lap, listening to the smoke-hoarsened voice detailing the position he might have for her. From time to time Asmita reaches for her glass of juice; from time to time Razel pauses, sips on a cocktail. Even from this distance she can smell his pickled boozy smell; all the fine Italian clothes and French colognes cannot mask his decrepitude. But his voice is steady, and pleasant, and his shadowy figure suggests a man once vigorous, now gaunt. Finally he asks her to talk about herself, which she does, briefly and confidently: her schooling, her work experience, her hopes for the future.

And marriage? asks Razel.

Oh, not yet, but eventually.

He nods his approval, with the avuncular authority which, to his regret, will characterize their relationship. Asmita, whose father has largely refrained from participation in his daughters' future (other than financial), is grateful, so she accepts Razel's role, and accepts the position he has offered to her.

Christian, on the wall phone to Asmita from Mahébourg, exclaims astonishment, looks out at the busy street; even now he is jostled as people pass him. His temper rises. You said yourself the man's a crook——

But he has primarily very honest dealings. And—

But how do you know he won't use you without your knowing it, get you involved—

—and the pay is twice what I would make anywhere else.

So that's all you care about—

It's not all I care about, but it's my future. It's a good position, personal assistant to the executive director. It has nothing to do with Razel himself. I won't even see him.

You hope.

Christian relents, wonders at the sudden violence of his disapproval—what business is it of his, after all?—and looks down at his fist banging the wall next to the telephone as if it were a thing detached. As if he knew better than she did what was good for her, what was right.

How were your tourists? asks Asmita.

They canceled. Not enough people signed up. Fran was ecstatic.

So I could have seen you?

Yes. But you wouldn't have got your new job.

Fate? says Asmita lightly.

Christian laughs. I think you know what you're doing.

A short silence, then, When can I see you?

Any day but Tuesday.

I'll have weekends off.

Saturday, then. I'll pick you up in Curepipe.

Christian is fishing at sundown off a natural promontory in the lagoon. He has caught a *vieille rouge* and a *dame berri*. His thoughts churn and swirl, eddies in rock-shadow. Asmita is among them, her identity now somehow confused, too strong, as if it were giving off an unfamiliar and not altogether pleasant smell. Christian cares so little about money that he cannot understand its attraction beyond the minimum needed for survival. Even when an egg on the black market in Bihać cost ten deutsche mark, he would pay without complaint, would have paid a hundred if that was the price of survival. Christian does not question the possibility that one day he might not have a hundred deutsche mark for an egg, in wartime, or ever. He lives with the affluent West's sense of entitlement. In Christian's case, this is not patronizing, merely ignorant, inexperienced. He lived for so long in a climate of utter deprivation, where only the generosity of nations kept people from starvation, that he has not yet learned the terrible destructive power of ordinary money in the lives of ordinary people.

Thoughts swirl, a fish bites, then escapes. In the end he is sorry there were no tourists yesterday; he might have enjoyed a change in routine. Fran was nervous and bad-tempered until they canceled; then she invited him for a drink at the Hôtel Croix du Sud across the lagoon. She was cheerful, full of laughter, and released little glimpses of her life. Her work in Hawaii; a winter she spent on Guam researching bird extinction; her two trips to Europe and the rotten time she'd had in Switzerland.

Christian then apologized for his country; not your fault, she reassured him; expectations are half of traveling. As of life. People who expect too much are always disappointed. And often unhappy.

As a delegate Christian had learned to have no expectations for himself; expectations—like money—were a luxury.

But when Vlatković promised to allow him access to the prisoners, or to turn on the water supply, or to let the convoy through, and then broke his promise—was that the disappointment of an expectation? How closely is disappointment connected to the self, to a personal goal?

There are not even words for what Vlatković did. Beyond disappointment, beyond deceit, beyond betrayal, beyond any emotion cataloged by human understanding.

His thoughts swirl into the darker eddies. At times the simplicity of revenge glints in the water, knife-blade clear. But what would be gained? Revenge would assuage his anger, make him feel that briefly he had taken justice into his own hands, canceled blood with blood.

A genial man, not much older than Christian. At first, Christian liked him. At first, he trusted him, took him for a legitimate soldier who was doing his job, fighting for his beliefs. He was easy to trust— all that geniality and laughter. On previous missions Christian had dealt with men who were so very different from himself: swarthy, sober men, turbaned and bearded; serious men, theirs was a holy war, and Christian was merely a tolerated, occasionally respected, infidel. So he had learned to hold his trust in reserve: difference implying distance, trust would be dosed accordingly. You learned to wait, until they proved their honor; that way, you respected your commitment to the innocent.

But Vlatković was an easy man to trust. You couldn't not like his laughter and good looks. And he brought gifts of plum brandy, distilled by his own grandmother in Dubrovnik, and if he'd had a few glasses himself he'd start to lament the fact that he could no longer visit her there, the Croats wouldn't give him a visa, and in his words echoed every schoolboy's refrain, What did I do wrong? They started it.

With smiles and brandy and grandmothers he won you over, gained the trust he did not deserve, and because he was not different— wore no turban, because he was *like* you, white and Christian and European—you assumed the unassumable.

The convoy blocked at the front line, engines steaming in the cold, medical supplies and blankets and food held hostage to shouts and laughter and drunkenness, and the man signing the order, Let them through, before Christian's eyes, sign in blood, sign in smiles, and Christian too smiling, brief triumph of the humanitarian over the inhuman. And a round of brandy for us all.

And the next day you learn that the convoy was seized, its cargo vanished into the countryside, or to be sold on the black market in

Belgrade, in Podgorica, and take those British convoy drivers hostage while you're at it, and haven't they got nice warm good-quality special-issue jackets, we'll have them too now, march these English fools at drunken gunpoint back into Alija's territory. What can I do— the man smiles, the same smile, but Christian is no longer smiling; What can I do, I give my men orders and they don't obey me.

No more brief personal victories, no victory in that war that was not a war, not a war Henri Dunant would have recognized, but a bloody game of bullies and warlords, a slaughter. Sign, Colonel Vlatković, sign and smile and make your promises that are not worth the brandy-rank breath they are written on.

But Christian liked him, once, the place of liking now filled with shame.

Asmita enjoys her new job. To her it represents a rise in status and responsibility. All day the hotel workers call or come to her asking for her boss, Monsieur de Froberville, and she can sit and gauge their need, and their status, and decide whether to let them through. She makes phone calls, arrangements, tracks down other people; memories of her hotel school training surface, usefully, and she thinks to herself, At last I am doing what I am meant to be doing; at last I am Getting Ahead.

So she feels extraordinarily grateful toward the fates, and toward Monsieur Razel. And when he calls one day, she chirps happily into the receiver: her gratitude, her delight. Good, good, *ma petite,* he answers, and sighs heavily, and if Asmita could understand his sigh she would see that it is a compliment to her, if only I were younger.

Sometimes she looks out of the office window at the line of filaos bordering the lagoon, and slips a daydream into her vision. In her daydream she is walking along the beach with Christian, and on his shoulders he is carrying a small nut-brown boy.

She does not think of pleasure, or the love Christian seeks from her. Her love is different, a way of life, a future. She suspects that the withholding of pleasure can be a tool: she hopes she is using it wisely, and that it will ensure that future. But there are times she wonders if she must yield to gain his love, to be sure of it. She knows that love takes different forms in the West, and she fears the division of cultures. At times she feels there is too deep a chasm between the two worlds, and the mystery of her own sexuality is a burden to her. She loves Christian and wants to trust him. Wants no one else to make her a woman. But her fear is great, for if she yields to Christian to gain his love, she will lose the world which has always been hers. She needs the security of that world, of its approval.

Asmita hesitates.

One afternoon a young Creole man comes into the office and tells her he has an appointment with Monsieur de Froberville. He chats easily with her while he is waiting; Asmita answers his questions stiffly, unsmiling. She thinks he is too familiar, and too curious. Where does she live? How long has she worked here? Does she have a boyfriend?

She does not answer his questions, then asks him, woodenly, Why are you here? Why do you need to see Monsieur de Froberville?

He grins, shrugs, shows her his palms. The new séga program. For the Grand Lagon.

You're a séga dancer?

Yes, come and see me, I'm good. Come, bring your boyfriend. My name's Jean-Baptiste.

Asmita sighs and looks at him with irritation. And what makes you think I have a boyfriend?

Comme ça . . . a pretty girl like you must have a boyfriend. In fact, I know you do. I've heard he lives out there on the island, with the mad American woman. La folle. But you can bring him. You can be my guests, if you let me know when you are coming. Okay?

He laughs shrilly. Asmita looks down at the papers on her desk but does not see them. His laugh has made her uneasy. Is this the same nosy fellow Christian has talked about? When the phone rings she lifts it with relief, then tells the young man he can go in now, Monsieur de Froberville will see him.

Perhaps, thinks Fran, I should fly to South Africa for a few days. There's a bird man I need to see at the university. Then, the usual reservation: can I leave the island to Christian?

She is sitting on the veranda; Christian is fishing down by the landing. She reaches for her glass of gin and tonic, and her notebook. The ink is drying in her pen.

She writes, *I would like to get away. To purchase distance, to look at my work here and understand. There are times when I feel that nothing has changed, that there is no progression—no* evolution—*that I am merely a custodian, a gamekeeper, setting traps for poachers.*

Two fledglings in six months: hardly a sign that the critical threshold has been recrossed. Hardly a sign that a minimum viable population has been reestablished.

She leans her head back against the cushion. Evolution, she thinks, is what makes loneliness bearable. If I can witness change, progress, a sign that what I give to life is transformed into energy, into motion of some kind, then I will hear something beyond silence. There is a music, a satisfaction in hearing some echoing vibration. In knowing, simply, that I am here.

The ink has run out, she tries dipping the pen in the gin and tonic, to no avail. Lets thoughts scroll, too fast without the restraint of written words.

Christian, Satish. Satish not loneliness but its opposite. Christian like a reflection of loneliness, glaring: his numbness, his sharp, perverted sense of humor (wet mongooses), which sends you away from him and into yourself. For all I loosened up yesterday, told him about myself, gave him the chance, yet again, to do the same, his only response was to apologize for Switzerland's coldness. As if it were something you can apologize for.

Three days or so in Cape Town. I could visit the ornithological in-stitute; look up that woman in the botany department who was so in-terested in the orchids. I could be back in time for the tourists. Play tourist myself in Cape Town, purchase distance, and empathy.

Leave the place to Christian; maybe, without me, he would under-stand its magic, learn to love it. Let a few days' real solitude burn off the numbness, melt the glaciers.

Fran will go, then, for a few days to South Africa. She needs a change, does not see the taunting of her loneliness. She will go to Cape Town, where she has acquaintances, if not friends; where there is the Western-world glitter and glaze of money and commerce, and a certain urban alienation from Nature, which will remind her of the good she is doing, if not in the world then for the earth.

And while she is gone, Christian will awake with a deep inhalation of pleasure, the knowledge that but for birds, insects, butterflies, tor-toises, and geckos he is alone on his own little earth-world, and that this pleasurable aloneness has nothing to do with his own sharpened presence, but everything to do with Fran's absence. Because he will, at last, be able to spend a night with Asmita. Her parents have gone to London for a week; her younger sisters are staying with an aunt.

He hopes it is only the lack of true privacy which is the real cause of her reticence, and that now she will yield, fulfilling the promise of her kisses. This maddening cycle of kisses, caresses, always halted, restrained. Now Christian succumbs to hope, to the sweet breathing of sexual anticipation: images rise and fall, rhythmic, and become a pulse of sensual longing. The world is made beautiful by the pulsing of tiny neurons: how does desire become a way of seeing?

Asmita has agreed to come to the island to see where he lives. She walks slowly around his lamp-lit room, touching things: his books, the shorts hanging on the back of a chair, the straw hat he wears to work in the bush. From time to time she lifts her eyes to him: she has come here to understand who he is and what he might offer.

She lies down beside Christian beneath the mosquito net. He has turned the jet on the camping lamp to a low hiss, and the light sends long shadows across the room. He touches her, she resists. Finally he murmurs, in quiet desperation: If you love me, why won't you trust me?

She draws small circles on his chest with the tip of her finger and says, Do you love me?

His hand closes and tightens around her shoulder, but he says nothing.

Did she ever ask him that question, Nermina? Did it need asking, when every gesture, every day they were alive was like a confirmation of their love for each other?

He remembers a time they were taking a break, somewhere, in a gray town, smoking in the street, and she was laughing at his poor pronunciation of her language, and the fact that he always confused the verbs for to want and to love, and how she had demonstrated, like a schoolteacher, saying, *I want a coffee, I love chocolate,* and he had mimicked her, laughing, but thinking that *I love you, I want you* were still one and the same in his vocabulary. *Volim te, želim te,* he muttered, and she threw her arms around him and tossed her head back and told him he was a bad student.

There is a long silence and the chirring of the insects in the night, and the faraway murmur of the breakers on the reef.

After some moments Christian again squeezes her shoulder, and returns Asmita's question: Do you love me, then?

She snuggles closer to him, as if she were cold, although the night is warm; then she says softly, I don't know if it is love, I've never been in love, but I want to be with you, all the time. Is that love?

Christian says nothing. Does not want to give her an answer that is not true, or a truth which will not be an answer. So he is silent, and they lie there in the questioning silence, barely touching, until he moves her, gently, and reaches out of the mosquito net to turn off the lamp.

Purple light, seeking blue; a man ferries a woman across a lagoon at dawn. Their forms are still gray against the purple night; the lagoon is a clear depth holding night, flashes of phosphorescence breaking loose on the wake of the dinghy.

Their short journey holds peace, an image blenched of time, that you could hold like a painting in your memory. But that would be to make them symbols—man and woman on the journey through life, the man steering, the woman trusting. But Asmita and Christian are no such travelers.

Christian looks behind him, into the swirling water. In the trick-light of dawn he sees the tendrils, long dark locks spilling, turning in the wake, a woman's face upturned, lagoon maiden, water sylph, her sad familiar features watching him as if begging for air. Don't you know me? It's me, Nermina. I have drowned, she seems to say, in your loss.

In Fran's absence Christian works. Clears another area of the island of nonnative growth. Cleans the aviary. Scrubs the floors of the house, does the laundry, patches the dinghy, repairs two broken shutters and the sagging seat of the armchair. Sews buttons on his shirts; uses the awl on his army knife to repair a loose sole on his hiking shoes. Pickles cucumbers, according to an old recipe of his mother's; writes to his parents and to Dubravka, who is still in Bosnia.

Dubravka. Croat from Croatia, but half-Serbian, she fled the violence in her newly independent country in 1991 thinking Sarajevo would be safe. On one level, it was: for a few more months she was able to speak her mind and not be accused of either nationalism or a lack thereof, for she no longer belonged anywhere. But when the war followed her to Bosnia she became a Yugo-nostalgic and opted for silence. She was tall and extravagant, and even at the height of the war she managed to obtain personal shipments of her favorite purplish copper hair dye through her contacts in the black market. She was a truly impartial worker at the Red Cross, bound to a strict ethic which enabled her to go beyond her paper identity. In the early days she tried unsuccessfully to seduce Christian, before he had met Nermina; he felt a brotherly tenderness toward her, called her Comrade. She always found a place for him to stay, and cigarettes, and later, on a few occasions, arranged his trysts with Nermina. She would stare longingly, as if awestruck, at Nermina. But she was loyal: her deep, raucous laughter like a signal to a cease-fire, a prologue.

Dubravka has feather-light handwriting, a smooth, looping Middle European scroll. Christian remembers the notes she used to leave for him at the delegation office. Now he looks at his own spare script and wonders if she will write back.

In Asmita's absence Christian's thoughts multiply. He would rather empty his mind of doubts or musings, but in the silence and boredom which accompany work he cannot stop thought from breaking in. Her face, the picture of her brown body stretched long and lovely next to his, the lamplight melting the thin layer of clothing under the mosquito net, playing tricks. But thinking of her has brought uneasy fears, whisperings of words better not spoken, words which impose time, remove illusion.

Do you love me? It was a gentle plea, a whole hoped-for future riding in her intonation; Do you love me? he answered warily, a future feared, something he did not want to think of.

No, Asmita, thinks Christian in moments of clarity (the awl has slipped, he has jabbed his thumb), I do not love you. I wish I did, but I don't and, for the time being, can't. And why can't I tell you this? Why do I prefer silence—am I waiting for a day that I might grow to love you?

But her body, he thinks, would give me the gift of forgetting. No doubt it is her body I love. My body loves hers for the forgetfulness it seems to offer.

Like a gift maddeningly out of reach, a forgetfulness in itself: a drug, a dizzying sweetness.

Fran is at a party hosted by a Professor Smits from the institute of ornithology, where she has been meeting professors and researchers and using the library. His home is in a residential neighborhood: vast gardens shaded by stately overhanging boughs, old homes gleaming with a patina of equally old European wealth, ideas, and traditions. And Fran wonders if the strangely jarring sense of entrenchment, of lives embattled by history, fear, incomprehension, is a residual molecular reality in the evening air, like the scent of a wild beast, or whether she is imagining this from what she has read, and heard, of this country. All evening she will try to find someone sober and serious enough with whom she might broach discussion of the new South Africa, of Mr. Mandela, of the Truth and Reconciliation Commission, but the guests wander from the living room to the veranda, then to the lawn, in search of drinks and chat and some other residual molecular scent of which they no longer have any olfactory awareness: sex.

Fran, the outsider, observes this, adds her own natural fantasy to the heightened awareness of others that her months of solitude have given her. Red-faced, white-maned professors leering over handsome, laughing younger women: it is all so familiar, so predictable, she could be back in Berkeley, at any time in her life there. Fran has never been "good at" parties: now, holding a glass of South African Chardonnay in one hand and a smoked salmon canapé in the other, she watches a woman her own age (thick silver-blond head of hair, ivory linen against a deep tan, lots of ethnic jewelry) conversing with a man Fran finds attractive (salt-and-pepper swath of hair, small wire glasses, large mustache—Turkish? Iranian?) but despises because he is so obviously taken with the silver-blonde, leaning toward her, moving his head from side to side. Fran thinks of the courtship rituals of seabirds—albatrosses in particular—who bow and nod and engage in a hilarious dance of outstretched necks. She waits for the woman's response: a sip from her glass (a white wine, to match the hair, skin, linen), then the woman leans forward, eyes flashing, and waves her head from side to side, slowly, in rhythm to her throaty laughter.

Fran feels a sadness welling, heavy with regret. She is in the middle of her life, her sexual attraction on the wane, and she has never known what it is like to be able to flirt. To detect the residual molecular reality on the air, feel the atavistic tug which animals find so natural. To flash her eyes, move her head from side to side, voice a mating call of throat-laughter. She had no instincts, no urges beyond the immediate logical urge aroused by someone else—her husband, a casual lover, sometimes her own intellect obeying a media-driven mating call. *Thou shalt mate. Thou shalt be Liberated Woman.*

Am I missing a certain gene, she wonders (the blonde is now whispering into the Turk's ear), or is it the power of my mind to repress? Her parents, deeply conservative, secretive about the ways of the body, taught her shame, only shame. Nakedness was sin. The body was a sin. She recalls the brown-paper packages her mother brought back from the store: intrigued, little Fran would ask, What's in here? (Hoping: a toy for me?) Her mother, evasive and embarrassed, would say only, I'll tell you when you're older. Oh, the mystery of being grown-up. Much later Fran learned the brown parcels contained pads for menstrual blood. Her mother's blood. (That's how they were sold, then: nowadays, thinks Fran, they advertise these things with graphic illustrations and tell you how wonderful—how *normal*—you'll feel if you use their brand. You can even flirt and whisper into the ear of a handsome man.)

Regret. Would I have been more attentive to my body's signals and urgings if I had grown up in a different country, or twenty years later?

It's all about society, she thinks; and that is why I belong on Egret. I can't play these games. I am misadapted. In any other species I would not survive. Obviously. Despite my mating, I was barren. Am barren. Perhaps I cannot flirt because my body has known all along its biological destiny.

At the edge of the lawn, in the darkness checkered by light from the long French windows, Fran sees a man moving, tall and thin, dark-skinned, dark-haired. For a moment she will forget her sinister thoughts of natural selection: all the world is not Darwin. There are other mysterious forces at work: she feels a tightness in her chest, a stinging in her eyes and throat as she looks at the figure moving silently across the lawn. She does not know him, his name is Sanjeev Gupta, he is a student from Bombay. If she knew this she would not be feeling how emotion quickens and moves the body's response. She would not, for a brief moment, succumb to memory's illusion, she would credit an obvious, racial resemblance. Instead she sees Satish walking there, in and out of light across the lawn, across her regret.

On the night of the day after Fran had kissed Satish by the landing on Egret, she sat out on the veranda alone, listening to her sounds, the familiar reassurances of the place to which she belonged. Waves, insects, perhaps the real or imagined echo of wind in the distant filaos; sometimes she liked to think she could hear the crackling of the cane fields burning. She tried not to think of why she was sitting there, legs outstretched on the old wicker sofa under a thin cotton blanket, to protect from bugs. Only imaginings, musing. All day Satish had avoided her, not angrily, but with a kind of hurt shyness. At the end of the afternoon he had asked permission to take the dinghy into Mahébourg, and she had granted it, feeling too much the boss. Feeling artificial, even. Yes, all her words artifices to deflect what she felt.

Now she could hear the sound of the outboard, its slow approach across the lagoon. She listened with a bemused anticipation, imagined that Satish would come to the house with a bag of supplies and greet her quietly and politely with a certain reserve, and ask her some questions about the next day's work, or tell her whom he had seen in town, or even what was happening in the world.

He emerged from the darkness into the dim gaslight which drifted

from the warden's house, his hair windblown; on his face he wore the
same expression of pained shyness. Fran drew her legs up. Sit, she
said, indicating the sofa. Have you eaten?

He nodded, and only when he sat down, his head against the cushion, his eyes closed, did she see his fatigue and disarray, a Satish she
did not know—he who was always fresh and eager, puppy-boy, she
often thought, sniffing out a world of joyful smells.

He began to talk, his voice low and grave and tired, perhaps he had
been drinking, and she listened and marveled at how the night, the
warmth, sounds, his voice merged to form an emotion.

He talked to her about his work, about how he loved the island,
how she had given him an opportunity that no one would ever give him
again. How important this was. How grateful he was. Fran listened to
his quiet, pained voice, said nothing: felt dread slowly taking hold.
He's going to leave, she thought, he's going to tell me he can no longer
work for me. He will say I am a bad woman. And he did begin to talk
about their relationship—how he looked up to her, how she had
taught him so much (here she tried to interrupt, but he ignored her,
went on speaking). And now he said he had a problem, and could he
speak to her about it, and could she help him with it?

For the first time he looked over at her, his eyes big enough to contain her, contain the night, contain all the hurt; a brief glance, then
down again, or away again. Fran nodded, murmured, Tell me, then
he was telling her that he had to decide, that he thought he would have
to leave the island, leave this work because he could no longer be with
her, because of what happened yesterday (only a kiss!), because now
he wanted her, the way a man wants a woman, and it wasn't right.

Not right?

Because, he said, still looking away, his two palms pressed together, fingers outstretched and spread as if in prayer or greeting, unless you want me, the way a woman wants a man, I cannot stay, it
wouldn't be right. And if you want me, our life will be difficult, I

think. Yes. And maybe that is not good for you. Not what you want.

He lowered his gaze, raised his palms to his forehead, closing the greeting, the prayer, tapping gently with the tips of his fingers, marking time, waiting for her answer.

In the fragrant African night, Fran remembers. All around her real shadows merge, men, women, talking, flirting. Less real than the simple words in her mind—But Satish, yes, that is what I want—raised again by the shadow of a young student from Bombay walking across the edge of her vision, across the center of her self. She looks again for him on the lawn, then on the veranda, then in the living room, but he has gone, so she will never know if she really saw him, or merely wanted to.

Asmita has never told her family about Christian, and because he wants to be sure that she will answer the phone, they have a prearranged time frame and signal (two rings, hang up, dial again). Now for several days, at a certain prescribed time, the telephone has been silent, or if it rings, it continues to ring, on into a third, jarring jingle. Mrs. Peerun calling for her mother; Mayila and Kavita calling for her sisters; Mr. Chawdhurry for her father, wondering if he has brought back the Manchester United mug he asked for. Asmita is sleepless and cross, yells at her sisters, doesn't answer her parents. Doesn't she want to hear about their trip? What is wrong with the girl?

She feels Christian is slipping away from her. She tells herself, glumly, that she is quite depressed. She closes her eyes, tosses her head back, feels his lips against her neck. In her mind she succumbs, allows the scenario to play on, past her Bollywood dreams, past the whisperings of her girlfriends and of her conscience. He is undressing her, he has his hands on her breasts, between her legs, she is about to discover something—that other sexuality portrayed in Western films and books. But more important than that, she is about to pledge her trust.

But how can she be sure? What if he is just like all the men she has been warned about? Poor Padma, who was in class with her in Switzerland, who got pregnant and was abandoned by her Swiss-German lover; she had to go to Britain to get an abortion, and now there were rumors that no one wanted her anymore, that she must be sterile.

A knocking interrupts her thoughts; she hastily composes her face, but her father, when she opens the door, sees only her confusion, her rebellious stubborn gaze.

Mr. Chawdhurry— She begins to speak but her father interrupts.

Your mother and I have had a visit from Mrs. Thapoor, he says sternly.

That old busybody!

Don't speak badly of our neighbor!

What has she seen now?

I think you have to come with me, your mother too is waiting for an explanation. Do you want to break our hearts?

The day before Fran is due back from South Africa, Christian sets out in the dinghy for Mahébourg. It is dusk, particles of light quickly dropping into the lagoon, into encroaching darkness. He has not been ashore (he thinks of Egret as a ship now, moving backward in time) since he ferried Asmita home at dawn, days ago, it seems; he has not called her because he is jealous of her job, irrationally, but also because he has wanted to isolate himself, to think. To decide whether he can survive without her. And he believes that he can.

Days of fruitful solitude: working, fishing, swimming, reading, writing to friends at home and around the world. Lying in the hammock listening to the shortwave radio. Knowing the world is out there—full of women, money, things, art, food, violence—and knowing that he does not care. No longer cares. He has become caretaker of a family of rare birds, who are doing well, and of his own broken-winged soul, and has made a place safe from predators, for now.

So he has discovered that Asmita, in her way, is a predator: she cannot mend his broken wing, she seems to cause a deep aching in him. Her spell has been broken. Through no fault of her own; because of the way he is. I am using her, in fact, he thinks, expecting her to make me better, but making it harder for myself. It is time to break.

A few stars hang in a moonless night, teasing light. Christian looks behind him, back toward Egret, and sees a flash of phosphorescence. And again. Not a moving or jumping fish, something too bright and steady about the light. Until he realizes it is not phosphorescence at all but the shimmer of a boat's lamp. A small, open boat, probably a pirogue.

Christian pushes the lever on the outboard and veers away from the Croix du Sud, toward Mahébourg. He looks behind him: the pirogue has changed course. He continues for a time toward Mahébourg, then veers again; the pirogue follows. His heartbeat quickens, but he stays calm, opens the throttle.

A few minutes later he looks behind him again and can no longer make out the pirogue or its wake: they have given up the chase, out-motored.

Christian slows, cuts the engine. He is a few minutes from shore; he lets the dinghy drift under its own momentum, then takes up his oars. Only the plashing of the wooden blades against the lagoon's silence. And then he thinks: They were fishermen, looking for a good spot. They weren't chasing me.

I'm foolish, and tired, he thinks; I still see danger everywhere, invent it, crave it perhaps. I adjust so far to normal life, then seize an opportunity to feel the fragility, the vulnerability, that so . . . enhanced my life then. No, *enhance* is the wrong word: refracted then, caused me to see everything enlarged, and slightly distorted, and in that distortion I seemed, curiously, to find the truth.

On an impulse he veers away and heads toward Blue Bay on the far side of the lagoon. He leaves the dinghy at the landing and walks over to the local hotel, where, he's heard, there is good séga dancing. Tables and chairs have been set around a small stage outdoors, under a palm-thatched shelter. The music is loud and amateurish, a cheerful blend of African and island rhythms. Christian joins a sunburnt French couple at a table and orders a beer. The dancers, two men and two women, wear flamboyant costumes; their bodies move in supple circular rhythm, miming some atavistic physical courtship, sensual yet restrained. Christian is mildly fascinated, yet refuses to join in when the dancers invite the tourists onstage for a lesson. He watches with dismay as the French couple perform a stiff and mocking imitation of the dance; he wonders how they can ever make love when they return to their hotel room at night, how they can fail to find each other ridiculous and superior. Yet at least they are joining in the dance, he thinks, while he sits there cynically criticizing. One of the Creole dancers is a superb young woman with long black hair and almond eyes; he cannot refrain from looking at her, yet his fascination strangely depresses him. The mere fact of it is further proof that he does not love Asmita. He finds himself wondering if the dancer is sleeping with the young man who is her partner—his hands barely touch her, yet seem to linger suggestively. Once, she moves close to the edge of the stage not far from Christian's table; she gazes at him, an openly hard, provocative gaze. Christian turns away, embarrassed; she must have seen him staring at her. When next he looks at the stage, she is dancing with the sunburnt Frenchman, who is gloating. Her smile is false; she looks bored.

Christian sighs and gets up. He shouldn't have come. Yet he wanted to see the local dancing, he had to try: he's become far too serious and conservative. Cheerful things depress him; his balance seems to depend on a measure of sadness in the world, the reality of hardship. This was not always so, but he can no longer remember a time, in his life, when he would dance with strangers.

He realizes, too, that he was hoping to see Jean-Baptiste, hoping to confirm to himself that the young man is no more than a friendly, curious local who likes to meet foreigners. Whose friendliness is hospitality, whose curiosity is a sign of polite interest. A séga dancer, nothing more, someone Christian can share a drink with from time to time.

But his absence seems to confirm Christian's unease, even when he tells himself that there are dozens of hotels, and Jean-Baptiste is surely dancing elsewhere.

Christian undertakes the long dinghy ride back to Mahébourg, hoping to get to the Dents du Midi in time to call Asmita. He finds his friend Bertrand the owner smoking on the terrace, and when Bertrand offers him a beer, he accepts gladly, a beer for thought, to postpone the necessity of what he is about to do. He knows it is cowardly to break with Asmita over the phone, but he does not have the courage to see her, to resist her smile, her soft skin.

He wishes he could confide in Bertrand, wishes the older man could provide fatherly comfort and advice with his cold beer and irascible good humor, but that is hardly the way of the Swiss, or even of men. It was not the way of Christian's father, who circled him in silence during the months, after Bosnia, when Christian lived at home wound tight like a clock upon himself. Except when he was calling Sarajevo, as often as he could bear it, the only activity on which he hung his hope and his defeat.

Bertrand rambles on, local gossip, scandals, projections for the tourist season, and Christian observes a sensation of division and distancing in himself: one Christian drinking beer (cold gassy bitterness, sliding down); the other on a perch high above everything, not unlike a bird, hearing only a sound like the distant warning call of a raptor, You must move, soon, from your safe perch, from the height overlooking your life.

Christian dials, listens to the ringing, hangs up, listens to his own heartbeat, disgusted at what he must do, dials again.

Her quiet phone voice, answering, Is that you? He pictures her walking with the cordless phone to an imagined part of the house: the courtyard-garden, or her room, or perhaps the front porch he has seen from the street. So at first he does not hear the urgency in her tone, a tremulous demand, until she says, I have to see you, now, it's terribly important.

Wait, Asmita, what's wrong, I can't—

Please, please—can you get the Land Rover?

Yes, of course, but can't you tell me over the phone?

No, absolutely not! I have to see you, what is wrong with you—you don't want to see me!

I do, I do, but—

On the corner, by the banyan, as usual. Please, please hurry.

Bertrand smiles, waves away Christian's fifty-rupee note. Next time, next time. *Problèmes de femme?*

Christian shrugs, shakes his head.

Ah, les Mauriciennes . . . Charles Baudelaire devoted a poem to a Mauritian woman, did you know that? You wouldn't be a bit of a poet yourself, by any chance?

Christian laughs his shy laugh, shakes his head. Bertrand sketches a male embrace, taps Christian on the shoulder. Come what may, you'll get a poem out of it.

Long, dark nighttime road to Curepipe; Christian drives slowly, full of dread. Why is this so difficult?

Asmita is waiting by the banyan tree and has never looked more lovely. A long, tight dark dress, split to the knee. Her thick black hair coiled against the sides of her face, against her nape, with medieval intricacy. (Christian does not know the sum she has spent on this appearance, borrowed against her new job.) She is splendid, and Christian would be lost, had he not hardened his heart in the terrible way of truthful, guilt-burdened men.

But he will be lost when he hears what Asmita has to say, when she reaches her long fingers to his face, to his neck, pulls him to her, her face streaming with tears, will be lost to the tumult of words and pleas, his heart no harder than his last unripe resolution.

Asmita is looking out the window of the Land Rover at the banyan tree. It is knotty and entangled, with its curtain of hanging roots struggling to grow both earthward and through its own shade toward the light. Next to her Christian is silent, his head back against the headrest, his eyes closed.

Finally he turns to her, reaches for her, a hand on each shoulder, his forehead pressed against hers.

Will you help me? she murmurs, and he nods. You won't let me down?

Her skin is warm and sweet, with a faint scent of cinnamon in the curve of her neck. Everything is changed. Christian can shed his guilt and forsake the truth. There are other things now, more important than truth. He will be an honorable man.

We can't stay here, murmurs Asmita.

Dazed, he pulls away, turns the ignition. They head for the hidden roads, among the cane fields, or the tea plantations, but everything is changed.

At the airport at Plaisance, Christian is waiting for Fran. She is glad to see him standing aloof and silent among the noisy and colorful crowd. He is wearing khaki bush shorts and a white T-shirt; his hair is uncombed, his cheeks unshaven. There seem to be new lines in his cheeks, carved out by the sun and the fresh air; of course they are not new, but she had not kept them in memory. Her mental picture of Christian was dated, coinciding, no doubt, with a moment when he had moved or angered her. Now she records a new mental picture: tousled, rumpled, familiar Christian—he has moved her.

He is shy and gallant, helping her with her case, asking her about the trip. It was refreshing and tiring at the same time, she says, and explains: it was good to see people, get new ideas—but that city life, the traveling, the crowds—no. I'm glad to be back.

It's good to have you back.

Later, in the warden's house, he turns to her and says, Are you very tired? Would you mind some company this evening?

Who were you thinking of—Sean?

No, actually, my friend Asmita. She'd like to meet you. She's got the day off, she could get the bus down to Mahébourg—

Fran does mind. Sean would have been all right—familiar, entertaining, mindless of her fatigue—but a young woman? This girl-friend? Am I envious, intolerant, or bored before I even meet her? wonders Fran. She looks at Christian, again feels strangely moved by him, the quiet expectancy of him.

So she says, That would be fine, I would like to meet her.

The evening is not going well. Asmita's loveliness depresses Fran, compounds her fatigue, stirs an atavistic jealousy. As if Christian were her son. So Fran broods while Asmita sits quietly emanating, and Christian strives: unprecedented efforts to please, to succeed. He prepares a delicious light meal of meat and mushrooms in a creamed curry sauce; he pours the wine, changes the cassette in the tape player, and talks nervously about the cuisine of Switzerland: Not all cheese, no! Some of the world's best chefs are Swiss! The White House had a Swiss chef!

They are polite, they laugh and smile and raise their glasses; pluck out ideas and words and sentences from the silence they feel within. Fran tries to understand the significance of the dinner party: is it for her return—but she was hardly gone a week—or for some other event of which neither Asmita nor Christian will speak?

She tries to ask Asmita about her work; a sinking feeling overtakes her, then, when she learns that Asmita works for one of the hotels belonging to Razel. She has heard about this Razel; there was something Satish once said. Now, looking at the luminous expression on the young woman's face, she tries to remember but finds herself confused by youth, and a curious sense of loss. Perhaps it will come back, later; perhaps it was nothing important.

Once, Fran intercepts a gaze. Asmita's dark eyes entrusting warmth to Christian, and his eyes searching elsewhere, somewhere beyond her warmth. An impression, naturally, but years of observing animals have given her an uncanny accuracy in reading the signals of her own kind.

Much later, lying sleepless in bed, she hears Christian return from taking Asmita home. Hears his step on the veranda, the striking of a match, the comfortable hiss of the camping lamp. Pictures him sitting on the edge of the wicker sofa, staring into the thickness of night. She could get up and join him, bring him her sleeplessness, share the night and the silence. She could do that. But then she sees again the lovely girl in her long dark dress, and Christian's searching gaze, and Fran thinks that it would not be right. Thinks that she has missed her chance, if ever there were a chance, to enter a shared territory of solitude with this man.

Then it comes to her, what Satish had said about Razel: that there had been an uprising among the cane workers, years ago, and Razel's parents had been killed, but no one had ever been convicted of the crime. That Razel had actually been the one to find his parents' bodies, and this had changed him. He, Satish, knew who was guilty, and would guard the secret with his life.

She's lovely, says Fran.

Christian is repairing a loose plank by the landing. He looks up at Fran, at her scrubbed, sleep-freshened smile. He puts his hammer down, stands up, folds his arms.

Yes? You liked her?

Well, I'm afraid I wasn't much in the way of conversation . . . I'm ashamed I don't really know much about Mauritius itself, apart from kestrels and macaques . . . the usual . . . not as much as I should.

The awkwardness is there again: as if Asmita had been conjured up by Fran's words.

Then Christian looks at Fran, shading his eyes from the glare of the sun, and says, We've decided to get married.

Fran struggles with words: Married, that's wonderful; I didn't realize—

Yet his expression is veiled: the hand above his eyes, his mouth set in a half smile. Fran says, You must be very happy.

He lowers his arm, looks away, gives a dry laugh, half sigh, half exclamation, Well of course I am.

This all happened rather fast, adds Fran. (She is thinking quickly now: Will he stay? Go to the mainland? Work here or not? Go back to Switzerland?) What are your plans?

I don't know, says Christian.

Now he is looking down, as if he has given her not good, but bad news; with his toe he is pushing against the strap of his sandal with a violence as if to break it. Still the set, wry smile, a rictus of boyish embarrassment, confusion, pride.

Why didn't you say anything last night? We could have celebrated.

We decided on the drive back.

I see.

(Fran sees: he is looking away now, in the direction of Curepipe, the long drive, ridged with darkness, their words sowing a future.)

Well, she says finally, starting to turn, That's great news. Let me know what you decide to do.

He watches as Fran retreats into the growth of trees. He gave her the news to test himself, to test the reality of his feelings, and something shifts inside, blocking light. He thinks and rationalizes, but is unmoved. There is no displacement of the numbness, no light.

~~~

They tracked snow and misery into the delegation office, and Christian looked at them with love. He took their words of death and saw birth; he cursed that the power he felt inside him could do nothing for them, could not stop the snow or their misery.

I'm going to have your child, Nermina had said, just minutes before. Beyond the window lay a field of snow, and in the distance, on a hilltop, stood a shelled church, its bells silenced. And Christian could hear the ringing of bells, the pealing of a message into a sky suddenly struck blue with peace.

What will I do now? writes Fran. My ordered little world, it seems, is only an illusion of order, thwarted by biology.

She has eaten supper; night is folding swiftly around her, a wrap of insect darkness and her own equally restless thoughts. She had not, until now, realized how indispensable Christian has become to her, how, unconsciously, she has come to depend upon him. She cannot envisage the search for a new assistant, the adaptation it will require, the training. All over again. I won't be so lucky a third time, she thinks; although Sean could provide her with a number of excellent students, she knows that what she needs for the work here is more than knowledge. Satish remains irreplaceable; Christian, despite her initial reservations, has proved solid, efficient. With this one, fatal, exception.

She will have to let him go, simply give him notice. His solidity and efficiency are required elsewhere now; he cannot spread himself so thin. Or so it seems to Fran.

In the last light she writes, *I take so much for granted, finally, and only realize what I have when it's too late. Even Satish; especially Satish.*

Does Mauritius have seasons? For some, the heat blurs all difference into an accumulation of days whose surface is too smooth to be marked by time. But Fran can mark the seasons by the subtle changes in her world: seasons for breeding, for flowering, for molting; almost imperceptible shifts in air and water temperature, in cloud formation, wind direction. And the drama of cyclone season, which begins with the influx of Christmas tourists: summertime gone mad, gorged on itself, an implosion of heat and sunshine, with the whirling, sweeping, gyrating of palm trees, rain riding horizontal across the hills. For Fran cyclone season is a time of fear, when small animals and birds disappear, fragile before the blizzard, buried beneath drifts of debris, avalanches of earth or wave. A cyclone, Fran knows, can extinguish a species, destroying its last habitat, killing its last fertile individuals; defeating natural evolution. The stochastic factor, or the act of God; Darwin's wink.

Fran had marked her year with Satish: the flowering of the flame trees, of the sugarcane; the courtship, nesting, and hatching of the pigeons and kestrels, the tropic birds and fodies, and her own splendid, precious mourner-birds; the visits of migrating sandpipers and plovers. And the cyclone season. It came upon them both slowly and as if without warning; in their defiance and joyful self-absorption they ignored the signs—and if one refuses to hear a warning, does the danger exist?

Now, sitting alone on the veranda, with hindsight Fran can see all the warnings. Can sense the slant of the day, the odor of the wind, that mark the season's beginning. She needs no calendar to commemorate; memory's reckoning is sensual, visceral.

She closes her eyes and inhales the night with its warmth and moisture, a salt-breath she has grown to love, a scent she would find niched in his body. She had turned to him and said, Satish, it is what I want. She stood up from that same sofa where she is now sitting; said yes and barely nodded with her eyes for him to follow, she did not take his hand, nor kiss him to seal their agreement, no, just a brief look over her shoulder as she turned, and he followed. In the house she lit a lamp and left it on the floor on the threshold to her room, where it threw shadows deep and strange against the wall: a chair piled with clothes, her body as she added more clothes to the chair, then his body double-shadowed in the room. A gesture (her hand parting the mosquito net), then another (his knee bending as he lowered himself beside her)—and now the sequence blurs, as it always does, and she can play it over and over but she will never be sure of how it really played, her hand, his knee, then the sequence of gestures, repeated over days and weeks and beyond counting, yet irretrievable.

Memory's reckoning: she sits on the old sofa and her lips part, her eyes close, his breath is in her ear; the sensation, oh, the sensation, there are no words for it, but as she remembers her body softens, opens, yearns.

The fish are sulking, thinks Christian. His line hangs limp into the water, connecting him to a placid, empty underworld. He closes his eyes, forgets the fishing line: sees for the first time visions of the future, faint yet clear: Christian as husband, then Christian as father. Acceptance yielding to possibility.

Like a flock of pink pigeons, were there such a thing, rising in frantic flutter above this island cathedral. Christian smiles to himself, remembering Fran's words: Possibility—that's what this place is about.

But what about Fran: what will he do now, live in Mahébourg and travel daily to the island? Find another field station on Mauritius itself? Give up the job and return with Asmita to Switzerland? He has not begun to think about this, he is only just beginning to accommodate Asmita in his life. His future-maiden.

There is a tug on the line; he moves his fingers, then hand over hand as if trying to rouse himself from his deep dream—too late to catch the fish. What will I do about Fran? he thinks again. There are times he does not consider himself to be at all indispensable to her, and thinks that she will easily replace him (his degree in botany has hardly been a prerequisite, his work more often that of a handyman than a naturalist).

Then there is the distance, the coolness between them; his suspicion that she is interested in him merely because he happens to be there, and that there is no real curiosity, no warmth toward the person she does not see. Nor does he know how to approach her. She has kept this hard professional edge pushed toward him, to maintain a safe, respectful distance. So he does not care; she seems to lack humanity, toward humans at any rate. He would not miss her; like Asmita says, she is a strange, hard woman.

He could find work back in Geneva; perhaps the ICRC could take him back on as an administrator, or for a training program.

He stares into the lagoon. He sits on beyond sunset, into nightfall. A sudden welling of sadness, a deeper turbulence. His own voice echoing to him from a place of darkness: *Any news?* That ritual; the crackling telephone line, the voice on the other end, Dubravka's familiar apology, *I'm sorry, no, nothing.* An almost daily ritual of restoring grief to its necessary place, like lighting candles to the dead.

Once or twice he allowed himself to daydream. Dubravka's voice would rise like a clear bell, chime with happiness and celebration, You've called! Yes, she's come back to Sarajevo, she's alive, you must come, Christian, she's waiting for you.

Although it was his hope and the reason he called nearly every day, he knew better than to believe in such happiness; he knew he was expiating his despair, finding a strange comfort in Dubravka's sad apology. Or perhaps the brief moment of hope, the interval between his voice and her answer, was what enabled him to go on, jerking forward in life, until the hurt would not be so great, until the dream disappeared altogether.

It has not yet disappeared, not entirely.

Christian pulls in his line, winds it around its block, stands and walks slowly back through the dark to the warden's house, remembering. There was once a rhythm to his dreamless sleep. He used to wake in the house in Rolle and think his mother was chanting to him, but it was his obsession, voicing the name of the wretched, beautiful city in the hills.

Sarajevo, he thinks abruptly. I must call Sarajevo, one last time.

He does not see Fran sitting on the veranda there in the dark, so when she calls to him, he starts. Catch anything? There is a tremor in her voice.

He mumbles something incomprehensible; Fran did not want a response to her question, it was only a greeting, a warning, I'm here.

A way to rouse herself from a place that is memory-charged, future-weary. Now she says, Would you like a glass of Scotch?

Christian is surprised, hesitant; he wanted to go to his room, to be alone with the geckos and his thoughts, perhaps have a drink of his own. But Scotch would make a good change from the cane liquor, and he accepts.

Get a glass, she orders.

In the dark Fran pours a healthy dose for him, then for herself. They say nothing for some time, listening to the night, then Fran, her voice blurred with drink or emotion, says, I'll miss you.

Again Christian starts. I haven't left yet.

But you will.

At first he does not answer, then says cautiously, I don't know yet. I won't necessarily go back to Switzerland. Maybe I could stay on here, live in Mahébourg——

No, no.

The flutter of her hand, like a pale bird catching light.

No, she explains, that won't work, I need someone living here. It isn't safe.

Are you sure——

(Even as he says this he knows she is right.)

I'm sure.

Anyway, says Christian hastily, I don't need to leave for a while yet. The wedding—— His voice falters. The strangeness of it.

Yes, have you scheduled the date? asks Fran.

Christian does not answer. It is as if someone had given him some distressing news; as if his earlier thoughts of marriage, of completion, belonged to some other still-dreamed part of his life. He tries to think of Asmita, to see her walking down the street past the banyan tree in her coral dress; closes his eyes and takes a gulp of whiskey, lets it burn, thinks of her lips on his body, her long fingers smoothing his worry lines.

I'll miss you, says Fran again.

Fran, I'm not going anywhere, not yet.

But you will. You'll have to leave. A few weeks to settle things . . . oh, I suppose legally I have to give you a month's notice.

Christian thinks to himself that she is a bit drunk, that her almost-angry insistence on his leaving is a kind of pique. Again he conjures up Asmita, his head back against the edge of the sofa, his eyes closed. Then he says, I'm sorry. I know it's inconvenient. I didn't mean for this to happen.

You mean she got pregnant.

No. Not at all. She's a virgin. She's in love with me, and her parents have found out that we've been seeing each other. Now it's the honor of the family.

Fran would like to laugh and say, It's a survival tactic, but even she tires of her ever-Darwinian explanations. Instead she says, She's a lovely girl, and you deserve each other.

What do you mean?

I mean, that you deserve the best. After what you've been through.

There is a moment of silence, a pause, while Christian considers what she has said. Then he stands up and says, You don't know what I've been through. That has nothing to do with it.

Well, it doesn't stop her being a lovely girl.

Good night, Fran. Thanks for the Scotch.

You're welcome.

Perhaps Fran cries. Perhaps those are tears poised at the edges of her lids, for in her thoughts there is real anguish. She is astonished at Christian's restraint, his sense of honor. This was the last thing she had expected: as if he were some relic from another era. A gentleman. She laughs, then her laughter intensifies her sudden anguish. An absurd catalyst to a stranger grief. No one can see how, in this darkness, she is surrendering to an old and sweet mythology. She is sorry

to lose Christian because his quiet, solid presence—nothing more—
acted as a barrier. There could be no ghosts. She might think, often,
of Satish, but Christian could always walk in, take his place, restore
Fran to the present.

She surrenders to the old, pre-Christian mythology, where Satish
has not died. He lives here still, ghost-soul of birds and lizards and
silent growth. A ghost-soul of love, in a myth of continuity.

Fran looks down upon herself as from a great height. She sees Fran the tour guide, leading her first group of gum-chewing camera-poking lotion-gleaming shorts-and-T-shirt-wearing safari-dreamers through Egret's modest tangle of bush. She leads, Christian follows last (make sure they don't straggle or pick anything or step off the path or litter or make noise).

Fran talks, her voice loud and confident as if she were once again in an auditorium. And her voice booms against her beliefs because to make herself heard to the tourists she must disturb the wildlife, shout down the twittering of birds.

She leads, the tourists follow. They are a typically passive group, a dozen or so, of nondescript nationality (they all look, dress, act alike now, thinks Fran, these Eurowanderers—only the Italians might still stand out, too talkative, exuberant, and unruly); if they do not understand her, they do not protest, and Christian, ready to translate into French or German if need be, merely smiles and watches.

Thus, as she stops to explain the origin of the giant tortoises, their history, their worrisome future, for comfort's sake she lets her gaze wander toward Christian. He is looking not at her but away, off into the trees, up into the branches, politely bored, like a daydreaming schoolboy. He is working a muscle in his jaw, patiently, unconsciously; she has never seen him do this. His cheek seems to quiver, and as she speaks—by rote, mechanically—she stares at him, as if she were seeing him naked, exposed, vulnerable.

But Christian's patient, unconscious jaw working is the result of his impatience, the urgency of the day's mission: Sarajevo, call Sarajevo.

He does not see beyond the picture in his mind: the phone booth on the wall outside the supermarket on a noisy, busy street; the distant ringing, often a busy signal, until he gets through, then his own darwin's wink ~ 133

voice, nervous, anticipating, the long war-worn corridors of the ICRC building in Sarajevo, Dubravka's voice, or another, to whom he will have to explain everything (and in explaining, relive it all, feel the constriction in his chest, even stronger). He does not see beyond that moment, does not see Asmita or his future self; does not see, now, the placid group of tourists, or Fran, who stares with such intensity at his cheek, at him.

First tourists, writes Fran. *It went okay. One bright-faced elderly English gentleman with lots of questions at the end; the rest a passive bunch of sheep. One American woman tried to tip me; I told her it would be a donation for the foundation. Oh, but you were so good! It was so* interesting, *she gushed.*

That shallow interest of the comfortable middle classes, particularly women: what is it? *They're* not *interested, but they gush because it's socially correct, a way of making you think that they're good and, in turn, interesting people.*

I'd forgotten that whole aspect of life in society—the necessary little daily hypocrisies. I suppose it goes on here too, on the mainland.

Perhaps, if they behave, these tourists will be a good thing. They will remind me, constantly, of how lucky I am.

If only Christian weren't leaving. Even now he's rushed off to Mahébourg to use the phone. It's odd though; most of the time he doesn't act like a man in love.

Dubravka works in another department now, you want to speak to Dubravka?

An unfamiliar male voice, with its rich Sarajevan drawl, sends a gust of nostalgia down the phone lines, but Christian replies, No, I just have a question for the tracing agency, just two names to check, can you look them up for me?

Go ahead.

Sead Numanović, says Christian, quietly.

Numanović, Sead?

Yes.

There is a pause, a clicking of keys, then the man's voice reading from the computer screen, again the thick drawl: Reunited with his family on February 23, 1996, in Tuzla, Bosnia-Herzegovina.

Christian's heart pounding, a warmth weakening him; then he says, quietly, as if it were some deep shame: Numanović, Nermina.

Didn't you just give me that name?

No, no, it's a different Numanović, his wife—

Again?

Nermina.

Again the silence clicking with computer keys.

Numanović, Nermina?

Yes.

A pause, then, Missing, since May 17, 1995. I'm sorry.

Christian is standing in the warm midday street like a man lost, woken from a long traveling dream. Cars blow their horns at him, a man on a motorcycle shouts at him. Somehow he makes his way to a spot of shade by a building; he leans against the wall, closes his eyes.

Sead Numanović: Nermina's husband. It was for his sake that she joined the local Red Cross, to be closer to sources of information, to be able to look for him in the crowds of displaced people, the camps, the hospitals, along the flight-roads which led to exile.

Sead Numanović is alive, *reunited with his family in Tuzla, Bosnia-Herzegovina*. Sead survived, somehow, and reappeared after the end of the war, and found his family, but his family does not include Nermina, still missing. Since the day I reported her disappearance.

~~~

I must find my husband.

Her voice quiet and poised. Christian looked at her, astonished that he had known her for weeks and had not known that she was married. She wore no ring, but in Bosnia that meant nothing: many people removed their rings, for fear.

It was dawn, and the convoy driver had woken them in the middle of the night, shipments of rice and flour and other supplies to be unloaded as quickly as possible. They had worked in silence, by torchlight, until the first gray light relaxed their senses, the work nearly done. I must find him, she said again, in response to no question, only an urge to confess. And this time as she spoke she looked at Christian as if asking for his help, or expecting his anger, or both. Because she knew already that she loved him, knew that they would soon become lovers, and perhaps this was her last attempt to remain faithful to someone who had cared for her.

Her breath faint against the dawn light. Her words a small cloud of uncertainty, her lips half-parted. He turned back to his inventory of figures, codes jiggling before his eyes. I didn't know you were married—what else could he say?—then she sat down on a box of supplies and her voice continued soft and poised. He—Sead—is much older than me . . . I was very young, he was a teacher at the local school, my history teacher, when I came back from the university, all those years later, he remembered me and came to me and very soon he asked me to marry him. I thought I was in love, yes, perhaps I was, I admired him so much, he is a very interesting man, he knew so much and I loved him for that, too . . . He's a good man . . . They took him away during those first terrible weeks. I heard from him once, through the Red Cross; he was in a camp. Then nothing. It's been over two years.

Her voice almost a whisper, carrying her fragile breath. Christian put his clipboard down and walked over to where she was sitting. Her eyes were wide, staring into space. She looked at him then, suddenly, like a surprised animal. Do you have a cigarette? she asked, and he reached for his packet, handed her a cigarette, cupped his hands close to hers as he held the match. Their fingers touched, her eyes, again, flickered toward him and away.

Sead, she said softly. It's like a dream. There's never been anything but war, has there.

The birds sit high on the branches of the bois d'ébène, looking down at Fran.
Mother-proud, she looks up at them, her two fledglings, grown into
fine, full-feathered young males. They blink at her, she blinks back,
proud yes but sad, too, that they are both males, doomed, perhaps, to
celibacy, unless she and Sean can successfully resettle them in Black
River, where there are other females. Demographic misfortune,
thinks Fran.

And if I needed to mate, she muses, I could emigrate to Australia,
or Alaska, where the ratios work in favor of women. But I don't want
a man, do I, not now, not anymore.

She looks up at the birds as if asking their opinion. They blink
again and one of them takes a little hopping bow, resettling on the
branch.

And if they never know anything else, will they become aware of
their misfortune? wonders Fran.

Christian's last month on Egret Island passes quickly. Fran pushes
him to finish small jobs; in private she curses him and the seductress
Asmita. She frets and radios Sean almost daily to ask if he's found a re-
placement for Christian. Sean gives her a few names, including Marie-
Chantal, Miss Mauritius runner-up 1995, but Fran shouts and says,
Sexual discrimination be hanged, I'm not hiring a woman. We're in the
Indian Ocean, not the bloody Channel Islands.

The tourists arrive every Tuesday; they bore Fran, and she is short-
tempered and bossy with them. (Please be quiet when we are near the
birds. Don't feed the tortoises. Stay on the path. Please don't pick
anything.) One day, a Wednesday after their visit, Christian comes to
Fran at the house leading a small blond woman Fran recognizes from
the previous day's tour. The woman sweats and frowns and glares at
Christian while he explains that he found her with a penknife in one

hand and a small branch of orchid bloom in the other. He places the delicate chain of tiny white flowers on the table; Fran looks at it with a shock reminiscent of her reaction to the dead mongoose. She looks at the woman, then at Christian, then at the woman again and says, You know we can take you to the police, don't you? You know you are trespassing, and poaching. But worst of all, you are contributing to the extinction of a species.

The woman looks back at Fran, glum and defiant. Her eyes are a very pale, ice field blue. In slightly accented Euro-English, the woman snaps at Fran, I will call my lawyer.

Fran laughs and says, Please do, there's a pay phone across the street, then she turns to Christian and says calmly, Why don't you show our guest where the pay phone is?

Christian smiles, reaches to take the woman by the arm; she pulls away, looks at Fran with icy hatred, and marches away down the path toward the landing. Christian follows, Fran shakes her head.

She is indignant, a flush of red across her brown cheeks; this is the Fran of whom Sean says, I love to see her like this, her eyes flashing. A Fran outraged by human folly—that a woman whose hobby, obviously, is orchids, would care so little for their survival, would break the law, no respect, no decency—

But now Fran's face is creasing, folding in upon itself, moved by something stronger than mere anger at a trespasser. She pounds her fist on the table, pauses, then opens her palm, both her palms, to hold her face, as if to hold back tears.

Once, Satish brought her a tiny chain of orchids, held it out to her, on his face a solemn smile. Fran looked from his smile to the flower and back to his smile, now gone; he had understood her shock. It was a present, for you, he said hesitantly; Fran shook her head. Satish, you mustn't pick anything that's so rare, you mustn't. Her voice was soft and she tried not to scold, but it was too late, the words were out and he was turning and walking away down the path.

It was their only disagreement, but one; this tiny chain of orchids, the last gift he would ever have the chance to give her.

On an afternoon heavy with the promise of storm, Christian sits by the lagoon, fishing. He is uneasy, ominous, like the weather itself. It makes it worse, knowing he should not be, knowing he should be happy, looking onward.

Instead he finds himself wondering, not for the first time, why he has not returned to Bosnia, now that the war is over. He could go and look for Nermina, try to find out what has happened to her, even if the news is bad; he might, at least, as other humanitarians say, find closure.

He is confident he could track down the soldiers easily enough, or even Vlatković; it is said that all the war criminals are in hiding, that the foreign peacekeepers cannot find them, but Christian would have a freedom of movement unavailable to the uniformed men who are supposed to bring justice to Bosnia.

Why doesn't he? Why does he push these thoughts aside when they rise—why this long, dubious attempt to bury his past in the future, with Asmita? Why has he taken his calls to Sarajevo at face value, without doing his own research? Why rely so heavily on the presumed efficiency and organization of the Red Cross itself? Bureaucratic, alphabetical lists of the disappeared, available on the Internet? Is life—or death—really that easily categorized?

When the answer comes, as it always does, Christian is overwhelmed by guilt and shame: he is so certain of his own weakness that he cannot feel worthy of Nermina anymore—even if he were to find her, he could not face her. And now he knows she will be back with

Sead, if not yet, then soon, if, if . . . She will be back with Sead, in a shared memory of suffering, in the same place in their souls. They are survivors, both of them.

I'm not a survivor, thinks Christian, not in that sense. I'm only trying to survive myself, and what I did, or failed to do.

He struggles briefly with the fish wriggling on his line, then frees it from the hook and tosses it back into the lagoon, watching for a moment as it flaps against the surface of the water, silver, gleaming.

There are times when Fran thinks she will ask Christian to stay after all, on any terms; then he is standing there by the table where she is working (writing a report, finally, for a scientific journal) with the keys in his hand and his pleading apologetic boyish smirk on his face, I'm going over to the mainland, and she thinks, Be gone, and good riddance.

But each time he leaves—walks away down the path, swinging his arms, his gaze slightly lowered—she knows what it will be to miss him. Each time his absence tightens around her, enlarging her solitude.

There are days when Christian wonders if it will be enough to marry and start a family in order to recover his dreams.

Had it been naïve, to picture his life with Nermina?

They would find an apartment in Geneva; he would go back to the ICRC as an office drone, letting others bury their idealism in distant countries, in cold-water dawn awakenings. Nermina would look after the baby and take French classes at the university. He could see her pushing the stroller through the park by the monument of the Reformation. On weekends they would hike on the Salève or in the Jura, the baby in a pack on his back. They would look forward, forward. All they would keep of their dark beginnings would be the love, that luminous flickering of life that had brought them through.

But he knows if he is to be happy with Asmita he must forget even the dreams, the naïve imaginings.

He wonders where the place of forgetting is to be found, whether it is within him, or in the bolts of colorful silk stacked high in the boutiques of Curepipe (Asmita tells him, her eyes kohl dark and happy, of her trips with her mother to shop for her wedding sari). He is wrapped, already, in the folds of gold-threaded gauzy silk, seduced, enchanted. Asmita instructs him on the purchase of his own wedding suit: off-white, high-collared, raw silk. Christian is at a loss with such elegance. He tells the salesman that he will look like a member of a sixties rock band. Where's my sitar? He laughs, but the salesman is puzzled. Do you play the sitar, really?

The wedding has been set for March, shortly after he leaves Egret. Soon he will meet Asmita's parents. His own parents are both delighted and dismayed by the news (So far away! A different culture!) but are making plans to come, trying to anticipate every major mishap from motion sickness to mosquito bites. They will stay at the Grand Sud, where Asmita works; Monsieur de Froberville has offered her the rooms. Christian knows that his parents, unused to such comfort and luxury, will grumble. If his friend Thierry cannot come all the way from Switzerland, he will ask Bertrand to be best man.

He walks through the preparations as if they were for someone else. He is an actor in his own life, playing to a script. He is astonished at how good he is, at how well his numbness serves him. He has no stage fright.

They are sitting in the cool thatched shade by the hotel pool, finalizing arrangements. Asmita talks, waves her hands, laughs and throws her head back. When she does, she draws Christian's gaze upon her fine neck; her words fade, become unintelligible, translated into his desire to place his lips against her skin.

Darling, are you listening—

He raises drowsy eyes to hers, reaches over, curls his fingers around her wrist. Her warm skin: a deep, intoxicating satisfaction comes over him, knowing that quite soon he will know all of her, will surrender himself to the gentle conquest of her.

She in turn places her fingers around his, squeezes gently. You're not listening!

You distract me. I can't deal with details.

You don't have to. I'll do it, just tell me which you prefer, blue or green, for the candles?

Orange.

Don't tease!

She leans over, kisses him full on the mouth. Each time, it's a new pact she seals; and each time he thinks, Perhaps the numbness I feel when I'm away from her is merely a normal apprehension, and when we're alone, with no barriers—

You're the tease, he says finally, when her lips release him.

Are you happy? she murmurs.

He nods slightly. *Happiness* is not quite the word, he thinks to himself, but does not know how to translate what he feels into a common language. Instead, he kisses her again, sealing yet another pact.

She is radiant. Heads turn; ordinary people—hotel staff, shopkeepers, passersby—bask in her passage. Christian follows, proud and puzzled, her prince consort.

One evening, Christian joins Fran in the kitchen, where she is writing in her field notebook. Headed out? she asks, not looking up. No, answers Christian, I'd like to cook dinner for you, if you don't have anything else planned.

Fran leans back, pushes her glasses up onto her hair, smiles indulgently. No, I've got a loge for *Madame Butterfly* at eight, but if you think we can eat before that—

Then her humor fails her and she sighs, and looks at him and says, Yes, dinner would be nice.

Christian makes a stir-fry dish with vegetables and a fresh fish he caught that afternoon. They have moved the table onto the veranda, where it is cooler; they eat quickly and quietly, slapping at mosquitoes. Words move slowly between them, weighted with what is unsaid. Finally Christian says, Have you found a replacement for me?

Sean is reviewing CVs at the moment. You'd be surprised how many people want to come and work here. Live here. Fran waves her hand dismissively in the direction of the lagoon.

Why did you pick me then?

Your experience. The desperate tone of your cover letter.

Was I desperate, really?

I'm teasing you, dear boy. To be honest, I really don't know why you were chosen. It wasn't my decision, entirely . . . It was between you and a grad student from the University of Glasgow. I think Sean reckoned I'd have difficulty understanding the Scottish brogue.

And so you understand me.

Fran pauses and looks at him, careful this time not to blurt out something blunt and tactless. His eyes are soft, troubled. There are those lines of sadness, of seriousness on either side of his mouth, lines which disappear only when he smiles.

No, Christian, she says gently, I don't really understand you. You're a—

She breaks off. Christian is not listening, but looking off toward the landing.

Are you happy? she asks.

A bit nervous.

Is that all? You should be happy. Have you decided what you're doing?

I'll look for work here . . . and if I don't find anything here we'll go back to Switzerland.

Is that what you want?

Christian has been turning a matchbox on the tablecloth, up-end, side, down-end, side. Suddenly he shakes the matchbox, then flicks it out of reach. He shakes his head, looks briefly at Fran, then away.

~~~

Will you take me to Switzerland someday, after the war?

If that's what you really want.

You know all Bosnians want to go to Switzerland! Isn't it beautiful, and rich, and safe?

It's not as beautiful as Bosnia.

I don't believe you. Don't tease me.

It's a cold, beautiful place. Cold and rich, and it has the soul of a bank vault.

She laughed, and he thought to himself, But I could live there with you. If I could keep you safe, keep you from the coldness, the wealth. If we could keep our little fire going, and warm ourselves with the safe knowledge of our unsafe elsewhere.

~~~

Christian lies in bed in the dark. A line from a Jacques Brel song claims his thoughts, insistent, repetitive, a mantra and a question. *Il faut bien que le corps exulte* . . . Affirmation, or fatalism? Does one allow the body's imperatives—its need for exultation—to rule one's life?

Christian meets Asmita's family. With him they are shy and respectful; among themselves they seem to talk volubly and nurture a congenial chaos. Christian sits formally in the garden with Asmita's father, talking seriously with the older man, about the work on the island, about the economy of Mauritius. He can hear Asmita and her mother and sisters laughing somewhere in the depths of the house. Small dishes of curry, dal, chatini, raita, and farata are brought; Christian thinks it is the best food he has tasted on Mauritius, and the spices seem to spread a warmth through him, melting the edges of his numbness, leaving him open to possibility.

They are handsome people, and utterly exotic to him—more exotic than Asmita herself, with her Western pretensions. They seem to like him; Asmita's two sisters, both of them still schoolgirls, look at her with amazement and envy, as if they did not know men such as Christian existed in the world, as if he were a new species.

They liked you, says Asmita later, in the Land Rover.

And I liked them, he replies.

My mother is so happy now—she can't stop smiling and pinching my cheek. I think they were worried you might be like some of the tourists they see.

Asmita takes his hand, curls it around her cheek, holds it there. Christian feels the warmth of her cheek and hand, the current which passes through him, connecting him to a source of well-being. With his free hand he grazes her other cheek. *Il faut bien que le corps exulte.*

Asmita is radiant. Christian has bought her a ring (not a fancy ring, really very simple, she will tell her friends, but quite expensive), a precious stone set in a gold band, but it is a confirmation, like the bolts of silk now set aside at Les Sarees de Paris in Curepipe for her wedding sari, like the lists her mother pins to the wall in the kitchen beside the refrigerator. Like her sisters' admiring glances as they follow her around the house, tugging on her skirt with questions and excited comments.

At the hotel people begin to comment and congratulate. Thus one day Monsieur Razel makes a sudden appearance, questions her politely on her wedding plans. Must I ask him to the wedding? she wonders; he kisses her on the cheek in parting, a tremulous mint-breathed kiss rather too close to her lips, his hand lingering rather too long on her arm. He has left an envelope for her on the desk: A small token, he nods, to help you prepare for the wedding.

Thus one day she again meets the nosy young séga dancer, and he too knows about her engagement. And he too questions her politely: will she continue to work at the hotel? Oh yes, to be sure; and her Swiss man, will he continue to work on the island? Asmita hesitates; in fact she does not know. Christian has suggested that he will look for other work, to be able to live with her on the mainland, but that is all he has said. So she looks at him and says, Yes, for the time being.

If Christian has not told Asmita the truth, that in fact Fran has given him notice, it is because he does not want her to worry about his income; but somehow he does not want to believe it himself. He cannot picture himself living in a room in a town full of traffic noises and the daily promiscuities of human life. He lies in bed staring at the geckos in lamplight and gauges time and the displacement of emotions against time, geological layers, silting up the open crevices, the wounds.

There has been some healing here, he thinks. A superficial scarring, enabling him to think, converse, work, find small pleasures in the island's wealth, and forgetful pleasures in Asmita's company. But the deep wounds have not healed, and in their inner bleeding they throb with an irrational sense of guilt—that others died, and he survived; or even that he survived because others died. Those wounds do not heal, and there are times when away from Asmita he can feel the throbbing like a pain made even sharper by the promise of pleasure.

Fran is annoyed. The heat irritates and frazzles her; she had not intended to come into Mahébourg so early, but Christian needs the dinghy and the Land Rover later this afternoon—it is after all his day off, and he wants to spend it with Asmita.

The town seems to press upon her with its heat and noise, an excess of bodies all trying to be in the same place, pushing and hurrying for a moment of cooler air, or a lazier time when they will not have to be running errands. Fran feels the falseness of her smile as she stands in lines, pushes past other waiting bodies. In fact, she does not need to smile at all, it is an American thing, this smiling, to oil wheels, to make people think well of you as you push and compete for space. And there are times she doubts whether the locals think well of her— no matter how much she smiles.

The bank is slow and tedious. The line does not seem to move. She is thirsty now in addition to being hot. Fans ruffle papers on employees' desks. There is a colonial, timeless feel to the place. As if it were a movie set.

She is late when she has finished at the bank, strides hurriedly through the streets. The post office is about to close; at the poste restante window she exchanges a few pleasantries with the young woman who is pulling Fran's and Christian's letters from the pile, one by one.

Oh, nice stamp, says the woman, pausing. Do you collect stamps?

No . . . do you?

My little brother does. You know, some people have a love for stamp collecting here . . . He would love this one.

Fran smiles, genuinely this time. Of course, she says, the Blue Mauritius.

The girl hands Fran a postcard. Two stamps, colorful, unusual indeed. Then the postmark seems to lift up off the color, dark and strong and faintly chilling, Sarajevo.

It's not my postcard, or I would give you the stamps, Fran says, regretfully, as she glances at the address, then the salutation, *Dear Christian*. A smooth, looping Middle European scroll, feminine. I should not read this, thinks Fran, looking away briefly at an Air Mauritius poster of the Île aux Cerfs: the otherworldly transparency of the tropical lagoon, a cliché; the otherworldly quality of a woman's handwriting.

The postal employee is looking at her expectantly, as if waiting for Fran to ask for something else, or to give her the stamps after all, as if some decision is forthcoming. Fran is caught somewhere between the unreal juxtaposition of that tropical lagoon and the city represented by the postmark on the card. Finally the young woman, exasperated, asks her, Do you need anything else? Fran stuffs the postcard along with the other letters into her handbag and smiles apologetically, murmuring an inaudible excuse.

Later Fran would wonder about things. Like coincidence, or fate. Why the girl noticed the stamps. Why she, Fran, and not Christian, came to the post office. Why an open postcard, and not a sealed letter.

Because it put her in temptation's way: the temptation to read someone's private mail. Because she realized she wanted to know what that message contained, as if it were somehow addressed to her too. Despite the fact that it made no difference, that Christian would be leaving the island soon anyway. She was curious, she wanted to know about his past. As if his past were a network of roots to which she might cling, and keep him from leaving.

Now she is surprised, even annoyed at her reaction. It must be the heat, she thinks, I'm addled.

She stands outside the post office and feels a burning in her fingertips. How easy it would be to reach into her bag and pull out the postcard. It is probably nothing, just a colleague of Christian's bringing him up to date on the Red Cross work in Bosnia. Someone who has his address, after all; someone with whom he is still in touch, to whom he has sent postcards, probably, of the Île aux Cerfs, for example. Probably nothing, and yet she is standing there torn between honest behavior and the power of her desire to know. More than mere curiosity.

When she returns to the island, Christian is waiting at the landing for the dinghy. Without cutting the engine she waits for him to climb in next to her, then she scrambles ashore. She cannot see his expression behind his sunglasses, but she senses he is angry because she took so long; he is eager to be off. I might not be back for supper, he says tersely.

She watches him pull away in the dinghy, looking toward shore. Too late, she remembers his postcard. Suddenly it no longer seems so important.

They are driving through a small town, past the sugar works, the smell of burnt sugar thick upon the air, like an element of climate. Christian slows the vehicle, maneuvering past men on bicycles, and women laden with baskets and bags. He stops to let an old woman cross the street; she is bent low beneath an umbrella to ward off the heat of a sun now hidden in cloud. Look, he says tenderly to Asmita, she doesn't even realize there's no sun.

Asmita opens her eyes. She has been dreaming. Now she says, seeing not the old woman but someone else, Oh God, no, there's that séga dancer.

Christian sees a flash of white shirt, a smile, a wave. He looks with surprise at Asmita, her dreamy smile. Interprets a complicity that is not there. You know him?

He works for Razel.

Yes, and he knows about us, remember?

He's incredibly nosy, isn't he. He always asks about you.

And the same here. I wonder what he's up to. And he knew Satish, apparently.

Satish who?

The fellow who was on the island before me.

The one who died?

Christian nods, watching Jean-Baptiste's rolling gait, his slow waltz across the street, the way he circles his youth around the old woman. His youth and insolence. Christian taps his fingers against the steering wheel.

Yes, he told me he was the last person to see him alive.

You know, says Asmita, stifling a giggle, the old gossips here on Mauritius say that your boss fed him to the birds!

Christian does not answer but accelerates abruptly. He looks again at Asmita: her dreamy face, her eyes closed once again. And he feels a sudden chill, like the first breeze before a storm.

The air is still; a sky of milk darkened with weather. Fran listens in vain for the bulbul's call, for the mynah's charade: the birds are silent, and she remembers ominous storm-warning times, and wonders if this is such a time. The lagoon has turned thick and murky. But the color is iridescent, mother-of-pearl; there is no depth. And when cloud comes, all the milky jade drains away, and only a dark gray-blue is left.

She swims, the only sound her gentle plashing. The roar of the surf is distant, then briefly louder on an imperceptible current of air, as if ready to break through the protecting reef.

They return to their love-road. Asmita is unusually soft, as if open, pliant. Christian touches her, dares a forbidden gesture or two. She murmurs and smiles, a knowing cast to her features. Now, he whispers, now that we will soon be married, what need is there to wait? He explores further, gently, wooing her trust.

In any case, she says suddenly, easily, almost flippantly, that is what they think.

They who? he murmurs.

My parents.

Think what? Again she moves beneath his hands, both offered and withheld, sighing, moaning.

Think what? he repeats. It is a tease, nothing more, so he is not prepared for her answer.

That you—that you have already made love to me. That I might be pregnant.

Christian pauses. His skin retracts. He is aware of the passage of rain on the roof of the Land Rover. He looks at Asmita: has she ever been more lovely? Her offered, dreaming face, eyes half-closed, lips half-parted. Her green dress raised on her half-opened thighs.

You, she murmurs, made love to me.

That is what you told them?

She nods, still not looking at him.

Christian sits up, looks out through the shimmering trails of rain at the blurred landscape. The implication enters him like a wound. You told them that? he exclaims. That's not what you said! You told me that someone saw us together—

Yes, Christian, that's what I told *you;* and someone did see us, our nosy neighbor Mrs. Thapoor, but my father was so angry, he wanted to know . . . so I told him . . .

She pauses, looks at him as if trying to gauge his reaction, then smiles, certain that her seduction is assured; misfires. Lightly she asks, How could I be sure you would marry me? Whether it was true or not, you violated my honor, the family honor, didn't you? Isn't that funny? And it wasn't even true. But it's appearances that count, you know, what people think . . . But now you can make it true—it's what you want, isn't it?

Her eyes call him. Two huge brown eyes in which you could lose yourself, in which he almost lost himself. At last Asmita is offering herself to him: she will release her own desire and succumb to his.

But Christian is turning the key in the ignition. He jerks the Land Rover onto the pitted road, drives into the blurred landscape as if to escape himself. He ignores her sudden tearful pleas, her excuses and apologies. They are like the querulous calls of a stranger, speaking a language he does not know.

Fran calls the birds and they come to her. The air is so still they must make their own resistance to find liftoff, almost imperceptible currents which lead them gliding to her. Like flight in a vacuum, in a tainted sky, where flight deprived of air would be impossible. Do they feel fear, or sense the darkening change of the sky as a warning?

She talks to them, coos to them, and they listen and nod, and she asks them what the sky means, what the wind-silence means, and they twitter among themselves—the lone female and her male, their pair of offspring. Fran looks to the mainland, where still darker clouds labor across the sky with a train of rain cloth, but here the air holds a threat of moisture, still uncertain. She wants to protect the birds and considers the aviary but then shakes her head, wondering what inculcated fearfulness this is, overprotective, desiring to control Nature. She asks them again what the wind-silence means, and the birds grow agitated, and Fran looks again to the mainland, where the top of the Lion Mountain has now vanished in cloud.

Twilight is premature, pulling the cloud-darkness over the face of the earth as it turns from the sun. Birds huddle and prepare to sleep with their heads tucked against their wings; small lizards return to their refuges. The cicadas are silent, confused by early nightfall. Fran watches the fleeing light and sees a solitary kestrel leaving a last dark sigh against the dusk. She observes its lonely struggle against airlessness and wonders at the illusions of flight. Her body feels heavy, defeated by an unusual gravity. But the kestrel too tugs at the sky with the span of its wings, as if the motionless air were in fact a heavy countercurrent impeding flight. Hurry home, thinks Fran; but you will not find lightness on earth, either.

She waits for the relief of rain and wind, but stillness prevails. She waits for something beyond, too, but cannot see past the stubbornness

of weather and Christian's imminent departure for his new life. Like a
sailor's wife she is bound by waiting, but she does not know why. The
sailor's wife scans the sky and sea and awaits her sailor's return, and
with it her feeling of security and belonging. Fran sees only a dome of
sky marked by the omen of a bird's passage, and wonders why she was
not chosen.

He left her by the banyan tree and thought how strange the light
was, how instead of being saturated with color as the rain bled contours into a shimmering abstract the street was winter-drab,
city-gray. And the woman now running down the street barefoot, in a
long drenched and rain-sodden dress, was a stranger to light.

I'll call you, he had said, and shaking his head as she had again begun to plead with him, he had not kissed her, and had not acknowl-
edged the graze of her fingers against his wrist.

Now Christian sits in the Land Rover looking out at the lagoon,
some miles north of Mahébourg, but does not see the stillness of the
water, the white vacuum of the sky. He feels only a sympathetic resonance within, carving hollowness. He fears for the island, for Fran.
Will she let him stay on? And if he stays on, can he return to the moment when he had known he must break with Asmita, before she told
him, the morning after she stayed on Egret, that they had been seen
together and that she was threatened with dishonor and her parents'
anger? Before his sense of duty and responsibility suddenly shaped his
perception of the world and altered his aimless trajectory? Will it be
possible to fold time back upon itself?

Far in the distance he can see the island, Egret Island, a tiny
thumbprint of whorled green against a canvas striated with sky and
sea. The only suggestion of color against the still, drained seascape.
Night is falling more quickly than usual. By the time he reaches the
dock it will be dark.

So he does not hurry but sits on and absorbs the colorless air, as if upon returning to the island he will be revived by color. As if the island's green holds some secret of survival.

Asmita sleeps, stunned by a potion her mother has made. Asmita sleeps, and her dreams are filled with questions which taunt her but are unreal, so they cannot touch her. Will you marry now? ask voices, some chorus of future-maidens, angelic and sad.

By the time Christian sets off from the shore in his dinghy, the colorless sky has turned to black, and the smudge of the island has disappeared. At first he rows, to give himself time to find his bearings, to avoid the pirogues moored here and there in the black water. Then he fires the engine and reaches in his backpack for his flashlight and compass.

This is routine. He has crossed the lagoon almost daily, has had an almost instinctive sense of direction, as if navigating by his urges as he crossed to tryst with Asmita. On occasion he might look at the stars, or the lay of the dark sleeping mass of island. Once or twice he might have used the flashlight and compass, on such a dark night. But he has always kept them in his pack.

But on this night Christian has lost his sense of direction, his navigational instinct. The closing sky has caught him unaware, his mind on other things. So when he does not find the flashlight and compass in his pack—which he leaves tucked under the thwart in the dinghy—he curses but assumes he has forgotten them on Egret, or in the Land Rover.

Christian lowers the throttle, strains to see. Come on, Fran, he thinks, give me a light so I can get home.

Perhaps he curses, *merde, putain de nuit;* perhaps he squints, props his eyes wide open, holds his glasses, tries every optical trick. Perhaps he prays to Saint Christopher. He cuts the throttle to a mere putter, and goes slowly in what he believes to be the right direction.

Fran lights the two gas lamps, although she usually needs only one. Spiting darkness, she thinks. Moments ago as she stood on the veranda she could see neither stars, nor moon, nor the lights of Mahébourg. Now she places one lamp on the table on the veranda. For Christian, she thinks, to light his way, and she imagines her small flickering presence guiding him back. Then another, harder self, asking, Why should you, what for? as if she ought to extinguish the lamp, to spite him too, spite his successful male adaptability. Then just as suddenly she reproaches her lack of generosity, her mean-spiritedness.

I am slowly going mad in isolation and in my will to play God. Talking to birds, envying kestrels at dusk. There is an instinct in woman to care, thinks Fran, an urge in man to be cared for. Is it genetic, is it a human construct, or is this my own interpretation? Why begrudge Christian his success—after all he has been through?

And she thinks, as he once reminded her, that she does not know what he has been through, that he has never talked to her about Bosnia. That she has drawn her own conclusions from what she has learned of the war from the media alone. And that from those conclusions she has on occasion interpreted his quietness or withdrawal as the throbbing of a wound, but she does not know.

She remembers the postcard in her bag, feels again the tug of curiosity, then thinks better of it, berates herself. I'll leave it in there and give it straight to him when he comes back, so I won't even have to look at it. It's none of my business.

She waits, listens. Once she thinks she hears a chug of outboard, then the sound vanishes. Once she thinks she hears a sigh of breeze, but that too disappears. Silence clings to the walls of the house, to the bark of trees, to the leaves, and soil.

She makes supper, disappointed. She will leave something in the pan for Christian. Food does not keep long in the heat and humidity, so they choose their fresh produce carefully. Fran has made a vegetable stew, which will keep for a while, but that was not the point. It is a kind of possessiveness, as if the reason for his failure to return is that even though Asmita knows she will marry Christian, she must still find ways to keep him from another woman's presence. Are they, at that moment, arguing over Christian's right to have dinner with his legitimate employer, or is he late because he had to have one for the road? My thoughts are coarse and bitter, thinks Fran, perhaps unfair. He even told me he might not be back.

She inserts the worn, heat-muffled cassette of *Tosca* into the tape player. But the batteries are low, and after some minutes the voices slow and become gravelly. Finally she switches off the tape player, and the silence seeps again into the shadows, coiled and expectant.

She washes up, makes tea, picks up a scientific journal. Pushes her glasses to the edge of her nose, then up again, tries to read, but the words scamper off, leaving her own voice droning on, querulous. Only a few more days and he'll be gone. Men. Maybe I should hire a woman after all.

Fran is hard. She has forgotten softness but is no stranger to it; she despises weakness and misinterprets the nature of softness.

So often astonished at herself, back then, in the Satish-days; how the hardness within her would liquefy, as if his soft brown gaze had such a power.

With hardness one forgets love, one forgets what is possible. She observes her birds: their brief pragmatic courtship, attentive parenting; their obvious fidelity. To Fran this model behavior is proof of a greater, nobler scheme than that devised—interpreted—by men. To attach love to the business of evolution seems a frivolous conceit.

She has forgotten, as she lies in bed waiting for sleep, that not so long ago she subscribed to love as to faith, a system of belief. Evolution as an end in itself—beyond the rational beauty of Mr. Darwin's discovery—then seemed barren to her. As she lay next to Satish, she would chide Mr. Darwin: without God or without love, what was the point?

Perhaps if the great man were there, talking to his disciple, he would smile, and wink at her, as if imparting a secret that only she would share.

But now she has forgotten faith, and her feelings have grown hard around a hollow place. There is nothing left, she fears, to liquefy.

She sleeps. Once she wakes and thinks, Am I alone? but sleep recaptures her before she can wake fully and look for signs of Christian's presence: the keys on the hook, his sandals by the door.

Her mother once told her about maternal love. That it governed sleep, that a mother always knew when a teenage child was not home, and would wake in the still hours to listen for the sound of the key in the lock, or the door opening, or the tooth brushing. And that the softest cough of a sick infant could wake a mother.

In the early days of Peter's betrayal, Fran would lie in bed and wonder why he was so late, why he had not called. And falsehood governed sleep: he would come, finally, so late, whispering lies, and she in turn would pretend to sleep.

After Satish died she could not sleep. She drank potent herbal teas from the market in Port Louis, which gave her hallucinations and a strange impression of sleep. Sean stayed with her from time to time, often pouring her into a Scotch-stupor of forgetfulness. She cannot even count the months which separated Satish's death from Christian's arrival. Although he does not know it, Christian has become the guardian of her sleep.

In the morning she rises sleep-muddled, pours water, stands on the veranda to wait for the water to boil. The sky yawns gray and thick with morning breath, close odors of life decaying in the heat. Fran makes coffee, then remembers: looks to the hook on the wall, but the keys to the Land Rover are not there.

Damn, she thinks, assailed at once with fear; unwilling to believe that anything so bad could happen twice in her life, she rejects ideas of catastrophe and opts for blame, How inconsiderate, all night with his fiancée, not even the decency to call. Not that he could call, of course. A simplified explanation, a female jealousy, learned with Peter.

So Fran goes to work, sets out at once with her field notebook and binoculars, takes roll call, measures growth, inspects for trespassers. Large fronds of pandanus and *bois de chandelle* hang limply in the languid air. As if the wind has forgotten the world and retreated behind the ceiling of cloud. And even the ocean seems to lie utterly still, except for a slow throbbing swell, which arrives from deep within and far away, like an echo of samba traveling far and faint to reach this shore. Fran looks out and dreams. Beyond the stillness there are cities and cathedrals, or samba dancers or stone streets filled with cafés and love, but she is no part of that; she has been abducted by stillness, confined to silence. Her dreams crash against silence, like sparrows against glass.

There is blood on his hand and in his memory. He seems to bathe in blood—warm, damp, his skin is blood and he must not move. The sky is white and sharp, like a blade above his head, prohibiting vision. He thinks not Where am I? but What am I? and he trembles against the hard ground and the hard light, and then the blackness comes again.

survival

Fran paces. It is early afternoon and still Christian has not come. She has eaten the rest of the vegetable stew, and now, on the veranda, she considers his absence and the closed white sky.

Islands carry romance but they also carry doom, like old spice boats sailing to a certain fate. Cap Malheureux, La Roche qui Pleure, Le Morne, Baie du Tombeau, Îlot du Mort. Fran thinks not of the romance—that is for tourists and readers of novels—but of doom. Island biogeography is a study of probabilities. *The smaller the island, the greater the likelihood of extinction.* This is Fran's basic math, it is why she has been on the island for five years, trying to transform negative probability into positive possibility; trying to flout Darwin, to laugh in his face, reverse evolution, abet the survival of the weakest.

Altruism destroys Darwinism, suggested a famous naturalist. Fran agrees, but without the dreadful intervention of man, stacking the cards against so many species, there would have been no need for the altruism of Fran and her kind. No splendid birds would have languished unto rarity at the court of Versailles; no sad and innocent dodo birds would have disappeared forever into the holds of ships, down the gullets of Dutch and Portuguese sailors. The dodo, she muses, became flightless because there were no predators in its world, before man.

But this place has become a prison, thinks Fran; I am trapped here, both now, in this moment, and forever, if I am to succeed. The entire chain of restoration, of conservation on this tiny plot of land depends on a human presence, as surely as the whale depends on plankton. If I leave, the island will survive, willy-nilly, with Sean or another naturalist—but what would be my place outside the chain I have entered? Where would *I* find my sustenance?

Near tears, Fran takes the VHF radio from the shelf and tries to call Sean. Of course there is no answer; their appointed time is later, at four in the afternoon; as it is, the batteries are low, the signal weak. Fran is near tears because she cannot understand her frustration, cannot pick it apart and say, This is why. It is more than Christian's absence and the knowledge that she has no way to get off the island. It is a huge unwieldy emotion, a massive unyielding jailer withholding the key; it is also her life, and it makes no sense.

Again the kestrel hesitates, hovers, glides closer, beats wings against a lethargy of air. From a treetop he looks upon his domain: the green promise of land, the dazed colorlessness of the lagoon and the sky. There is something wrong with the picture, and the kestrel knows this with the wisdom of its bright-eyed instinct. In the distance are mountains, canyons, steep ridges which offer shelter. It is a long way to go, and the kestrel too is by nature a homebody. But the bird can smell the blood of mammals, and that smell is an alarm. He rests, considers his choices, then at last rises upon the sluggish draft, into exile.

Fran swears, pounds her fist against her thigh, looks again at her watch. Still too early to call Sean, but too late for Christian's absence to be normal. Where is he? she shouts, as if anger would restore normalcy: he is drinking beer with Bertrand, or shopping for his wedding, or fucking. He has lost his watch. The outboard engine broke down. He ran out of gas. The irresponsible, clueless idiot; the dear, doomed dodo-brain.

Then a sound of wings, loud against the vacant sky. Fran looks up and sees the kestrel overhead, as on the previous day, and she shivers. As if this time she knew it were fleeing: something in the urgency of its propulsion, pistons driven by feather and bone, burning air. She watches as it heads out over the lagoon, leaving her behind.

At five minutes to four Sean steps naked out of the shower. Marie-Chantal sits wrapped in a towel at the edge of the bed, frowning. What is it, love? asks Sean, touching her shoulder with the back of his hand.

I don't know . . . I didn't want to sleep with you. What happened? Why did I?

Ah, lass, you didn't want to *intellectually*. But you've always wanted to, physically. You fairly quiver with desire.

But you're my professor.

Was your professor. You've graduated. You're a grown lass, you can do what you like.

He sits down, leans over, lifts her mass of black braids in his palms, kisses her neck. You think too much, he murmurs.

No, Sean, please. Stop. I have to go.

Go where? Stay here. There's a cyclone warning. Stay here, I've got a deep, well-stocked cellar. It's cool, and it's a fine place for making love.

His lips move down to her shoulder, his hands tug gently at the towel. Again, he whispers, before we have to go to the cellar.

Marie-Chantal abandons her token resistance. Oh well, she thinks, I tried. Despite herself, she concedes her lust, throws off all barriers.

The flight of the kestrel has filled Fran with an irrational fear. Again she calls Sean, and when he does not respond, in anger she hurls the radio from the veranda into the brush. Then regrets it: there is always the emergency channel. Am I in danger? she wonders, retrieving the radio, calmer. She switches the channel, hears the faint signal from Port Louis, then silence.

How long should she wait? It will be dark in a few hours, too late to begin a search; if she does not call now, she must wait until morning, when it may be too late altogether. But why? she thinks; too late for *what*?

The night Satish vanished, she was not afraid, not even suspicious, until they found the dinghy. He could have been anywhere—with friends, with family. That he did not have many friends was not something Fran considered; not until later did she learn, through Sean's careful parsing of local gossip, that most of Satish's friends had abandoned him, suspicious, envious. Perhaps that envy was even responsible for his death. That night she did not worry, was not alarmed.

But there were other things that had caused her to lose sleep.

She decides to wait until morning before calling for help. She is afraid to seem foolish, overanxious. Her story will carry more weight if more time has elapsed. She refuses to consider disaster. Twice on one small island is unreasonable, against the odds.

Fran does not consider that it might not be a question of odds, of random determinants, stochastic factors. Refuses to see that others, too, can play at God.

She tries to read, a battered copy of *Lord Jim* that Christian found for her on one of his trips to Port Louis, but the prose is dense and resists the efforts of her distraught mind to grasp more than mere words. *In the destructive element immerse.* So she dozes and wakes with the mosquitoes. She listens to the silence, translates the quickening darkness to a need for light, but then resists, and sits on in twilight, thinking that light will change nothing, that Christian will not come, that she will be awake most of the night. Plays a game with fate: if I light the lamp for Christian, he will not come. If I give him up for gone, and sit on in darkness, he will come.

His skin records the recession of light, warmth evaporating from his body, leaving him in shadow. Gone is the impression of damp ooze. Slowly he explores, first hands then arms, then he rolls from his stomach to his side, massive aching, but no intense pain. And finally he is able to sit: he reaches trembling for his extremities, lifts his palms cool and dry and questioning, as if holding all of experience in this moment when he understands he is not dying.

He stands, unfolding rigid, aching muscles; reaches out to hold the branch of the red ebony; listens to the pounding in his head, which gradually gives way to silence. And begins to walk, one foot after the other, unsteadily, along the edge of the island. Each step brings darkness; now and then he stumbles, or stops to look at the murky, moonless waters of the lagoon. There is no way to navigate; he knows he could be lost again all night, wandering in the tangle of growth; he could stop now, find shelter to curl up and sleep, but although his feet are uncertain, some unseen beacon draws him on.

Was it dark when Christian came stumbling to the veranda of the warden's house? Later, Fran cannot remember; her senses merged to give sight to sound, his footfall was hesitant on the wooden floor, but she saw him as if at that moment the island were lit by lightning. He will later swear it was pitch dark; she sees him.

She bathes him, cleanses his wounds, and feeds him. She soothes his trembling with her quiet voice. He tries to tell her what happened, what he thinks happened, but she silences him, tells him to lie back and try to sleep, and he will tell her in the morning.

During the night he calls out and she goes into the room, parts the mosquito net. In the fractured beam of the flashlight his gaze wavers, upon Fran, upon a shadow behind her. She brings him fresh water, holds him up by his shoulders to drink, to swallow some aspirin.

Christian abandons himself to Fran. There is a womblike comfort in her care: he knows, in any case, that he has no choice. In a lull between two attacks of fever he senses her power. And his hitherto inexperienced fragility: in the war he had an awareness of the proximity of death, its unlimited potential, but never of his own body's surrender to that potential. He does not know if he is in greater danger now: he fears her power, and respects it. He wants to obey.

She feeds him a thin broth with noodles, or a sugary water. She places cold compresses on his forehead and limbs. From time to time he is roused from a troubled sleep by a burning sensation: she is cleaning his wounds. Infection, she murmurs.

When she has finished she sits on the floor beside his bed, her arm propped on the mattress and her head resting against her arm. He cannot see her face but he can hear her murmured words. Sometimes she seems to be talking to herself. About the bird, about Darwin, about a storm. As the hours pass her voice grows fainter. The roof is rattling against a rising wind. Sometimes he thinks they are in an airplane: a still yet tumultuous vibration. Are they moving?

The sky circles, dark, then light again. Fran sleeps, guardian of his dreams. In the morning she closes all the shutters to make night. She talks about broken glass. The terrible noise on the roof has not stopped.

At times he struggles to hear her voice, to make out the words. I'll tell you a story if you're good, she says. He has tried to be a good patient. She makes it easy: no injections, nothing unpleasant, except the stinging wounds; he hopes she cannot see his tears as she touches him there.

I'll tell you, she begins, the story of my life on the island with Satish.

Satish—he struggles to remember. There is something he must tell her, a warning.

Sssh. Be quiet. Listen.

He will think afterward that he must have slept, and perhaps he dreamt. This stern, nurselike woman, this general fighting a war, tells him a love story. How she and Satish became lovers, and it was like being residents of a final Eden, and they had to keep it a secret from the world.

But then he died, as you know, she murmurs. Again there is something he wants to tell her, but she continues, shaking her head. I want to tell you what happened on that last day. I've never told anyone, and I live with it.

Her words fade in and out of the storm, and shape a dream. He sees Fran and Satish, now clearly, now as faceless specters. She will tell a story, a last day.

The mourner-birds mated, and Satish was happy. He went daily to the hidden place where the birds had made their scrape, close to the ground, vulnerable in another world yet safe, still, in theirs. He watched with pride as the male sat on the eggs.

Then he came one day to Fran and said, What will happen? Will we have children?

She was sitting at the table on the veranda, writing a report; she took off her glasses and looked at him, astonished.

No, Satish love, you needn't worry—I'm protected.

What do you mean, protected?

I mean, I'm using birth control.

Why?

Because I can't have children.

Why not? If you stop using birth control, can you have children?

No, I mean, I don't want to have children. Not now, not—

You mean you can have children but you don't want them?

She sighed and laid her hand upon his wrist. Satish, she said softly, I tried, for many years, with my husband. Nothing. Now I'm too old, it wouldn't be wise—

Your husband was a bad man. You said so. And you're not too old.

She withdrew her hand from his wrist. The skin on his hand was smooth and firm; she thought of a fruit—mango, peach—gorged with juice. Her own hand, a pretty freckled color but dry, tiny wrinkles irrigating the skin with time. She looked up at him, his puzzled, closed face.

Satish, what is it?

You're not too old, he repeated. My mother was almost your age when I was born.

What are you saying?

He was looking away into the trees, as if her gaze were suddenly too bright, and to look in her eyes would burn him. Softly he said, I want a family someday. I want children.

Fran looked down at her hands, where the fine wrinkles caught the light and shone faintly. Satish, someday I will go back to America, and then you will take a wife, and you will have a family. You will be young still.

But it is your child I want.

No, Satish.

She must have whispered this, so touched and desperate did she feel; did age change everything, remove all possibility?

Satish, she continued finally, I too want a child. But—

She must have thought of the barriers. Her age. His youth. Her status. His origins. Perhaps briefly she envisioned what might be possible: cutting the island adrift, sailing off into a world where they would be the only inhabitants, the chosen survivors of a cataclysm.

But the island was rooted, like their past.

You think I care what they say? said Satish with a sudden violence, thrusting his hand toward the mainland. I don't. I don't. They have given me nothing. You give me everything.

She must have reached for him then. She remembers holding him, as she said, I don't know if I can give you this. I don't know.

Fran said nothing to Satish but did not stop using birth control. And if he knew this, he said nothing, and Fran did not have the courage to intrude upon his silences, which seemed more moody, and thoughtful.

Then he would seem to forget, and time would be as before, a distant concept. There was the love, which made them playful. And there was the work, which brought its own rewards: the germination of the native plants, the nestlings' small cries in the still morning.

There were days you thought you could hear the island growing, the quiet murmur of stem and leaf urging toward the light, of bone and feather toward the sky.

There were days Fran wanted to be part of that growth, and thought of the lost years, given to illusions of career and marriage; she now knew that the truth was here, and that she, surely, had arrived too late.

So she learned to live with joy and with acceptance, and knew that as time went on there would be less and less of joy and more and more of acceptance. And wondered why it should be so; and thought that perhaps joy was only a lure or a reward, attendant to procreation; that acceptance was the place where one learned to reside outside of Nature's dictates.

How long will you be here? he would ask. She had no answer, did not tell him that there were times when she worried that they would lose their funding, or that the island would be sold to a private company. Nor did she tell him that one day she might have to retire and return to America, and that she had pictured him as her successor. Though why she should ever retire to America when she was content on the island she could not imagine: unless Satish were to go away, leaving behind seeds of loneliness. It was a game they played, for she would ask him, How long will you be here? thinking, Before you tire of me; before you want to start a family; before you realize where you are and who you are.

Neither would answer, or they would make up pretend-world answers, like Until every gray pigeon on the planet has turned pink, or until the tortoises have all died of old age, or the *oiseau-languit* has learned to sing Puccini.

~~~

From time to time Christian seems to nod, or smile, his eyes closed. Once Fran discovers that she is holding his hand curled in both of hers, and she looks at it like a thing detached until she understands that he has given it to her willingly, because he is listening.

~~~

She did not know it would be the last day—how could she know? The ordinariness of that day, with no sense of any future different from the present: they awoke, made love, went to swim in the lagoon, came back for coffee and breakfast of toast and jam, of mangoes and coconut. Fran went to check on Satish's nestlings: ugly little crumpled balls of feather, growing toward certain beauty. It was all so ordinary, and now when she looks back on that day, indistinguishable from those which preceded, it seems to belong to an experience of dreams, beautiful and fragile.

(By Christian's bedside she worries the past like a dog with a bone, eager to apportion blame or forgiveness. If she finds the phrase that changed everything, she might be able to understand the workings of fate, and move on.)

Shadows lengthening across the heat-parched day; Fran dozing on the sofa on the veranda; an occasional breeze would brush her skin like a caress. Once she opened her eyes to see Satish sitting beside her, stroking her foot, Satish like a breeze. For some minutes they did not speak; then he announced in a quiet voice, I am going over to Mahébourg.

Good. I'll come with you, I need to do some shopping.

No, it's better if you stay here.

Satish, I need to come. I need to pick up some flashlight batteries.

Then you can go tomorrow. Or I'll get them for you.

But why can't I just come with you now? For Christ's sake!

Satish shook his head, said nothing.

Fran reached over and held his wrist. More softly: Satish, I want to come, she said, but again he shook his head, then looked at her, a warning gaze which told her to stay away, yet was sad, too.

Why not? said Fran.

I cannot tell you.

Satish, you have to tell me. I'm sorry, but I am responsible for you, for the dinghy, for everything on this island. If you take the dinghy to go to Mahébourg I have to know why.

(She knew this was not true. She knew these were the sudden words of panic, thrown needy and thoughtless at him; control-eager, love-anxious.)

No, Fran, he said softly, you own the dinghy but you don't own me.

I don't own the dinghy! The foundation owns the dinghy, and I have to answer to the foundation!

Then trust me, Fran. I am working for the foundation too.

You cannot tell me because you are ashamed! You don't want people to see us together! They've been talking, is that it?

No, Fran, that is not the reason. You know I don't care what they think.

Then let me come.

No.

Then tell me why.

(Why did Satish not simply lie, why could he not say, I'm going to see a friend or relative; I'm going to the cinema and it's in Hindi and you won't understand; or even, I have a surprise for you and if you come it will spoil it. But he said none of these things, because he was honest and he could not tell her the reason for his mission. For her own good.)

Go, then, she said finally. Go and do whatever it is that's so bloody important that you won't take me with you. Go.

Satish looked at her now with sadness. Do you need anything else, besides the batteries?

No, no. I'll go tomorrow, on my own.

Fran—

It's okay. I'm sorry. Just go.

She sat on the sofa with her eyes closed and she did not see him go. She lay there and thought of how she loved him, and that she was her own worst enemy, and that when he came back she would apologize and make everything right again, and they would go on as they had before.

~~~

In the darkness Christian cannot see Fran. She has been sitting on the floor, her head against the mattress; now he moves his arm through the mosquito net and his fingers graze her hair. The room is strangely quiet, without her voice, as if the storm has become a familiar, normal thing. The strange quiet of shared loss is upon them, and all these months he had not known, had not even suspected. Christian reaches again for Fran's hair, feather-soft, and strokes it. Her story, in its way, has comforted him; with his febrile touch he returns comfort.

He was hurt, says Fran finally. So he went and got drunk. He was angry with me. He was drunk and fell off the dinghy.

It was not because of you, says Christian.

Why else would he get drunk? He had no reason to drink.

Christian does not know if he has an answer. He lies near sleep, and feverish thoughts surge and ache, close to truth.

Fran, he murmurs, it was not your fault. He didn't fall from the dinghy.

What do you mean?

The same, as me. For some reason . . . He struggles to tell her, but he is still too weak. Something is pulling him, something stronger, into sleep and memory. If he can sleep and his thoughts are still there in the morning, he will tell her.

Fran is so eager for sleep that as she lies on the cool wooden floor beside Christian's bed she does not feel its hardness. She loves sleep, loves its woolly warmth, its irresistible forgiveness. To her it is neither unconsciousness nor a waste of time; it is a sensual journey where sometimes the source of dreams is discovered.

She could have returned to her own bed, but here she feels needed. Christian's breathing is loud and uneven; from time to time he calls out to her, and she awakens only long enough to answer, I'm here.

Later she will not remember how she learned the story, whether he told it to her in his gravelly voice, or she went with him to the source of his dreams. When she asks him, he will say, I never told you, you're imagining things.

But is it true?

Yes, that's what happened.

The colorless sky had closed to black, and the smudge of the island had disappeared. He set a course, what he believed to be the right direction. He looked for a horizon, or the welcome of a light, but saw nothing. He fought away thoughts and fear, told himself he had been through worse things in life, that there are times when any kind of navigation is impossible. Once or twice he cut the engine, to listen, thinking that the voice of the reef could guide him, the roar of breakers. But its voice seemed to come from all around, like a strange murmuring chorus. He could hear his own heartbeat, a compass without a needle.

Then the light: far, far away, mere pinprick but unmistakably the lantern on Egret. He raised the throttle and felt an answering lightness; there was no danger, he would be there soon.

He was going quite fast, confident, guided by Fran's lamp. He thought, as he steered, about Asmita: wondered if he should mention what had happened to Fran. She might hold him responsible, in some perverse way; then again, she might be glad to have him stay on. He thought of his promise to Asmita, the grave consequences of his with-drawal, then weighed that against the implications of her deceit.

Too late he heard the shouts as the dinghy hit something hard, and flipped. He felt the rush of water embrace him, a warm salt turbu-lence as he fought his way to the surface. He was shouting, gasping, trying to swim and grope for the dinghy at the same time; trying not to panic, to ask for help from the voices he had heard. And still he could see nothing, so he shouted, *Ici! Une lampe! Une lampe!*

He heard shrill laughter, and someone said, *To pou gagne to lalampe!* and a spotlight suddenly shone bright in the darkness, searching the surface of the water until it found him. In the glare he heard the roar of a powerful outboard, growing louder, coming toward him.

The light was too bright as it approached. Christian curled upon himself and dove back into the water, just as the boat passed overhead in a ghostly swirl of bubbles and turbulence. He came back up for air, heard again the laughter and the voices—*Aïo bon Dieu, cot li été?*—voices that wanted to send him to the bottom of the lagoon. He waited. And that is when he thought of Satish.

The boat swung around, the searchlight scanning the water. He dove again. The boat made another pass, a few feet away, then leaned into a graceful curve, to search again.

He does not know how long they tried to find him. How many times he dove from the searchlight, suspended in the dark lagoon as if some principle of death had been reversed, and life now resided in some murky underworld. But his lungs were bursting, and when fi-nally the boat gave up and motored away toward the shore, Christian lay floating on the water as if there were not enough air in all the in-visible sky to ease the pain of breathing.

Somehow he made it to the shore of the island, so eager for land and so exhausted that he did not feel the coral opening his skin, felt nothing as the wave drove his forehead against the rocks. How he wandered into the night, lost, his head pounding and bleeding until finally he succumbed to a fainting feverish sleep. Until the late-afternoon sun and the insects inspecting his body woke him again, and somehow he was able to fight his way through the undergrowth and his own fever to find the house.

At first, he takes them for hallucinations, delirium, the spirited workings of the fever upon his mind. Where are these walls charred with gunshot and mortar; who are these people walking head bent and mute along an aimless road? And who is this dark-haired woman smiling down on him with sadness, as if he were wounded, and whispering, You are not my brother. And you are not my father, you are not my son, you are not my husband, this is not your war.

In the mounting storm Fran sits and listens, and it is as if she is watching Christian's dreams. The sounds of storm become the sounds of dreams, and remembered images, silent yet eloquent, replace the black night.

~~~

It was springtime and blossoms defied the war, opened in an exuberance of white and pink in every garden and orchard. Even those trees which had been hit covered their char wounds with a profusion of hopefulness.

Christian and Nermina were working in a village near the front line. A fragile cease-fire allowed the villages to breathe, a tentative harvesting of the warm spring air. Children reappeared, with soccer balls and battered limbless dolls. So lifelike, those dolls: They're war victims too, said Nermina to Christian one day, and he sensed her fear, and moved to stand beside her.

Regularly he would ask her to leave with him; it would be safer, for her, for their unborn child. But she always shook her head: You're dreaming. We're not married; they would never let me out with you. And besides, even if you found someone who could arrange it, I'm not going. They need me here.

Your child needs you more, he would insist, but she was adamant. And she would shame him and say, And you're needed too.

And Christian would not reply, but thought to himself that he was replaceable: so many had already left, disgusted or despairing, and there had always been others to take their place, idealistic young men and women with their innocence and conviction, certain that they could help, and that their presence would change things for the better.

In his moments of deepest cynicism he would argue with Nermina that the aid workers were merely helping to prolong the war, helping the Serbs by feeding their victims, helping aggression by refusing to take sides, and by adhering to their vows of impartiality and neutrality—helping, even, with ethnic cleansing, every time they filled a bus with Muslim or Croat refugees to send them out of Serb-occupied territory to safety.

But Nermina would always disagree, saying that was the larger picture, seen by the West, seen by the cynics, and it did not take individual lives into account. Her eyes dark and sad, she said, You would have them die, these grandmothers and these children? The Red Cross is the only thing between life and death: if you were not here, they would be killed. Or starve.

Because she refused to see the larger picture, refused to enter into the political or moral debate. Accepted the suffering as inevitable with a fatalism which infuriated and fascinated Christian. As if there were another dimension to her life which gave her a deeper understanding; an intuition for life's fragility which gave her a greater skill, a hunger for the moment, an instinct for joy, because pain was so constant and close. And it was not only Nermina: he saw this in so many of them: the grandmothers and children and soldiers alike. A strange talent bequeathed, perhaps, by history; a gift for living that could not be learned. As if, endangered, she were closer to life.

Petals fell from the fruit trees as the fighting revived. Pink blossoms bled their color into the ground. The wind changed direction, and there were those who knew that this would be the last summer of the war, but that for the war to end, many more would have to die, and they would not be only soldiers.

On a morning tender with warmth and the scent of growth, Nermina came running to Christian with the news that the Serbs had taken a group of civilians hostage in a neighboring village. He struggled from his chair, from the desk where he had been writing a report; struggled from his apathy, his sense that he had heard it all before; struggled to regain consciousness, to overcome his feeling that he was captive in a recurring nightmare, and could not awake.

He knew the Serbs at the checkpoint, and they were jovial, even friendly, waving him through with a mock salute. He should have been suspicious, that they had asked for nothing—no cigarettes, or fuel. He should have asked who the commanding officer was. But he obeyed the familiar urgency that came of outrage and adrenaline, and drove on to the schoolhouse where they had told him he would find the commanding officer.

A group of women had gathered outside the entrance to the school—wives, mothers, daughters. Someone had placed a bouquet of wildflowers in the grille of the fence. Christian thought of Nermina as he pushed his way through the crowd of women. Somewhere in a school like this she had met her husband. Now schools had become barracks, or prisons.

Some women clutched his arm; others looked away. He tried to ignore them, knew the false sense of reassurance his red-and-white badge gave them. He shouted above their anger to the soldier behind the gate. The soldier shouted something at the women, something Christian did not catch, and they grew quiet suddenly, threatened, chastened. Christian slipped through the gate, and the soldier nodded with his head toward the entrance to the school.

Tattered children's drawings still lined the walls of the corridors, pictures of boxy houses with flower beds and smoke curling from chimneys. Dogs and hens and horses. Sketches of an unreal life: Christian had seen the drawings the children now made, since the war began and the schools closed: the orange and yellow bursts of flame, the black coils of smoke from windows, the rigid simple figures lying on the ground in pools of red crayon. He did not want his child to make such drawings. He wondered how safe his child was in Nermina's womb, if what she witnessed or her anguished thoughts would find their way to its embryonic soul.

The officers were seated on tiny chairs; for a split second Christian thought they were squatting and he wondered where he was, whether he was back in a part of the world where chairs were not the custom, and where men sat on their haunches low to the ground like conspirators. Then he saw that they were comical, these massive soldiers in their combat fatigues and boots, with their assorted bandannas and caps and vintage headgear, sitting on remarkably sturdy kindergarten chairs. Christian would have liked to laugh at them, would have liked to stand at the door to the schoolroom and tell them how ridiculous they looked, overgrown schoolboys with their—if only—toy guns and their dress-up Chetnik insignia. Instead he felt that he was the teacher arriving late and reviled, despised, come to scold them, and they would mock him and humiliate him.

One of the officers turned, and Christian recognized Colonel Vlatković, and something in him moved with a flutter of hope and revulsion. If Vlatković was in a good mood, Christian might get what he wanted; but if he was not, Christian might, unwittingly, only make things worse. It was a cat-and-mouse game with him; the feline grace of the man.

Christian did not hesitate, stood above Vlatković and shouted at him, You've got civilians here: let them go. You know it's against—

—the Geneva convention, article kiss my ass, paragraph fuck your mother, Red Cross, answered Vlatković. He laughed, rose to his feet, looked at Christian. His gaze seemed to wander, hard, impenetrable. He shouted at the other soldiers to leave the room, then walked to the teacher's desk, pulled a bottle from a drawer, poured two glasses of a pale yellow liquid, and handed one to Christian. Then they sat on the little chairs, hunched in sunlight.

Živjeli. Christian returned the toast, then said quietly, without drinking, Colonel Vlatković, somewhere in this building you have a group of elderly civilian men—

They are terrorists and spies, said Vlatković. They are helping Bosnian army. One Serb soldier was killed in the village last night. They are Muslim traitors. This is Serb village but we leave them alone, let them stay here, and this is how they thank us. They betray us.

For half an hour Christian argued and pleaded. Sunlight filled the room. Vlatković wiped the sweat from his forehead with a large embroidered handkerchief. He reached into a cardboard box at his feet; Christian tensed, until he saw a small gray-and-white kitten dangling from Vlatković's long fingers. The Serb chuckled and sat the kitten on his knees and stroked it, while it mewed plaintively in a mixture of fear and delight. Christian could feel the sweat trickling down his back. Words seemed to fill the space of their own accord, words learned, rehearsed, memorized. But he was elsewhere—in the motes of dust circling in the sunlight, in the glass sheen of light on the bottle before him. He knew all the words, but the passion in his voice could not match the indignation with which Vlatković cloaked his boredom. Muslim threat, terrorists, you could not trust them, you were kind to them and they thanked you with a knife in the back.

All right, said Vlatković at last; all right, Mr. Red Cross: Maybe I will let your people go. Why do you all love them so much? All the foreigners, you come here and you don't love Serbs, you love Muslims.

He paused, glanced briefly at the sleeping kitten, stroked it slowly, then narrowed his gaze on Christian. You love Muslim woman, for example.

Christian's concentration suddenly sharpened as if he had been hit. Motes of dust, sunlight in a clear glass bottle came into focus, his retina singed with words.

What do you mean? he said, and watched the smile spread across Vlatković's face.

Listen, said Vlatković, lowering his voice, leaning toward Christian across the little table. She is beautiful woman, I think. And she is hot, no? You know what they say——

I won't talk to you like this. I don't know what you're talking about.

You love your Muslims so much, I will give you a whole roomful of them——

Now, insisted Christian.

Čekaj, wait, only one thing more.

Vlatković's voice dropped almost to a whisper. One whole room of Muslims for one hour with your Muslim woman. It's good deal, okay?

Christian stood up, kicked over the child's chair. You're mad, he shouted. You're drunk. I'll come back when you have something reasonable to say. Let those people go, they've done nothing to you or to anyone. They're old men. Let them go.

Vlatković sat back on the little chair and began to laugh. Christian walked down the corridors and could hear his laughter. He walked past a closed door guarded by a soldier, and he heard coughing, and a moan, and Vlatković's laughter. And the kitten, mewing. He could still hear the laughter as he left the building. The blood pounded in his ears.

At the gate the women clutched at him, circled him, tried to stop him from climbing into the Jeep. Some were crying, others were angry, shouting and shrieking. Christian shook his head, back and forth, his cheeks burning. *Kasnije, kasnije,* he shouted, Later, later. He would try again later.

As he drove back toward the checkpoint, he passed the UN vehicle, similar to his own. Maybe the UN would have a better deal for Colonel Vlatković.

She held him and kissed him and put his hand against her belly. Someday this will be over, she whispered. She took her faith and that part of her which had moved him to love her, and she offered them on a shard of hope.

Later that day he learned that Vlatković had let the hostages go, unharmed. Christian was relieved, but puzzled. It was not the usual way; usually, the Serbs wanted something in return. He refused to consider what Vlatković had said in the schoolroom, those oil-coated, despicable words. He tried to give him credit, the benefit of the doubt: that he was human, that he could be a man of honor after all. Maybe the UN had made a deal. Or perhaps in the larger world of the politics of the war, for once a decision had played in the victims' favor. It was not something you could predict or expect. Christian was there, mostly, to pick up the pieces.

He was tired. He wanted to go home. More and more he saw the red cross on a white background as the unsatisfactory negative of his national flag. He longed for peace. He longed for the air of the Alps, so still that a call could carry across a valley in an echo.

~~~

Fran listens. She hears a deep rumbling: have the guns of Christian's dreams come to echo beyond boundaries?

The house seems to shake with fear. The darkness concedes sounds: this rumbling, and the wind weaving a seeping draft through all the rooms, from the eaves to the window frames and doors. Fran feels it upon her skin, and shivers. It is a wind from elsewhere, bringing foreign tales.

~~~

Again Christian pleaded with Nermina to come away with him, and again she refused to consider it. She gave no explanations but retreated into a chilling silence, a lover's silence of anger and hurt. If you loved me you would understand. And although Christian could not understand the dread which shadowed him, he knew that lovers' quarrels had no currency in a war zone.

But later he would understand it all: Nermina's silence, his own dread. She could not speak to him of her struggle to stay faithful to those she loved. To leave Bosnia would be to abandon their memory, to choose the path of ease (cross two borders and you are in Western Europe, in peace, people having dinner parties and skiing trips, drinking wine and eating tiramisu and talking about film festivals). And she did not want to resent Christian for such a choice. So with her silence she bolstered her love, kept it as a shelter where she could go, briefly, to escape the war.

And Christian's dread was not of the shells that were falling once again with increasing intensity as the days grew warmer, nor of his own death. It was the dread, the fear of loss, of a void where Nermina would be taken from him. As his love grew, so did his dread.

Hey, Swiss man, you are so quiet.

She lay beside him on the single bed. The guns were silent and you could hear the stubbornness of crickets. Christian moved his hand upon her in response. He could not speak of the source of his silence.

But she knew, she had a sense for these things. If I die now, she said, I will die happy. I would not mind to die now.

Shhh. Don't speak like that.

And you? she continued, would you not die happy?

No, Nermina, I don't want to die, I want to live and have children and feel this joy many times.

I am glad to have had such joy in my life. I don't know if I can expect more.

Of course you can. That's just your Balkan blues.

Oh yes? And you, gloomy Swiss man! You are not happy now because you worry about being happy tomorrow. Where is your joy!

He pulled her closer and said quietly, My joy is very quiet, and very deep. It's not something you can see.

He held her for a long time, and perhaps they slept, and made love again. And the joy was there, so quiet and deep that to come away again in the morning was to experience a brutal loss.

The sky became a place of violence. Streets emptied; sounds became the strange and terrifying orchestration of war. You heard only shouts and screams and lamenting. And the constant incursions of burning metal: a clatter, a whistle, a thud. Christian spent nearly all his waking hours at the hospital, helping with the wounded.

The Bosnian Serb army was surrounding the town, and Christian realized they would have to evacuate. His dread encased his heart like a wound. He filled his duffel bag and would not look at Nermina. She prepared to join him. There were dark circles under her eyes.

Vlatković had sent a message to Christian saying that the Bosnian Serb army could no longer guarantee the safety of international personnel. To the south the government forces had launched an offensive to recapture Serb-held territory. Christian no longer knew where he was. The town had become a no-man's-land, neither Serb nor Croat nor Muslim, a place without identity. Soldiers shouted in panic at civilians to leave. Suddenly no one cared who you were, there was no time left for that, your nationality was alive or dead.

In the Jeep Christian and Nermina joined the slow convoy of people fleeing toward a zone of safety. Serbs fled east, Croats fled west, and the Muslims fled south. With Nermina in mind, Christian headed south.

Put your badge on, he said suddenly.

What?

Put your badge on. They might think you're a refugee otherwise.

I am a refugee.

Don't argue, put your badge on. You're Red Cross.

They rode in silence. The sky was dark, streaked with low gray stratus, like the smudge marks of passing projectiles. Christian tried not to look at the people struggling with suitcases by the roadside. At this moment he could not help them.

Once he had to stop the Jeep. A herd of sheep blocked the road. The animals moved in circles, confused and frightened, pushing an ever-tighter circle around one another until they were locked and could not move. Christian blew the horn, nudged gently into the woolly mass. Old women shrieked at the sheep, at Christian, waving their arms. A shell landed at the edge of a field, and the beasts scattered and fled.

Christian's heart was pounding. He stepped on the gas. A few drops of rain fell on the windshield. Nermina pulled her hair back and tied it with an elastic.

There was a row of poplar trees in the distance at the crest of a low hill. Christian could see a tank and an armored personnel carrier sheltering in the trees. From time to time the tank fired in the opposite direction. Shit, he said, aware that when they passed the poplar trees they would be in the line of fire. It was too late to turn back. He did not want to be caught by Vlatković's troops.

As they drew nearer Christian could see a roadblock, some fifty yards before the tank. An old man on a tractor was waiting with his family behind him in a cart: his old wife, a younger woman, two small children, and a white goat. Christian looked at the soldier guarding the roadblock, praying that he might be government, but fearing, from the direction of the tank fire, that he was Serb. As they drew up behind the tractor, the soldier walked over and gave Christian the three-fingered Serbian salute.

Christian recognized one of Vlatković's men who had been sitting on the kindergarten chairs. A young man with an earring and a small dapper beard and long curling hair. A poet soldier. The soldier was about to raise his hand to wave him through when he seemed to remember something, and paused, and called to his superior.

Christian looked at Nermina. Her eyes were closed.

The officer strolled over. A big man, red-faced, clean-shaven, and wearing a Chetnik cap, he was chewing gum, spewing a rancid odor of chlorophyll and plum brandy as he leaned into the vehicle.

Who's that? he shouted at Christian. Documents!

Christian handed their papers to the officer. He took them and stood to one side with the young soldier. Christian looked at Nermina.

Her eyes were wide, looking at the men, listening. Go! she whispered to Christian. Go now! Drive on, quick!

Christian looked again at the two men. They were laughing, not looking at the Jeep, pointing to Nermina's photograph.

If he had sleeping dreams, this would be one, recurring, familiar, the place where he would rewrite his life. The poplar trees, the gray sky, the tank with its turret pointing south, the armored personnel carrier squatting by the shoulder of the road. Two soldiers, their faces unforgettable, the faces of fate-workers, indifferent, jovial. Ahead of him the family on the tractor, faceless, universal, bearers of their country's pain. And his own inertia, his pounding heart, his hands sweating on the wheel.

He could have done what Nermina said, pulled out, driven around the tractor, around the barrier, past the tank. Perhaps the tank would have fired. *Two aid workers killed in Bosnia-Herzegovina as their vehicle came under heavy fire.* Did Christian foresee his own death, a headline, a statistic? He did not want Nermina to die. He heard her quiet urgings and he did not move. One last time, he believed the red cross would protect them.

The officer came back, walked around to Nermina's side. Get out! he shouted. Nermina did not move. Christian began to argue. Let us through. She's a Red Cross worker.

She's a Muslim whore. Out!

No! cried Nermina, leave me alone! I'm half Serb! My mother is a Serb!

Christian looked at her in astonishment, wondered if she were making this up, but Nermina was shuffling in her bag, frantic, until she found her birth certificate and shoved it out the window.

Look! Radmila Janković, she was born in Novi Sad. Leave me alone, let me through, I've no quarrel with you!

Then why are you trying to leave? shouted the officer. If you're a Serb, why are you going to Alija?

I have work to do, just like you!

Christian sat breathless and stunned, watching her, and her hand reached out to grasp his own, tight, as if she were falling.

The officer had opened her door and was pulling her by the other arm. The young soldier walked around to Christian's door and laid the barrel of the assault rifle on the edge of the window, toward Christian. Get out, he shouted at Nermina. We have orders. Get out.

Nermina began to scream. Christian tried to shout, tried to reason with the officer, dreadful blunt words about the Red Cross and international law, then one last, blind attempt: Who is your commanding officer?

Colonel Branko Vlatković, answered the officer.

Well, I have orders from him to evacuate myself and all my personnel from this zone. He can confirm that. He won't like it if you hold my personnel without permission.

The men laughed. Won't like it, repeated the officer. I have orders from him too. I have orders to detain this Muslim whore. Colonel Vlatković said you made a deal with him. You didn't keep your part of the deal.

That's a lie! I never made a deal!

Nermina was slipping away. He grasped her hand and looked at her, and his eyes pleaded with her, begged her to believe him. She did not look at him. He could not read her gaze, could not read the unfocused darkness of her eyes, could find no sign of anything.

Suddenly she was gone. He had not been strong enough to hold her. He watched, as they led her toward the armored personnel carrier. She held her head back, chin up. A few strands of hair had escaped from the elastic.

He opened the door and began to run after them, shouting. The young soldier turned around and fired into the air. *Ajde,* get going, don't try to fuck with us! Get in the car and go back to Geneva!

And still Christian followed, and the soldier aimed, this time at the ground, past his feet, into the side of the Jeep, bullets spattering like hailstones, causing the family in the tractor to duck and scream.

Through the noise and screams, as if from a very great, hollow distance, Christian could hear her say, Go, Christian, please, just go.

~~~

The night sky spins around him, centripetal force bearing memories to a center, a core of helplessness.

Fran sits for a long time on the edge of his bed. Why, only now, has she found the vision to read his dreams? He sleeps and the room is silent. But outside there is the tumult of the sky, too small for the jostling, thrusting air.

She struggles to open the door and goes to stand on the veranda. She sees that she has been away and that in her absence a wildness has captured the island. She cannot distinguish the crashing of waves from the force of the wind: sounds merge and birth a third element, a violence of rain. Blue flashes of lightning show her the change and the danger. She does not know where her birds have sheltered, or if they are safe; her own safety becomes an afterthought, and she is surprised to find herself clinging to the pillars of the veranda, fighting the wind. There is a crash behind her as something in the kitchen falls. Now an armchair is lifted and flung from the veranda into the night.

Why does she feel no fear? How is she able, so calmly, to turn and grope her way back into the house, where she closes and locks the door? In the kitchen she sees the lamp was knocked over but still burns, singeing the tablecloth, coaxing flames; calmly, she rights the lamp and douses the fire. She closes all the windows, extinguishes the lamp, and returns to Christian's bedside.

His cheeks are red with fever. His eyelids twitch; his breathing is rough, as if puzzled and searching for air. And there is such a tumult of air, all around; Fran sits on, watching over him, hears the storm but does not listen.

Suddenly there is silence. An eerie absence of sound, of wind, of storm. The eye, thinks Fran, her heart pounding. Then the metal roof seems to sigh, the house creaks, subtle, relaxing sounds. Fran shivers with a strange anticipation, as if in this moment, anything could happen.

The cyclone comes again, a second, stronger flank of wind and rain. Sucking, whirling, seething, hurling branches and leaves and waves in a confusion of anger against the sky. Fran sits on the floor by Christian's bed and wonders how the house has not yet risen from the ground. It shudders and creaks and resists, but with each thump and groan it seems as if they will lift into the sky, cloud-bound for a new existence.

Christian sleeps, still feverish, his breathing uneven. From time to time he mumbles incomprehensibly: quiet, resigned statements that fill Fran with dread. She has searched the house and has nothing left to give him for his fever. There was never anything stronger than aspirin, and now that is all gone.

The room fills with a liquid gray light; swirls of rainfall crash against the windowpane. Slowly Fran gets up from the floor, stiff and cramped. She walks to the window and places her palm against the glass: it is surprisingly cold, and the vibration of the storm runs through her in a violent shiver. She recalls the kestrel she saw—how long ago was it? How many days, weeks?—and realizes that the bird knew about the hurricane. But her instinct, for the first time, failed her, preoccupied as she was by Christian's absence.

Now it strikes her as strange that he has not mentioned his marriage to Asmita in all these hours of lucidity and confusion. As if telling the story of Nermina had erased Asmita from his mind, or heart.

Fran stares out into the rain. Does she understand better, now? The lure of forgetfulness, the need to drive away the pain of loss. Asmita's receptive, warm beauty. The possibility she offers. How can she, Fran, blame him now? I blamed him once, she thinks, because I did not know. I saw only a besotted maleness, its eagerness to breed, regardless of the heart. No. It is life itself that has contempt for the heart—suffering continues, our pain does not go away. So we seek comfort, we continue to hope. I should have known that, but my hope for comfort has faded over the months; I have built a fortress instead.

She shivers. She thinks again of how Christian stumbled toward her: a ghost as he came forward in the night. As if, somehow, this ghost had taken Satish's place, where Satish, less fortunate and weakened by alcohol, did not make it ashore.

Fran looks out into the rain, her fingertips against the cold pane. He should have survived; he should have survived.

Christian is dreaming. He is in a white, colorless place, a depth of water, or a thickness of cloud. He is breathing, he is light. Now color enters the edge of his vision, and movement: someone is coming toward him. Walking, swimming, flying—he is not sure. The person comes closer and he sees it is a woman with long dark hair; now he sees her face and it is Nermina. Joy colors the dream, greens, blues, intense reds; he reaches for her and discovers that they cannot touch, that there is an invisible wall between them. Her lips are moving, and he cannot hear her. He struggles against the wall, feels nothing, no glass, no hard surface of resistance, yet still he cannot reach her. He is shouting now, as if his words could break the barrier, the silence. His own shouts wake him. He is in his bed on Egret Island, surrounded by the gauze of the mosquito net; he reaches for the cloth, and it is soft and yielding. He feels heat and does not know if it is the air or his own body. He hears the tumult of the storm, as if an angry crowd were trying to break in. He tries to sit up and finds he has no strength, tries to speak and has no voice. His shouts were in his dreams, then. His body aches and burns and defies him, and sleep taunts him with visions so real that on awakening he no longer knows on which side his life belongs.

Fran stands by his bedside and gently calls to him. There are tears on his cheeks, and he struggles for speech. So she kneels by him, reaches to touch his arm with the gauze of the mosquito net between her palm and his wrist, and she talks. Says anodyne, cheerful things, nursery things like You'll be getting better soon, already I can tell the delirium has passed, you'll be fine, the fever is dropping. And as she says these cheerful things she is not sure she believes them, for he is still terribly hot, and she has nothing for the fever or the infection, only water and her presence.

She pushes open the door against the wind. She struggles to hold the basin to fill it with rainwater. She is drenched in seconds, shivering yet revived. The veranda is strewn with storm wreckage; even now branches, leaves whirl around her in a frenzied ballet—a mocking dance, her fragile achievements so quickly undone. Then she returns to Christian's side and places moist compresses on his forehead and his limbs. He seems to smile with pleasure as their coolness seeps hope into his blood. He closes his eyes, murmurs Thank you. Fran again sits on the floor and lays her head against the mattress. His fingertips reach for her shoulder, make contact, gently. She closes her eyes.

Fran is writing. She is sitting at the table with a single candle, and the long shadow of her pen flickers, hesitantly. A dark flame.

Wednesday

The cyclone has ended. Quite suddenly. A burst of blue and it was gone; and the wind dropped. The air strangely quiet, as if the land were catching its breath. He is getting better. There were beads of sweat on his skin. I took a cloth and bathed him with fresh rainwater; at first he resisted, as if ashamed, then he lay back and closed his eyes.

He tells me a dream, tells me he has not dreamt since Bosnia. Tells me there are times when the visions inside seem to pound on the walls of his brain, struggling to get out, and his whole body grows rigid in protest. But now this dream. How he saw Nermina; how he could not touch her. Vivid she was, alive, still.

Later.

I slept for a long time. When I woke up he was not in his bed, and I found him on the veranda, his legs dangling over the edge, his upper body awkwardly collapsed against the floor. He was so weak he had fainted. I helped him sit up, and his cheek was marked by the seams of the wood.

His body is firm and solid, but as I touched him there was something fragile, too; as if part of him were insubstantial, given over to the recovery of dreams.

It has been four days, I think. It surprises me that no one comes. But then, why should anyone come? Sean will when he suddenly remembers, between two spasms of eccentricity. It could be days, yet. We have water, but food is dwindling. I can fish.

I sit by his bed and his fingertips move toward me through the gauze of mosquito net. We have begun to talk. As if the two defining events of our lives suddenly opened us out onto each other. We sit and talk and I watch him grow better, incrementally, healed by words.

Sometimes, she is saying, it's as if there is a black hole in my life. In my past. As if my years with Peter were so . . . stalled, and wasted, because they led nowhere. I put my career on hold, I hoped for a child, I tried to be a good wife, and he left me. And now there is nothing I can salvage from those years.

You are hard on yourself. There were good times. You were living. You were in the present moment.

But it never felt like the present moment. It was always, always striving for the future. To have something. To acquire, to do.

Still, I am sure something good came of it——

My Darwinism, she laughs. He left me for a younger, fertile woman.

Do you think Darwinism can explain everything?

It explains a lot.

It's a cynical faith. It doesn't leave much room for hope, or change.

You're wrong! It's all about hope and change. Hope fuels survival. The human race is getting better.

But it isn't. It isn't getting better, and your "fittest" survivors—where is justice, fairness? Darwinism says there is no justice—so who will strive for justice anymore? If the younger, fertile woman always gets the man? It's fatalistic. I am surprised if you have any feminist ideas that you can accept this kind of fatalism. Why fight back if evolution will always win?

Because there are many different ways to survive.

What do you know about triage? he is asking.

(It is dark, she cannot see his face, hears rather the heaviness in his voice.)

Sean had a case. Before I came here: the foundation told him to abandon his work on another rare bird on the mainland. There were only a few individuals left, and it was costing a lot to try to keep them going. So the foundation selected them for extinction, only Sean refused. He never told them. He used his own time and resources and rescued the birds. They're thriving now. And that's what I'm trying to reproduce here.

And in war? You know what it is in war?

The same, no, deciding who to save, who to abandon?

I saw it sometimes, in Bosnia. People, still conscious, and you would walk by them, and they put their hands out—like this—reaching for you. Like a prayer. And you knew that they were going to die. You could do nothing. And after a while you realized there was no logic, no justice, it was random, all of it. It could just as easily have been you lying there.

There is a long silence, then he continues:

You made other pacts. With the lesser evil. The Serbs wanted something and you gave in because if you didn't it was going to be hard for everyone. You let some die so others could live, or so you hoped. You became an accomplice.

Don't blame yourself.

(He ignores her words, as if she had not spoken.) You know there are soldiers who commit atrocities because their officers order them to. Because if they don't, they'll be shot. And you never learn who were the ones—if any—courageous enough to resist, to call their bluff.

And die a martyr?

No, not even a martyr, because to be a martyr you have to be known. They died anonymously.

I didn't do enough. I didn't do anything—to save Nermina.

There was nothing you could do. You would have been killed.

I don't know. Perhaps my badge would have saved me, saved both of us. I didn't try hard enough. The roadblock—

Shh. Shh.

I would have liked to have been beautiful. Really, really beautiful.

Why? You are a fine woman—

Because in my Darwinian scheme, beauty is the ultimate survival tool. All men, I mean all men except homosexuals, want the most beautiful woman. She is always chosen. Men dream about beautiful women.

(He laughs.) That's ridiculous. Superficial and ridiculous. I can't believe it is you talking.

You're a man. You've no idea how a woman's identity—and a woman's survival—has been tied up for millennia—forever—with beauty. I would like, in another life, not to have to worry about that.

Fran. Nermina was—lovely—and because of this—

He breaks off and looks at her, and she is shaking her head, looking away. I'm sorry, she murmurs at last. I never think, do I.

Sometimes when he sleeps I look at him. The childlike space around his sleeping eyes, full of innocence, lashes against his cheek. And I want to protect him. I see the darkness, I want to stop it from hurting him.

Other times I want to keep him where he sleeps, under the mosquito net. The faint quiver of his breath against the veil: he could be my prisoner.

I walked through the island. It is worse than I had feared: the aviary is totally destroyed. The nursery too: young shoots crushed, trees and plants uprooted, defoliated. And a silence in the trees, no sign of the mourner-birds anywhere.

This storm was God's work—let him rebuild. I've worked to undo man's destruction, but I'm not about to take on God.

Or is it that simple? Is it not all one and the same now—God, man, Nature—who is responsible? Who must cherish life, and who can decide when death, or extinction, is necessary? Triage? Or is there no scheme, no logic possible—only this storm-victory of chaos?

This morning we sat for a while on the veranda. It was cool, overcast, with a breeze. Wreckage from the storm everywhere. We have to sit on the edge of the veranda. We began to talk about the mourner-birds, and I broke down. I don't know if I can find the courage to rebuild, to begin again. My bird has disappeared.

I told him this, and he held me. It was strange, to be held; I'm not used to comfort. He held me, and although he was silent and promised nothing, it gave me faith.

We ate rice boiled with lemon juice and curry powder. A flush came to his cheeks and he reached across the table and took my hand beneath his. You've been very kind to me, he said.

He has become a friend. Now his flat little jokes and his rueful smile have a resonance.

He is getting better, so I took him swimming. We almost never went to-
gether, before. As if there were an uneasiness: all my doing, my American
prudishness, tyrannical modesty, invincible to this day. But he took his clothes
off, and I thought in a detached way—yet full of wonder—There is a fine
man, and I have tended him when he was sick, bathed him, touched him. But
then he was a patient; now he's a man again, and strange to me.

He is asleep. These moments alone, just candlelight, paper, and pen, are
magical. Stillness on the island, after the storm. The absence of birdsong sad-
dens me, but I have not lost faith. The cicadas are returning.

Fran looks up from her page. The candle has nearly burnt down. The
moon circles and dusts the window frame with silver. She rubs her
eyes, listens to the clicking of the tropical night, then writes on, hurriedly.

How secretive he is! He is not going to marry Asmita after all!
We were eating our rice and I suggested that she must be worried, and that
it was strange she had not come to look for him. He looked down, said slowly,
matter-of-factly, No, I can't marry her. He paused for a moment, as if hesi-
tating to tell me, then he said, She lied to me. Implied to her parents that I had
abused her, then offered to marry her.
And you hadn't—
No! I already told you. I respected her modesty, her religion. For what? For
nothing. She was the one who was dishonest.

Christian looked at me and said, I can stay on if you like. I can help you
rebuild.
That is the faith holding me.

The Madagascar fody has returned. Sweet chirping at dusk, as if to say to
the others, Follow me, it's safe now.

Lately I imagine a conversation with Charles Darwin. I tell him about the storm, the mourner-bird; I tell him about my life. The great man nods, agrees; we become quiet companions. And when I ask him for some comfort, something in his scheme for those like me, he begins to stroke his beard, pensive. I wait, expecting to hear his deep, earnest voice pronounce words of thoughtful wisdom; instead what shakes me from within my dreamy musing is the sound of his full-hearted and unrepentant laughter.

Perhaps Fran has been dreaming. In the predawn stillness she thinks she hears the mourner-bird's cry: she rises from her bed and rushes out into the late darkness, her hope like a light.

She stands and listens with all her senses, concentrating so hard on the echo of what she has dreamt that she does not hear Christian come up behind her. So when she turns, he is there like a sentinel in moonlight, and she starts and cries out, even berates him, What are you doing here? Go back to sleep.

You shouldn't come out alone—

I can look after myself.

Fran.

She stares at him in the moonlight. Even in the darkness she can see a cast of gentle madness on his features, as if he too had been aroused from a dream, a desperate one. A shadow of stubble on his cheeks, his arms hanging restless and apologetic; his naked torso; his baggy shorts.

How Fran must appear to him: her hair ruffled with sleep, her body hidden by an oversize T-shirt. It drapes from her shoulders like a square sail waiting for wind above the two short masts of her legs. She too has a mad gleam in her eye.

Christian reaches for her, his arms slide around her shoulders and draw her to him. Fran relaxes against him, feels his warmth, his skin. He smells of sleep, a sweet musty smell that comforts her. They stand like that for a moment, in the silence broken only by the distant roar of surf. As if listening for each other's thoughts, or, reluctant to part, waiting for the moment to break of its own accord. Then Fran sighs, an involuntary spasm, strain rising to the surface; she looks up at Christian, sees a curious half smile play across his lips. As if he already knows he will lean down and kiss her, a very hesitant, questioning kiss, Is this all right? he seems to ask; yes, she murmurs in reply, with her lips against his, soft beneath the prickle of mustache. They kiss slowly, restrained by astonishment, This cannot be happening, why suddenly now, why us? then as they begin to understand, Yes it is happening, and why not? they become bolder, their hands begin to move, to touch. Then they suddenly pull apart and look at each other. It has grown lighter, and each can see now the mad desiring gleam in the other's eyes. Fran laughs. They hold hands, chastely, and return quickly to the house.

The next morning, Fran imagines a new field notebook:

Last night. Moon not quite full. Weather calm. Moon-drunk, we mated, the resident male and I. The pleasure was intense, unexpected. Male virile, attentive; female (me?) fertile in response, anyway, given advanced age.

Breakfast. Watery coffee and dried biscuit. No appetite for food, turned to mating instead, here in the kitchen. Sensation outside the realm of words or field notebooks.

Lunch. Rice again; again little appetite. Feverish recourse to sex instead, sofa on veranda.

Extraordinary responsiveness on part of female; male easily aroused, despite heat.

Evening. Rose late after long sleep. Swam naked in the dark off the pier; made love in the lagoon, typical lek of the human species.

Female's breasts (mine) swollen. Belly tender. As if in heat.

Fran is blooming, seems to emanate a softness, a tenderness she can see in the mirror. Her features grow gentle, seductive.

Christian sheds his dour, melancholy moodiness; he hums to himself, he sings to her. Teases her with a yodeling folk song.

Good sex, thinks Fran, is always just that, in the beginning: good sex. You could describe it, graphically, and you would get an erotic, nay, pornographic description of a function. You would get field notes.

It becomes interesting when it is no longer mere sex. At the point when I look at Christian and see no longer a partner but a lover. This will not take long: the time, merely, for another chemistry to take over.

Can physical sensation, and its attendant, unexpected emotions—an instinct for magic—be chronicled in any way? Yet chronicle she must, if for no one else than her own memory—as one must when one is overflowing.

When you've been alone for a long time you forget how good it feels. You take a superior attitude—that you can live without it, that you are not someone who is governed by appetite. You find ways, you rationalize.

Because when you are reminded, you wonder how, this time, you will trick solitude. This time. To make up for all the other times, when you were outside, looking in at those who celebrate and flaunt their gift: how you have envied them, or condemned them. (The women, especially the women: young, with their long hair and short skirts, they scarcely need to move for it to be there: the display, the call.) Yet there should always, always be enough for everyone. A realm where Nature, perhaps, was fair. We are all capable of delight, we all have skin, and senses.

My mind is detached, sky high. Bird's-eye view on my life. My own body—yet how did I become so detached?

There are times I am afraid of our connection, and I tell him so. And he looks at me and says nothing: his eyes are warm while his silence is a warning. What would I have him say? Why want words at all?

I should know. Nature is a place not of silence but of senses. Words are a thing detached, like my mind. Silence is broken when our bodies meet; my body understands this language, but when we are apart my mind again struggles to place words upon the language, so that I can comprehend.

There is nothing to comprehend. Perhaps that is what some people would call love.

Sometimes he pauses and looks at me, and smiles, then buries his face against my neck. He sighs and his breath is warm, his hair is soft against my cheek.

Is there meaning?

Who is he, in the end? Why do I still feel I do not know him?

The wind cools the sun upon his skin. Salt drying, pulling. This is where he washed ashore that night; he wants to understand, to find an answer.

The lagoon is empty. On the far shore he can see a movement of people, then a gleam of light as a vehicle on the road catches the sun.

He thinks about Fran, about the comfort of her, the ease of her. She is uncomplicated by visual beauty; her beauty is in her simplicity, her honesty. He will not compare her to Asmita, or Nermina; she is a vessel of solace and sensuality, pure and safe. He loses himself in her. She reveals curves and softness he would, earlier, have denied her. Now in the sun and his thoughts, his penis stirs. Yes, the simplicity of her; her salt-speckled skin.

But someday the future will call in its bets, and he will lose this desire. He knows this, and it fills him with sadness. Because he will hurt her then, and he will betray, so unwillingly and merely by virtue of his manhood, the gift she has given him.

Their mating ritual is simple. She looks at him, silent, a tense and inviting sharpness in her gaze. He follows her as she searches the island. They make love against trees, on the scented ground. The island steams with decay and rebirth. Their fears leach away into the soil; when they rise they are covered in sand, leaves, tiny insects.

Later Fran will think the bird led her to Christian. That its disappearance is only an outward illusion, that it continues to fly and sing in the secret corridors of dawn, guiding her to the places she might otherwise have forgotten about.

Fran picks up the island field notebook. She has made no entries since the time of the storm.

Briefly she writes down the dates of the storm, and its figures; now absent from the island: kestrels, mourner-birds. Only the larger, more prosperous populations have returned: pigeons, fodies, tropic birds, bulbuls, ramiers, barred ground doves, mynahs.

She turns to her personal notebook and sees she has nearly filled it. She writes hesitantly, as if governed by space, but not space alone:

And happiness—where does it fit in with the scheme of things, Mr. D? Does happiness keep us healthier, fitter to reproduce? Or is it mere trimming on the cake?

Hackneyed words. No one much believes in these embarrassing words anymore: bliss, joy, beatitude. Closer, at the moment, is serenity.

She underlines it, *serenity.*

I stood by the lagoon—he had just left me—and spread my arms out to the sky. A brief infinity of not-joy: as if with my fingertips I could weave a vast blue dome over the world, that would contain serenity.

They begin to work again, assessing damage, planning recovery. They are thin and light-headed as they move through the strong sunlight. They work separately, and when they come together they examine each other for signs of change.

Fran thinks about islands. Not the geography of them—bodies of land surrounded by water—but their symbolic nature. Is an island a prison, or a refuge? The times when one is held there, for lack of a boat, or by bad weather: is one imprisoned, or free, detached from the demands of the rest of the world in one's own fortress? And is there something about the nature of living on an island that is different— does one become insular? Is one safe? Or is it like living surrounded by mountains, enclosed by Nature, cut off?

One day she asks Christian for his opinion. He nods slowly, then says, No, from an island you have a view, you can see the horizon, you can imagine elsewhere.

But the notion of barrier is still there, no? You must have a boat, or wings?

Yes, but the horizon is open, and this is what can make you want to leave.

Why want to leave?

Men have always wanted to leave. Marco Polo wasn't from Switzerland, was he. He was born on an island.

Any day now, soon, says Fran, Sean will come. I want him to come, because I'm hungry and worried about the birds, but I don't want him to come because—

She breaks off, looks at Christian. This would be saying too much.

He reaches over, holds her cheek, rubs it with his thumb. It is a rare gesture. There have been few signs of affection between them. Only their bright, hard desire; the giddy contact of cells. Now she realizes this, in a rush of emotion. A first weakness.

Fran writes, seated at the kitchen table.

He is looking away, out toward the lagoon, through the tangle of trees toward the pirogue which does not come. How does he see his life now?

And yet there is so much possibility in him, in us, but I hardly dare think about it. I don't want to love him, other than as a friend. A dearest friend. He plants his seed in me, useless, fruitlessly.

But now my body has begun to transform his gestures, the chemistry distills emotions. Wretched, wretched emotions.

Why, Mr. D? What do they have to do with it?

Fran sits awkwardly on the old kitchen chair, looking at Christian; he looks away. This is not the old Fran, brisk and sealed. She is waif-like, uncombed; she is younger, more fragile, and if she sits awkwardly it is because she is pleasantly sore. But the ache within will make her still softer, more vulnerable. She will plead with possibility, grow defiant in the face of patterns and inevitability.

It is dusk and they are sitting on the veranda, at either end of the old sofa, facing each other. They raise small glasses of cane liquor in a toast to Christian's full recovery. His left foot is upon Fran's right, her left is upon his right. A current passes. Before they drink, Christian reaches over, loops his right arm through hers, and when they are linked he instructs, *Schmolitz,* in Swiss German. It's an old European tradition: it means we can now say *tu* to each other.

Fran looks at him ironically and says, You mean, all this time we've been saying *vous?*

He smiles and looks away. You can be very formal.

You mean distant.

They drink, awkwardly linked. Another current passes, then Fran frees herself. Christian leans back and closes his eyes, cradling the small glass in his palms.

You know, he says, when I worked for the Red Cross, I would wake up in the morning with a good feeling. A feeling that I was useful. I thought that was why I was here, on earth—so I thought it was a good enough thing to want. By helping others I was helping myself too.

And now?

Now, most of the time in the morning . . . I haven't felt anything. I don't know how useful I am anymore.

You are, Christian.

But I don't feel it. You're so competent, you don't need *me,* anyone could take my place.

He pauses, then adds, And you? Do you know what you want from life?

Fran looks away, trapped by the question. Then says, I want to feel that I belong.

Don't you?

No.

Belong where—to what?

To society. To other human beings. I feel like I'm outside of the larger scheme. Of Nature's scheme, even.

Are you? Does there have to be a scheme? What's wrong with being a thinking individual? What about all the harm society does?

Because . . . Fran hesitates. She is not sure she wants to reveal her loneliness. Although he too may know it. She feels it as a stigma, a source of shame. So she shrugs, reverses the problem and says, I enjoy human company. I'm human.

Christian smiles, then says, And why are you here? Your purpose?

I have no idea. I could say it is to save the mourner-bird. My life's mission. Like yours in the Red Cross? But we're not succeeding very well, are we.

Is it only about success?

It shouldn't be, but then nor should it be about failure.

And is trying good enough?

Perhaps. Perhaps that's all we can do, try. There's so little one has any control over. All you can do is chip away. A few more mongoose traps, a few more letters sent to foundations and politicians. If you save one bird—

But not the species?

—at least that one bird will have had its life. Even if it is the last one. It will have taught us something, no? Is that worth it?

Christian smiles. He knows he does not need to answer.

Fran looks down at her body—her protruding hip bones, her sunken thighs. I've lost weight, she thinks. There is rice for three more days, and a few packets of stale tea.

Christian has gone fishing, thank God: there will be something to go with the rice, to ward off hunger.

She goes onto the veranda and looks toward the lagoon. Squinting into the distance, she waits for him, speaks to her hunger. At first she does not see the small boat heading across the water; they have become so isolated that she cannot conceive of her island as a destination.

But soon there are voices on the path and her heart pounds, tuned still to the stories told during the storm. Then the relief as she recognizes those Irish tones, and Sean's arms are around her. I've been worried sick, woman, look at the state of you, you're a wraith. It is all she can do to keep from crying, to withhold the emotion and the stories, but Sean is steering her to the sofa, and gesturing to Bruno the boatman to unload the basket of provisions he has brought. Fran's hands shake as she takes the glass of cane liquor: it burns as she swallows, and she coughs and laughs, holds on to Sean's arm as if to keep from falling.

I didn't know, she exclaims. I didn't realize—

Hush.

She leans back, closes her eyes. Hears Sean telling her that it has been ten days—only ten days!—while he has been digging out from the cyclone (you wouldn't believe the damage, girl, all over the island) until he finally realized that he had not heard from the Egret field station.

So I thought I'd better have a look, right?

The mourner-birds, Sean—

I know. I was up in the gorges yesterday: not a trace.

Fran finally opens her eyes. The air seems too bright, as if someone had switched on a powerful spotlight.

We must go and get Christian, she says. He's fishing—

She breaks off, and then, her voice lowered so Bruno will not hear, tells Sean about the attack, and Christian's illness, and her fear; she does not tell him more than that.

Now there is secrecy, a barrier, between her life and the world.

Later, when Sean and Bruno have left, Christian looks at Fran, as if expecting an answer to an unvoiced question. So she says, I didn't tell him anything about us. I didn't even tell him about you and Asmita.

Christian nods, says nothing. His eyes, behind his glasses, are distant. Sometimes Fran thinks this is an optical trick, the effect of the thickness of glass. So she suddenly reaches over, removes the old tortoiseshell glasses he now wears in place of the wire ones, lost that night, and looks into his eyes. She reads a confused sadness; he lifts his hand, gently holds her by the neck. The suddenness of his gesture causes her to shiver.

Christian sits on the far side of the island, facing the wilderness of ocean that leads unbroken to the South Pole. He is as far in mind and body as he can be from the warden's house. He has a need for vast, impenetrable space; the world entered, became small, with Sean's visit, as if he were all of convention: government, morality, religion, commerce. There was a fug about the man, unaired, oppressive.

There are whitecaps on the horizon. The blue of ocean hardens to gray; the sky on the horizon is ominous, with a dark, ship-threatening haze.

He stares at the whitecaps; imagines himself in a small sailboat, alone. Frightened, but alone. As he steers his small boat he thinks of Fran, and instantly he misses her. The shelter of her. Come about, trim the sails, he thinks. Head back for the pass, to her comfort.

To be her passenger and follow her to a destination he has not chosen?

He looks down. Sand crabs scoop miniature tablespoons of sand from their refuge holes, then scurry along the small white patch of beach. Salt dries, crackling, on his skin. Why journey to arrive, to succeed? That is a Western notion. Fran, in her patience, has learned otherwise: that existence is an end in itself. Mere survival the lot of most creatures. You can watch the trees grow, here. You can hear the quiet unfolding of a feather; it is a beauty you can protect.

Back there, Nermina: I was not able to protect her.

Fran's beauty. The simplicity of her. She would not betray him. You can watch the pleasure rise from her skin.

The shelter of her; perhaps there is time, still.

When he finds her again, much later, in the first coolness before dark, she is planting, on her knees with a small bucket of dirt and a trowel. He drops down behind her, moves his arms around her, holds her breasts, first gently, then harder. Buries his face against her neck, breathes in the scent of warm earth on her skin.

They feast. They eat the bounty Sean has brought until they can eat no more, their bodies gorged on the ripe flesh of mango, of papaya. They have not spoken, as if it is a game.

She watches him. He is sitting back, his eyes closed, his hands upon his stomach. A sly smile curving around the sides of his mustache. She could be bold, cross over now, straddle him on the rickety wooden chair, lift off his glasses. But she does not feel bold, only full and sleepy. A drop of juice glistens sticky-sweet above a corner of her mouth.

Alone, I would become a mad bird woman, she thinks. All potential concentrated into frail carriers of air and dreams.

Is this a last chance to be something else? To follow old, appropriate instincts?

During the night it rains. Fran awakens and listens: after the hurricane this rain seems absurdly gentle. Domestic, healing.

Christian lies next to her, curled against her back. This too, continues to surprise her. They say nothing, but there are times when they look at each other and know that the slight smile is one of surprise— and that they have been caught out by the unexpected.

In the morning the earth steams in the heat. The lagoon sparkles through the trees. Clouds wait, sit snagged on top of the mountains.

Fran and Christian are clearing away the damage to the aviary, so they can begin reconstruction. They work quickly and silently, until it is too hot and Fran calls a break. They share a drink of water, their lips are cool. They look at each other as if they are aware of this, but hesitate: should they act on the coolness of their lips?

The moment passes, lost, yet stored, as future fuel.

Fran sits, almost elegant in her linen dress, in the bow of the pirogue. Christian has shaved; he looks boyish, younger. Sean has sent for them from the mainland, and Bruno the ferryman is telling him about the damage to Mauritius during the storm; Fran cannot hear over the noise of the engine. She feels like a young girl on an outing; they will do their errands in Mahébourg, then go for a drive up to Curepipe, where there is a good restaurant. Then Bruno will ferry them back again after dark.

The town is a riot of sound and color, of market-day crowds, the streets a clutter of bicycles, vans, trucks, and people; somehow all manage to move toward their various destinations without colliding.

Men linger in conversation at places where beer is sold; women weave briskly among the traffic, shopping bags in hand or bundles poised on their heads. In their midst pale round tourists move without a destination, as if confused by the bustle and their own aimlessness. Fran feels stiff and strange among them; in another life, another place, she would like to take Christian's arm to guide her. They stand to one side as a woman walks by with an enormous bundle on her head.

Let's go first to the police, says Fran, I want to get that over with.

Fran feels she is on a movie set as they sit in the police chief's office: the long-bladed ceiling fan, swirling air; the old-fashioned blue uniforms, starched and pressed; the burnished wooden furniture. As they wait she reads a curious quotation on the wall: *If language is not correct, then what is said is not what is meant; if what is said is not what is meant, then what ought to be done is not done.* Even these words make her uneasy; she has not been here since Satish died. That was over a year ago, but a year was not long enough; the officers remember, are polite but insincere. Then, very quickly, Christian takes over in a calm, professional way which impresses the police chief. Fran sits quietly, answers a few questions.

We are not out of danger, she thinks. Whoever, for whatever reason, attacked Satish, then Christian, has not gone away. They will try again. For all we know the policemen may know very well who the assailants were. My foundation does not factor in an allocation for bribe money; corruption is not part of the philanthropic system. We cannot bribe these men; we can only hope they'll do their job honestly.

Christian signs his statement. The police chief is solid, reassuring. Fran smiles but does not believe him. Nothing will change.

We'll get things done faster if we split up, says Fran. Why don't you do the hardware store, Chen Li's, and the pharmacy; and I'll do the bank and the post office.

Christian walks away and she watches: her yearning is his shadow. A dark shape of dust, until he blends into the crowd of dark-faced, white-shirted Mauritian men. How easy it is to lose someone in a crowd; there are places on earth where you could lose someone forever.

She feels exposed, vulnerable. A man standing next to a taxi is staring at her. Not impolitely, but with an open curiosity that is acceptable. She finds it hard to be alone, suddenly.

It's all routine, the part of her exotic life she likes least, the part which tries to remind her of life back there in the so-called real world. Banks and post offices with their invisible connections to responsibility, society. The twin poles of finance between which everyone must navigate: greed and generosity.

She checks that the regular foundation deposits have been made, and withdraws a small amount of cash for their immediate needs. She goes through the gestures automatically, thinking how these are learned, unnecessary maneuvers; that the natural earth was not meant to succumb to such man-made absurdity. Ten days earlier she would not have thought about it like this; it is what the storm and their isolation have shown her. What is important.

In the post office she waits patiently, still philosophizing, deciding that post offices are less insidious than banks, because they enable communication, which seems a greater value to her than money. Birds, after all, communicate; all living creatures do. She stares at the poster of the Île aux Cerfs, and a sudden warmth comes over her, a curious sense of déjà vu that has to do not at all with the routineness of her trips to the post office but with the last time she came here. Of course, that postcard for Christian. She'd forgotten all about it, with the storm and everything that has happened: to him, to her; between them.

She opens her straw basket and peers inside. There is a small pile of letters and brochures next to her wallet that she hadn't even noticed when she was getting ready to come to town, hadn't noticed at the police station or the bank.

Someone is asking her what she wants, it is her turn at the window and she has been lost in thought. Confused, she asks for her letters from the poste restante. It is not the same girl as the previous time, who asked her so politely about stamps. This woman is a tired civil servant, practically throwing the packet of letters at Fran, before shouting at the next customer to state his business. Fran bundles the letters up and shoves them into the bag on top of the old pile.

Fran is at a point of no return. A threshold, open and waiting, yawning, to receive her into her future.

Everything has changed since the last time she came to Mahébourg. If she had given the card to Christian that day on the landing . . . might he have changed his plans there and then, depending on the message of the card? And how did she manage to block it from her thoughts so utterly and successfully—as if she had a sixth sense about the evolution of their lives, as if there could be no looking back?

Because now she is afraid the card might contain news she does not want to hear: something that could take Christian away from her. Even if he is here physically: something that could cause him to shut himself off. A path to memory.

She could destroy the postcard, unread; she could toss it into that rubbish bin across the street, where even now some schoolgirls are tossing the wrappers of their ice-cream cones, with casual gestures amid peals of laughter.

Fran looks from the rubbish bin to the girls and back again. As if she could pretend there were no postcard, no knowledge. The way it has already been for ten forgetful days. Not so much a second chance as a way of changing the switches, and derailing fate. Because she can hide or destroy a postcard: it is only a small thing, easily tossed into a rubbish bin.

That would be dishonest, she protests to herself, even criminal. She feels pangs of conscience, invokes an appeal to decency. Her upbringing, her Anglo-Saxon values of fair play.

But her right to happiness? Must she toss that into the rubbish bin?

She has a few minutes, before she sees him. A few minutes to plead with fate and conscience, and strike a deal.

She waits in the sun by the Land Rover. Christian is not there yet, and she looks anxiously down the street, shielding her eyes with her hand. Past the same two long-haired girls in their blue school uniforms, still eating their ice creams, interrupting the hushed confidentiality of their words with the occasional giggle. Past the two men unloading crates of fruit from a small truck. Past—and through—the luminous air buzzing with insects and an almost tangible fragrance. The fruit, mango and papaya.

The sunlit air holds a scattering of dust and wonder and expectancy. Then again she thinks of the postcard, and thoughts falter, confused. How long has she got? A few hours, until they return to Egret, or perhaps only minutes, if he should ask, Was there any post for me? Can she lie? Will she lie?

People lie all the time, she reasons. It is a spontaneous, basic instinct. Perhaps lying is an evolutionary survival tool; adultery entails lying, for example.

But what of upbringing, conscience? What of our own humane and wonderful evolution away from our baser instincts?

Now Christian is walking toward her. The sunlight catches him, sharpens his smile. Sharpens her longing. Intensifies and concentrates time and inevitability; all her future, like the past of a drowning man, is compacted into that space of sunlight, that time measured by Christian's steps, as he approaches. She must choose. There are two scenarios, two futures. The sunlight is a prism, refracting her reason, causing her imagination to dazzle with hope.

She cannot read the gaze behind his sunglasses. This troubles her; now more than ever she needs to know what he might be thinking. But he smiles, a long smile, and raises his hand, grazes her arm with his fingertips, an intimate greeting.

They drive north to Curepipe. Christian thinks of the hours he has spent on this road: the green, moist familiarity of it. Yet changed, as if it were long ago, part of a dream life. Asmita: her silken presence.

He glances at Fran. She sits beside him, unsmiling, looking out the window. Brooding. He would like to ease her trouble. At the police station there had been mention of Satish; she must have felt she was reliving the anguish of that time, strangely mirrored, since he, Christian, had survived.

Who am I for her? He reaches out, places his hand on hers, briefly squeezes it. A current passes; she smiles. He knows a place where they could pull off the road, shelter the Land Rover. He hesitates, then thinks better of it. They have a reservation at the restaurant, and there is little time. He questions, too, Fran's spontaneity, when she is not on her island, away from this world, out of time.

They are shy. Candlelight casts shadows upon their faces. They are not used to being in society together. A secret couple. The food is wonderful, after a diet of rice and noodles; they sigh and look at each other and let a game begin. Looking, eating, silence; thinking, above all. Private yet shared fantasies; thus they retreat into their own place, as if they were still on the island.

Later, driving back to Mahébourg, he says, Fran, I want to be honest with you. I am staying on because I don't know where to go. You've given me a home. An opportunity. I'm still rebuilding my life; I don't know what I want in the future. I cannot promise you anything; I don't know how long I can stay.

She is silent for a moment, then says very quietly, I'm not asking for promises. I'm not that kind of woman. I want it to be the right thing for you. I want to help.

But you see, I don't know if I want your help, either. I don't, I don't want anyone—you, or before, it was Asmita—to become too involved in my life. In me.

She waits, then says, Christian, you are free. You have always been free.

I know that. I know you understand that. But I need you—how to say—to measure my freedom for me. Because I am a good man and I will give you everything if you ask for it.

Fran laughs softly. And modest, too.

I would have married Asmita, even though it meant the end of freedom. But she was not honest with me . . .

Are you sure?

Maybe I should have married her no matter what. Maybe there was a sort of truth in her behavior: her truth. Her family's truth. Society's truth. Maybe she wanted to believe so badly in a future with me that she acted unconsciously. But I didn't love her enough. I didn't love her, no.

So her dishonesty was an excuse? A way out?

He is silent.

But Fran has her answer.

It is not too late, she thinks. In the morning she can begin the day, empty her straw bag—Oh look, Christian, I forgot, a card for you. But for now she does not want to spoil the evening. The card, whatever its message, could only take him into the past; she needs to believe, however briefly, that he is a part of her future.

Blue light, seeking black; Bruno ferries Christian and Fran across the lagoon by moonlight. Their forms are dark against the blue night; the lagoon is a clear depth holding night, flashes of phosphorescence breaking loose on the wake of the pirogue.

Their short journey holds peace, an image blenched of time, that you could hold like a painting in your memory. But that would be to make them symbols—man and woman on the journey through life. Someone else, however, is steering.

Christian looks behind him, into the swirling water. And in the trick-light of the moon he sees the tendrils, long dark locks spilling, turning in the wake, Nermina's face upturned, lagoon maiden, water sylph, her sad familiar features watching him as if begging for air. I have drowned, she seems to say, in your loss.

That night Fran is imprisoned by Christian's tenderness. She cannot escape the gentle sorcery of his touch; it goes deep within her, releases chemicals that soften and bind. She returns his touch and sees in his eyes the same spell, the same surrender.

In the morning Fran reaches into her straw bag. Very slowly, with a painful deliberation, she places the small pile of letters before her on the table. Maybe she imagined the postcard; maybe it will not be there. But it is—she looks briefly at the photographic side of the card: a cobbled square with a fountain, people sitting in cafés; in the background, a minaret, hills. To trivialize its presence she sorts through the rest of the mail: personal, business, Christian. She gathers his other letters— Swiss postmarks, all—into a separate pile and then slips the postcard in the middle. She reproaches her beating heart, questions again the source of her anxiety. Surely it is nothing; surely it is everything.

Then she goes more carefully through her own letters: scientific reports, letters from the foundation, CVs from students who want to work with her. And a note from Professor Smits in South Africa, inviting her to give a talk at the university. Perhaps she'll go; it would be good to get some distance. It's very short notice, but they'll pay her airfare.

When she has finished she takes the small pile of Christian's letters and places it on the chair, in his room, the way she always does, when she sorts the mail.

From time to time as the afternoon wears on she will wonder at the outcome of her act. She cannot doubt that she has made the right decision, on the side of honesty and goodness, but there are times she wishes things could be otherwise. That she could stack the cards in her favor, defy fate. I am only human, she murmurs to herself, and weak, like most people—and don't I have a right to be happy?

And what of Christian's right to happiness? How can she, even for a moment, wish for something for herself at his expense?

The stochastic factor, the random determinant. A postcard from Sarajevo: why should it even be important? Important messages don't come on postcards. That scrolling, Middle European handwriting: could it have the power to change everything, irrevocably? But she does not know, and now she will have to wait for Christian—for a sign, an explanation, reassurance, or the inevitable confirmation of her worst fears. Sarajevo: Princip's bullet, killing the Archduke.

Later that day she finds a feather. Iridescent, dark blue capturing fragments of gold. Iridescent feathers are not used for flight; merely for show. Hence, for mating. The male mourner-bird. She holds the feather for a long time, turning it in the light. The diamonds of the bird world, flashy, superfluous.

He has gone to Grand Baie, writes Fran. *There's a wealthy Englishman who's selling his yacht and all his gear; we might get a dinghy. Ours was never found; it must have blown out to sea in the cyclone. Bruno will be sorry: we've become his best customers.*

Why am I writing this?

Because the dinghy will reconnect us with the world. Because the last ties to the wildness that was the storm and what followed will be broken. Symbolically.

Even if the birds are still missing, even if we still make love. Our isolation, literally, will be no more.

Every day I search, and find nothing. No little corpses, no signs. Only that one feather. Like a postcard from death, or from their new, hidden life.

Perhaps they've migrated: to the mainland, or to other islands: la Passe, Phare, Fouquets, Marianne. With the dinghy we'll be able to search.

What I wanted to write. This morning he held me for a long time, in silence. My thoughts raging and pounding, and he was so quiet.

I wanted to think it was something like love. A wanting to be there always, a resonant longing, unfulfilled yet possible.

On a sun-violent morning they pack the new dinghy with a picnic and binoculars and a jerry can of fuel, and head out into the lagoon in a northerly direction. They skirt the edge of reef, buoyant on the deep blue cushion of water, the swell adding a rhythm to the dinghy's progress. Spray flies over the bow: Fran laughs at the pleasure of its coolness. Christian smiles, his hand on the throttle. He feels it too— the freedom, the knowledge that once again they can go where they want, that they are no longer confined to their island.

They reach a small bay that is the landing for the Île de la Passe. Fran is quiet and somehow aquiver, looking not only with her eyes but with all her senses, as if she indeed had a sixth sense which could show her what was not there.

He follows. The island is open to the wind; there are few trees, and it is barren, coral, inhospitable. Only tropic birds nest here; even now they circle overhead, graceful exclamations of white against the sky. Fran shakes her head; her birds would not come here, this is no refuge for their kind.

The next island is similar, equally open and desolate. Again she shakes her head, removes her cap and wipes her brow. I should have known, she says. There is nothing for them here. It's not their habitat. Let's go to the next island and we'll have our picnic.

Fran walks ahead of him across the rocks, stepping easily, goatlike. He follows, oppressed with heat. A sudden, more general weariness comes over him. He envies the passion that makes her so light of step, and wonders if he will know that passion someday—indeed, if he has ever known it. It is nothing physical, and yet it is a key, unlocking other mysteries of the organism. The spring in her step, the deter- mined frown, her nervous hopefulness. She glows with well-being.

He admits desire. The heat, his hunger. Her taut body ahead of him on the rocks, its angles, its supple movement. Weariness suc- cumbs to desire, a simple way out. Here, now? She won't want it. The landscape is brutal, unsheltered, and she is on a mission.

Still, before they climb back into the dinghy he reaches for her, holds her, buries his face in her neck. Her skin smells of sunlight and salt. She laughs, then slowly removes herself, turns to face him. He cannot see her eyes behind her sunglasses. She raises her hand, runs the back of her fingers along his cheek, then turns toward the dinghy.

A bird cuts through the cloth of sky. Fran raises the binoculars to look, follows with the heavy lenses. Wings flapping, not gliding; flash of blue.

Then Fran admits she has imagined this vision, willed it. There was a bird, but it was not blue, only white, a tropic bird. In her will there is defiance, and a touch of the irrational. At times she wonders if that is what distinguishes the brilliant naturalist from the competent one. There is no reason to suspect she will find survivors of her species here, but she applies visions, urges intuition.

When things began to fall apart with Peter she tried to apply visions. Long scenarios of how they would be reconciled, and fall in love all over again. Romantic dinners and walks along the beach. She saw it, she willed it. And each time he came to the house on Shasta Road she opened the door with the first vision ready for fulfillment, his abject apology, his words murmured into her neck as he held her. It never happened.

Why should it be different with the fate of birds?

She turns and looks at Christian, standing some ways off, staring at the sky with his hand to his brow. High cirrus cloud, wispy, sign of wind. She sees no visions there, for Christian. He is present. She remembers the postcard and feels a twinge somewhere within. He has said nothing to her, nothing at all; but earlier, he held her. A strange, needful embrace. She pulled away; the moment was wrong, for her. They do not think of themselves as two people in love; such a moment is dangerous, a license to change.

Briefly, she trains her binoculars on Christian. He looks restless, unhappy. But he often looks like this—as if to wear a smile would be insincere, because his life has been shaped by sadness.

She will often remember him thus, as she sees him through the binoculars. The black space enclosing him in a circle of light; his sadness, his far-off gaze.

He has not told Fran that on his way back from Grand Baie, with the dinghy strapped to the roof of the Land Rover, he stopped to see Asmita. It was an impulse, a coincidence of timing; he knew that she would be on her way from the hotel to the bus stop, heading home.

He saw her from a distance, recognized her gait, that rhythmic elegance. Her clothing, he thought, seemed sharper, more businesslike. He pulled up alongside and called to her, and she turned and for a moment he thought that it was not Asmita, that he'd been mistaken, but then her features came into focus. Her features, too, were sharper.

She looked at him. Asmita, he called, can I talk to you? She looked around as if hesitating, then opened the door. She climbed in next to him and said nothing, did not look at him. She was stony. He drove a short way further and then pulled off to the side of the road.

I shall miss my bus, she protested suddenly, her voice tense and hard.

I'll drive you.

I have to do some shopping. I haven't much time.

Where do you need to go?

Curepipe, near the bazaar . . .

They drove in silence, then finally Christian said, I know I've hurt you. I'm sorry. But you were dishonest with me . . . I just couldn't go through with it. I know I should have called you. I was sick. And the cyclone—

She looked at him sharply, then away again, and said, Yes, you should have. We waited for days and days, and you didn't call, then finally . . . My parents went to a great deal of trouble and expense.

I'm sorry about that too. I'll try to make it up to them.

Some things you cannot make up, she said flatly. Then she turned away, and Christian thought she must be crying: she was fumbling in her sack, sniffling.

Christian drove on in silence. Questioned his own madness that he had ever thought he could marry her, then was overcome with self-loathing, how badly, indeed, he had treated her, selfishly. His bad faith was as great as, if not greater than, hers.

I will write to your parents, he had said. That was all.

There were other things he could have said—how he had used her as subconsciously as she had used him, expecting her to heal some-thing that could not be healed. But he sensed it would not make things better, or be any kind of consolation, to either of them. He wanted her to think well of him, not to hate him, and when he pulled up out-side the bazaar to let her out, he looked at her with an intent gaze, willing her to forgive him. But she never looked up, and barely mur-mured good-bye as she slammed the door.

Now Christian looks at Fran in the shade and the dappled light of a filao tree shimmering in the breeze. She is reaching for a sandwich. She is flushed; they have been walking to find this spot of shade by a curve of lagoon. He fears for her, wants to protect her. She turns to look at him, and smiles.

I'm thinking of going to South Africa again. They've invited me to give a talk. They'll pay all my expenses.

Christian looks down. The recent image of Asmita fades; an older one takes its place: her visit to the island, the first time, when Fran went to South Africa. Long ago; another Asmita.

You could come with me if you like, Fran is saying now, and he looks at her, suddenly aware of her words, of their implication. More images drop through him in layers: memories, split-second projections.

It might be interesting for you, she is saying. Cape Town. You could hear my talk, meet other people who are doing similar work. The theoretical side of it. And see a bit of the country.

She is right, but he feels reluctant, and tries to unravel his reluctance. Perhaps the idea of traveling with her, being in her presence among others. In her shadow. He recognizes his own sense of inadequacy, tells himself it does not matter, that he admires her; tells himself too that his feelings for her are fragile, and might not survive such a challenge.

She is handing him another sandwich. Their fingers touch, and he knows instinctively and immediately that he must not go with her.

I'll think about it, he replies, finally.

He won't come, writes Fran later. *I've given him half a dozen perfectly good reasons why he ought to come, and it seems with each reason he retreats further into a gentle obstinacy.*

He looks at me and gives a half smile. Then looks away and says, No, Fran, I'd like to stay here. And gives me reasons why he ought to stay, and all of them are good reasons too, but then the one overriding reason is absent. The one important reason, to come with me.

Unless, of course, it is something to do with that postcard.

So our reasons cancel each other out, and it has become a matter of will, and I sense his has become the stronger.

There was a time when I could have persuaded him to come. When it didn't matter so much to me; when things were merely professional between us.

There is a new weakness in me. Perhaps he has found it, and it is enough for him to resist. And in pushing against his resistance, I feel this weakness increasing, expanding.

Fran hurriedly prepares her departure for South Africa. A small event: she will be gone only four days, but she anticipates it with curiosity and apprehension. There are times she feels that without that date she will lose her sense of time altogether, and that without time she will lose her sense of belonging. A tenuous link to convention, and thus to humankind.

(The island keeps its own time. Christian has severed links, rises with the sun, forgets seasons, lives by satiety and appetite.)

As she prepares her talk, the hardest part is the disappearance of the mourner-bird. She struggles with her notes, shuffles pages, realizes that she is trying to deny what has happened, trying to rearrange Nature in a way that fits in with her human, academic scheme. In the end she writes a blunt, factual paragraph, a sort of afterthought which in a few lines seems to negate the entire thesis of her discussion. She has no explanation. She is hoping someone there might have an answer, or consolation.

Christian drives Fran to the airport, waits with her by the gate, awkwardly. They are not used to crowds, he cannot say the things he wants to say, and realizes it is too late. He should have said something in the Land Rover, never thought time could be so abruptly compressed. Fran frowns at him, as if she does not want to leave. When the flight is called, he gives her a peck on the cheek, swiftly; she squeezes his fingers.

On the following day Christian goes to Bertrand's restaurant and orders an early dinner of *bol renversé*, then finds he has no appetite, pushes the rice around his plate, drinks his beer, too quickly.

Alors, Baudelaire? Bertrand stands before him, even redder and sweatier than Christian remembers him. Christian points to the empty chair; Bertrand sits down slowly, releasing a sigh as his heavy form settles, as if he were his own cushion, releasing air.

Still having woman trouble?

Life trouble, more like it.

Ah, now that's serious.

As in the past, Christian wonders if he should confide in Bertrand. His beer glass is empty; he points to it and says, Got anything stronger?

Bertrand shouts to his daughter to bring the bottle of cane liquor and two glasses.

An old Mauritian remedy, he says, winking.

Christian drinks too quickly, feels the alcohol spreading through his body, dislodging thoughts, nudging speech. Suddenly he is talking, talking, things he might once have said to Fran but no longer can, because there is a wall of respect between them; because he does not want to hurt her.

So he tells Bertrand. How he likes it out there, likes that island, gets on well with Fran, but at the same time, he can't explain, he feels trapped, as if his life were going nowhere. What kind of future does he have there? He isn't making money, he isn't making a career, he is just trying to forget or to escape, but he isn't fucking escaping, it is all still there, and he is going round and round on that little island and it is just him and his thoughts and his lack of a future . . .

Bertrand nods from time to time, refills their glasses. Christian goes on, never telling the whole story, Nermina, Asmita, Fran, as if the women are only part of life, that part which he wants to forget, or which could enable him to forget. Finally Bertrand says, You need something of your own.

My own?

Look at me. I'm not exactly a successful businessman, we're ticking over, good year bad year, but the wife's still good to me after all this time, the kids are healthy, I'm cardiac but what the hell, the place is mine, you know? That's what you need. Your own woman, your own place, a few kids, a dream to work on.

Christian is silent for a moment, then says, I had that once, and I lost it. I don't know that I can trust life that far again.

It's not life you want to trust, it's yourself.

Then I can't. I don't trust myself.

What happened?

Christian stares into his glass, as if he could read the past, an inverse clairvoyance, and explain what happened. As if there were an explanation. A way around the roadblock.

On the ceiling a large-bladed fan stirs the air in the silence, a whir, a thrum. In the distance he can hear the Mahébourg night: the shouts of children, music, a motorcycle, a television. Dogs barking. In a deeper silence he can hear his past, the sounds more real than the visions, a booming beyond the hills, voices in anguish. There was a time when Fran had seemed to offer a cure, a hope of real silence. She has gone and the sounds have returned.

He shakes his head, glances at Bertrand. Forget it. It's in the past, it doesn't change now.

He will stay the night at Bertrand's, in the guest room. After the fourth glass of cane liquor the room has begun to soften and curve; a numbness comes over his anguish as if it too is softening. Their words take on a knowing, male intimacy; Bertrand tells stories. He is gifted: long tales of ordinary adventures that he has surely often told but that with each telling acquire a polish, an expertise, a sense of timing to elicit laughter and exclamation. The next day Christian will remember no details of those stories, only Bertrand's hovering red face, the pleasant, shared drunkenness, the soothing effect of the stories, as if they were echoes from an Alpine valley; someone else's memories, an accent, elsewhere.

At night, in the guest room at Professor Smits's house, Fran imagines she can hear the two oceans pounding as they meet, swirl, and embrace. But the real sounds are of insects and wind and faraway traffic, and a dog barking. She misses her island. She misses Christian, yes. She has been gone scarcely twenty-four hours, and her body reminds her of what has become a sweet habit.

Then she thinks of Satish. It is as if he had stepped back and urged her to go on without him. She has forgotten his body; he has become her child, strangely innocent, deeply mourned, yet safe. Yes, safe from her longings, her regret, the power of emotions to stifle his clearer image. He is once again the boy bringing gifts: the orchid; seashells; once, a butterfly with iridescent wings.

Christian has no such childlike gifts for her. He does not bring her things, apart from her dreams of possibility. His absence of gifts is itself a gift: he tames longing.

Fran has just given her talk. Her voice rang pleasant and self-assured into the depths of the auditorium, as if it were not her voice at all but that of a gifted impostor, untroubled by doubt. Anonymous attentive faces turned toward her, respecting her words, writing them down. The echo of applause, a hollow ringing in her head: they praise her, but the mourner-bird has gone.

Now their questions come, after a quiet, polite rustling: What are her plans? How will she expand her search, or encourage the birds to return? Is she discouraged?

This last question, from an older man, perhaps a professor, surprises her. She pauses, looks down at her notes, grips the podium, lets out a speculative sigh. Her words rescue her, but inside she feels a cold, slow pain, as if, left alone, she would easily begin to cry.

Of course I am discouraged, she says. I'd be lying if I said I wasn't.

Six years of work, of progress, destroyed in one day of cyclone?

But the nature of the job is discouragement. Because you're trying from scratch to rebuild what was destroyed. And you're not using your own tools, you're using those of mysterious forces. To persuade two birds to mate—

She breaks off. There is polite laughter. The older man is frowning, skeptical.

Fran looks around her, desperate. Then continues, We can control the deterministic factors, to some degree, as I've explained. Regulations, nature reserves, reproduction management, measures against poaching, and so on. But the stochastic factors . . . we've got no control over them. Even statistically, even trying to make sense of the decline in bird population, in trying to impose a pattern on it, I'm not sure—

Again she breaks off. She has said too much, talked herself into a corner.

But the fact remains, she says sadly, that if man had not interfered in the first place, destroying the island's ecological balance, preying upon the bird population for his own purposes, we would not have had the dire situation we have now.

A young, male voice from the back of the auditorium calls out, half comment, half question: So you reckon the mourner-bird is the new dodo?

She smiles. She is gracious, and heartbroken. No one expects her to take this so personally. Her eyes sting with tears.

Yes, she answers. In one respect, yes. But I'm not ready to declare the bird extinct. That's an alarmist attitude, downright pessimistic.

But statistically—

Fran knows what she wants to say. Intuitively, hopefully, irrationally. Unscientifically. Because only her determination will find the bird now. But this is a hall full of young scientists: they are rigid, untried, dogmatic. So she shrugs, folding away her notes to signal she will have nothing more to say, after this: Experience has shown me that you cannot rely on things to be the way they seem. To use the old cliché, you have to expect the unexpected. In Nature, anything is possible.

In the heat of the morning Christian sets out in the dinghy to return to the island. He has been to the market, bought fresh fruit and vegetables, and a warm baguette. The sun is too bright, seems to vibrate in his head together with the throb of the outboard and the memory of alcohol. He has decided to take the day off, in Fran's absence, to sleep and read and swim, perhaps catch a fish or two. It has been hard to justify solitude or inactivity to Fran now, recently—she wants to be with him—or to himself in her presence.

He ties the dinghy to the landing. From the path he can see the warden's house, its familiar, pleasing simplicity, its faded time-worn elegance. The veranda. A hanging plant Fran has hooked to the corner of the roof. The ragged wicker furniture, still serviceable, even enticing, at this distance. He pictures the British officers who lived there once, bored and indolent in the heat of their colonial outpost, sipping gin and tonic, passing the time with endless discussions in plummy voices of war and women. He wonders that they did not go mad with boredom, that their ghosts do not wander the island still searching for a secret exit. He does not think he and Fran have ever been bored; they know the secret exits of the island, into worlds of insects and reptiles and fish and birds and now, each other.

He is musing in this way, confused, not unhappy, despite what he said to Bertrand the night before—which he now ascribes to a moment of panic at Fran's departure (something he could not confess)— when he looks onto the veranda and sees something wrong with the picture. No British officers, unexpected ghosts, but traces of a visit all the same.

Sheets of paper are strewn across the veranda: handwritten sheets, Fran's notes, littering the old sofa, the floor, the ground, a few sheets caught in the blades of the pandanus down the path. The door is wide open. Christian runs into the house, his heart pounding: inside there is more paper, but also their clothes, books, the stuffing from their pillows, their mattresses, rotting vegetables, plates, glass, all strewn, torn, slashed, stripped, squashed, smashed, pieces of their life.

Madly for a moment he thinks, the Serbs, then remembers where he is, the absurdity, the impossibility, lets out a cry in disbelief, swears, drops down onto his haunches and holds his head in his trembling hands.

He is lying on the wicker sofa on the veranda, and the breeze brings him messages, random pages torn from notebooks, in Fran's neat, sometimes hurried script. He has no heart to begin the cleanup, so he lets the messages come in the idle, childish hope that one of them will provide an answer, tell him what he is to do.

This quickening—and he is only a figment?

What chemistry is this; where does the brain play God, creating flesh where there is none?

All his efforts, he thinks, have been in vain: to escape his memories, to rebuild his life. This new destruction like a mockery: the words of her life—her loss and loneliness—scattered like the photographs of those who fled.

He sees Jasminka; he sees Nermina the first time he showed her the child's photograph. She imitated the little girl's missing-tooth smile, and they laughed; she was gently mocking of him, touched that he had made such a gesture.

His body is firm and solid, but as I touched him there was something fragile, too; as if part of him were insubstantial, given over to the recovery of dreams.

She's writing about me, he thinks. It's true, she gave me back my dreams. Because she was there, listening; because I was able to tell her—she gave me that confidence.

He refrains from reading entire pages of Fran's notes, respects a random privacy. If there is something vital, fated, he will read it, and know that he was meant to. That its meaning is revelatory, some order in chaos, some direction. Like stabbing at a page in the Bible, chapter and verse. Merely a game, he tells himself, his head throbbing, a philosopher's luxury.

Unsettling, the fact that Christian's young woman works for Razel. The wealthy recluse; Sean had a run-in with him when he first began to work here. Satish didn't like to talk about him, he said it was an old story, better forgotten.

What will I do now? My ordered little world, it seems, is only an illusion of order, thwarted by biology.

He makes a very strong cup of coffee from beans which were miraculously spared. Then he begins, disheartened, to clean up. The exhaustion is not so much physical—it is a small house, and it is small, light things which have been flung at random around its space—as it is mental: where does this go? The fact that this bowl is now broken—can I mend it? What else can be saved? Listlessly, he rights the chairs which have been knocked over, makes piles of unrelated things—books, letters, envelopes.

With Nermina, once, he had come upon an elderly Bosnian man whose house had been looted while he was away visiting relatives. The man had run out into the street in front of their vehicle, slammed his fists on the hood when they stopped, begged them to help, to find the perpetrators. His voice was shrill, desperate, breathless; he held his chest as he spoke. Christian had wanted to drive on—the man was in no danger, and they had been on their way to a local clinic to deliver long-overdue supplies; but Nermina shouted at him, insisted that they give the man enough of their time so that he would have the courage to continue. We must give him courage, that's all, she said. A little of our time, and courage.

He remembers the house—its smell of time, of a hundred thousand meals and of all the family and neighbors and friends who had added their breath and sweat with their jovial curses to the air, saturating carpets and walls; and how the simplicity and ordinariness of this widower's life had added up to so much detail and meaningless (to them) clutter. Ugly mementos: a plastic Eiffel Tower, a Venetian gondola, brought no doubt by relatives as souvenirs, now crushed and irreparable; plates and *rakija* glasses and embroidered wall pictures of Dubrovnik and photographs in smashed frames; and in her national costume (which nation?), a smiling doll, her wig pulled from her head.

The old man had wept and thanked them, still holding his heart with one hand, his black beret with the other, as they drove off. Nermina did not dwell on it. She had been efficient, quickly folding the old fellow's clothes, pulling away the soiled sheets and making the bed with fresh ones. In the Jeep she was silent, looking straight ahead. He knew what she was thinking: of the others, of the times they had not been there.

Now he looks down at the object in his hands and realizes he has been standing there immobile, unable to make a decision or even recognize what he is holding. The object has lost its name and its function in the brief time it has taken him to recall the old Bosnian man.

And Nermina. Suddenly she is there beside him, and she is whispering, gently mocking, It's a teapot, *dušo moje,* and it goes on the shelf above the sink, look, what a miracle it's not broken. It's a sturdy thing, this teapot.

At the end of the day Christian clears the last broken fragments— a windowpane—from the floor in his bedroom. He finds the limp body of a small gecko among the shards of glass, a surreally beautiful creature, green with red markings and a blue-and-red face. He makes no effort to wonder how the gecko died. He holds its little body across his palm, caresses its spine, as if tenderness might revive it.

He walks to the lagoon with the gecko still in his hand. A patch of sand will serve: he scoops deep into the earth. Memories occupy the void he has created: picnics by Lake Geneva with his parents, he was a child digging deep, wishing he could find a secret escape in the intricacy of tunnel he had created. His parents' silence left him pensive and unhappy as a child. Now he places the gecko into the hole and fills it slowly, his blank pensiveness a sort of prayer. Has he learned, too often, to seek the darker side of life, or does it, for some reason he has not yet learned, seek him?

He thinks of Fran, how her work is being systematically destroyed, and yet she does not give up, or lose hope. Still there is light. Her skin is full of light, she radiates that warmth, that hopefulness. He thinks of her, and his desire is abrupt and sweet, yet pointless: she is not here.

Beyond the dark volcanic skyline the sunset boils red, briefly. He lays his palms over the small mound he has filled in. The sand is cool, its coolness rises along his arms. He lies down, his body along the sand, and lets its coolness soothe, like a skin.

He walks back to the house in near-darkness. On the path he sees a patch of white in a pandanus bush: a last page of Fran's notes. He picks it up, will add it to the others he smoothed carefully into a pile on her dresser.

There were her clothes, too. He folded them neatly, bemused by the feel of them, empty skins of this woman he now knows intimately, in her nakedness. Yes, her scent lingered: he lifted a T-shirt to his face, breathed in.

In the lamplight he catches her words as he lifts the page to the pile:

What I wanted to write. This morning he held me for a long time, in silence. My thoughts raging and pounding, and he was so quiet.

I wanted to think it was something like love. A wanting to be there always, a resonant longing, unfulfilled yet possible.

He does not know, cannot tell from the paper or the handwriting whether this is a recent entry or older: is she writing about him, or about Satish?

He goes to the kitchen to pour himself a glass of cane liquor and then realizes that as he was cleaning he saw no sign of the bottle. He searches anyway, but of course it is gone.

In the darkness he sits on the veranda and thinks of what he has just read. His desire for a drink is overwhelming. He thinks of taking the dinghy to Mahébourg. It is urgent, as if, somehow, he will not be able to understand the import of Fran's words—if they are meant for him. As if the alcohol would make it clear somehow: whether she was indeed writing about him, or what is meant by her words. Has he even thought about her love? Love: when does the physical become something more—is it just words?

If he were drunk, or even only slightly so, he might see some poetic truth in the fine simplicity of their coupling—like Fran, he might see its possibility. But he sits in silence and sobriety in the thick stillness, and instead the mosquitoes feast, grow drunk on his blood.

Fran is sitting in the shade of a magnificent tree in Professor Smits's garden.
With her host and his wife she has had a late and copious breakfast,
talking extensively of birds but also of South Africa until suddenly,
rather wearily, Professor Smits says, I'm so bloody tired of politics,
aren't you?

Fran shrugs and smiles. He continues, We're very fortunate, you
and I, to be bird people. Don't you think that leaves us somehow free
of all that bloody nonsense? As if like our birds we can simply rise
above it?

Fran thinks of Berkeley, what heresy this would be there; then of
her own island, a state unto itself—and under siege. She hesitates,
unsure, then ventures an opinion. That's what I thought, once. It was
blissful to suppose you could get beyond not just politics but society.
That's what I thought. But society is very suspicious of individuals like
me. They've made my life very difficult over recent years. Recent
days, in fact.

Mrs. Smits looks at Fran wide-eyed: she is a quiet woman, birdlike
herself, feathery and flittery; she has said little, but now she turns her
pointed face to Fran and says, as she deftly pours the tea, How indeed? In what way?

Fran waits until Mrs. Smits has put down the teapot, then says quietly, Some of my birds have died, I don't quite know why. Freak acci-
dents. And before that my assistant drowned. And now my new
assistant—

She breaks off. She feels suddenly weak and anxious. The man and
woman opposite her are strangers; they seem grotesque in their wide-
eyed curiosity. She finishes quickly: He nearly drowned, too. Someone
collided with his dinghy. It all seems too much—

Professor Smits shakes his head, then says, A lot of people don't
like what ecologists are doing. We interfere with people's personal
interests. Their livelihood, their gain . . . selfish motivations, often.

242 ~ alison anderson

They see us as selfish too, I suppose. It seems altruism is not a gene we all carry, so to speak.

They sit on in silence. High in the branches of the magnificent tree a Cape bulbul looks down on them, casually yet cautiously, then settles again on its branch.

At the airport Fran finds a small Zulu sculpture in a gift shop. For Christian, she thinks, so he'll know I thought about him. Missed him.

In the plane she removes the sculpture from its tissue paper and rubs her thumbs along the wood. It is smooth and hard, but its roundness suggests skin, a curve of muscle. She can think of Christian, and a soft weakness seems to pull her toward earth. She has been gone for four days; her body feels bloated with absence, expanded with longing, like a fruit forgotten on a branch.

He is dreaming. In his dream Fran is holding him, and her grip is strong, and when he tries to pull away a deep pain shoots through him. She is silent, but her words swirl in the air of this undefined space, the handwritten words of her journal, flocks of black ink letters, meaningless yet accusatory. She is silent, but he knows she is angry, and will not let him go.

What do you want from me? he says, but she does not answer. He wants to grasp the letters as they pass, What-do-you-want-from-me? but her grip is too strong, and his spoken words fall upon deafness.

The bird's song awakens him, and he lies watchful and alert, waiting to hear it again. Its sorrowful cry, long absent. Where has it been?

Chilled by his dream, he waits, and thinks of the fidelity of birds. How they often mate for life. Is it calling for its mate? Where is the answer? Is this one a sole survivor, or will there be a pair for Fran's ark?

Again it comes, no twitter or trill or shriek, but a long, sustained questioning note. Is there a bird form of loneliness, or grieving?

There is no answer.

Before driving to the airport, Christian stops in to see Bertrand. It is not a good day, Bertrand is busy with a group of Austrian tourists, all men, red-faced and laughing and rolling into rotund middle age. They look not so different from Bertrand himself, only Bertrand is not laughing. You know why they're here, he mutters grumpily to Christian. My wife is so angry she won't wait on them.

Christian raises his eyebrows.

Mail-order brides, hisses Bertrand. The men are here to pick them up, it's part of the package. Flight, hotel, bride.

And where are the brides then?

They meet them tomorrow. Over at the Grand Sud.

Asmita's place, thinks Christian. Then he turns quickly to

Bertrand, places a hand on his arm to restrain him, and says, What do you know about Razel? I mean, was there any reason why Satish would have had a connection with Razel—

Ah, *mon vieux,* you want to stay out of all that—

Bertrand, the last time I came here, and stayed over, you remember—

But Bertrand is not listening; the Austrians are waving to him, pointing at their empty beer bottles.

Christian sits patiently, finishes his *bol renversé,* waits expectantly for the small glass of cane liquor Bertrand always brings him. He looks at his watch; he will have to drive fast, it is nearly time for Fran's plane to arrive.

Bertrand continues to make polite conversation with the Austrians in his bad German. Already the men are drunk, and their questions about Mauritian women—their future brides—cause Bertrand to grimace, even to look helplessly toward Christian. Like farmers at a cattle fair, thinks Christian; he understands the anger of Bertrand's wife. But then he thinks of Asmita and wonders again at her deeper motivations: can he blame the women who agree to meet these men as future husbands? Should he blame instead the Austrian women who, presumably, would not have them—or was it the men who chose to look for foreign brides to begin with, to gratify something in their imagination which would enable them to feel more handsome, more powerful, than their own women would allow them to feel?

Christian looks despairingly one last time in Bertrand's direction, then leaves a few rupee notes on the table. His question about Razel and Satish will have to wait. He waves to Bertrand, who shrugs and gestures in reply; Christian points to his watch, then steps out into what seems an aggressively bright sunlight.

He is holding her hands, squeezing her fingers, but they do not embrace; the light in the arrivals hall is too bright, inquisitive, like the crowd milling around them. Beneath Christian's faint, wry smile Fran reads a frown. She squeezes his fingers in return, then pulls away.

They walk to the parking lot, and their conversation is formal, as if rehearsed, as if spoken by their other, previous selves. How was it? asks Christian; Fran describes her talk, hears herself saying things as if by rote, when the real shapeless words in her mind are Here you are, with your dark shock of hair and your strong arms, your left hand holding my case, your right one searching for keys in the pocket of your dusty shorts, and your cheeks unshaven this is new and why that frown earlier and your eyes distant why will you not look at me—

In the shade and silence of the Land Rover, Christian pauses, does not turn the ignition. He looks at Fran, then away. What is he seeing? she thinks, and reaches over to him, kisses him on his unshaven cheek, murmurs, I'm glad to be back. Almost says, I missed you, then thinks that is giving away too much.

He begins to speak, and what he is saying is not at all what she expected to hear, no, any number of existential problems but not this. *The house was ransacked, Fran, everything upside down, it took me all day to clear*— No, what is he saying, and she lets out a moan and leans back, closes her eyes, sees her island, and her life violated once again, her work scattered and destroyed.

But you're all right, she says finally, again reaching over. That's the most important thing.

This time he holds her hand, tightly: I stayed the night at Bertrand's. I needed a change. Perhaps if I had been on the island they wouldn't have done anything. I'm sorry, it's my fault, I—

No, Christian, you might have been hurt, please don't blame yourself.

He turns the ignition and does not answer. They drive in silence toward Mahébourg, alongside the empty cane fields, past groves of mango trees. All the deep familiarity of home. But this home has become unsafe, and that knowledge raises deep disquiet. His silence worst of all.

Perhaps, she thinks, closing her eyes, it is something to do with the postcard from Sarajevo. Perhaps he's made a decision.

Fran looks around the house, like a prospective buyer, her eyes keen to note details, changes. Christian stands by the table, waiting, his eyes downcast. Finally she shakes her head and says, Actually, it looks better than before. You've cleaned and tidied.

He shrugs. It was all I could do.

She goes into the bedroom. He hears the rustle of paper, a low exclamation as she sees the stacked sheets of paper. He can almost hear her thoughts, Did he read this? and wonders if it matters. If the strange strength of their lovemaking has not been the silence of emotions. Hers hidden away on paper; and his own? Has he even thought of them?

He moves to her side. She looks distraught, confused; he stands behind her and takes her hands, buries his face in her neck. I'm sorry, he whispers. He kisses her neck, breathes her in, holds her. This is all there is, finally: her skin, her warmth, the possibility of her body. His apology.

In the peace which will come he will think, This is what she gives me: peace. A white silent sky, flutter of doves' wings.

But the future must be more than a mere lack of war, or absence of pain. It must also contain a chance for love and growth, and maybe, happiness.

So it is not peace, after all, he will think. A mere cease-fire, a resting place.

The sweetness in her body is melting like a soft light in her features; the serenity of it.

But there is his silence, and her wondering. Imagination is a deadly weapon against the serenity of emotions; the struggle has only begun.

Christian does not tell Fran about the mourner-bird—how one morning he thought he heard its song. Although he is almost certain of this, he does not trust his ability to make her believe, and he does not want to disappoint her, if the birds do not return.

So there are times when she looks at him with an unspoken question, and he wonders what she suspects, or knows. Partitioned by silence, they imagine different things.

Fran works. Rereads and reorders her notes; spends long hours in the hot sun with a new field notebook and binoculars. She searches for droppings, climbs trees, crawls through the bush until her arms and legs are covered in fine lacerations, some of them bloodied. She writes letters to foundations and associations; she holds long conversations from the post office or Sean's bungalow with Professor Smits and other ornithologists at the institute. She takes her faith and optimism and pours it like a fuel into everything she does, as if only in this way will she be able to conjure the return of the *oiseau-languit*. As if only some magical sleight of hand, sleight of mind, will work the trick.

Christian observes her. Imitates her application at other sites: on the coast of the mainland, and further inland, wherever there is a scrap of hospitable habitat an exiled bird might colonize. Climbing trees, rappelling down steep mountainsides, to look for nests. He spends a great deal of time with Sean, learning new techniques, but also talking about Fran. If he cannot give her love, he can give her a certain loyalty and devotion.

I'm her slave, he says one day, jokingly, to Sean.

Be careful, lad, she'll come to rely on you for everything.

The inflection is subtle, but Christian hears it. He hesitates, then says with an equal emphasis, She already does.

Sean raises an eyebrow, then chuckles. And you're all right with that?

Christian wonders, as with Bertrand, whether he should confide in him. Seek his advice. But it might get back to Fran, and hurt her. So he shrugs and says, She's good to me. She took care of me when I was sick.

Aye, she's a good woman.

But something of Sean's irony works its way into Christian's thoughts and remains there like a reproach. Perhaps it was the word *everything*. As if it implied, already, too much. As if in some male pride he shares with Sean, he should be above this. It is an old double standard, to be sure; he has noticed with no little irony of his own the presence of young women like Marie-Chantal in Sean's life. Everything.

Then he realizes where the flaw lies, and it has nothing to do with male pride. (As he is driving through the interior wilderness of tea plantations—their soft curves, their damp greenness breathing a cool mist.)

To rely on me for everything. Yet the one thing she really wants I cannot give her. There would be no suggestion of reproach—no male shame—if I could give her that. If I could be with her in an honest way. If I loved her.

He pulls over by the side of the road. Sits back and closes his eyes.

I cannot, he thinks, continue to be the Red Cross delegate. As if it is my life's mission to fight other people's pain and unhappiness for them. Fran is strong; she does not really need me. I am slave to her loneliness. And she cannot help me because I do not love her. That is not her fault.

My life's mission. What of my own pain and unhappiness—who will help me fight it? Or has it become such a part of me that I cannot let go of it; it is my mission now.

Christian sits for a long time in the Land Rover. It is almost dark: Fran will be worried.

I shouldn't have gone to South Africa, writes Fran.

She is sitting on the veranda, stretched out on the sofa, her notebook

propped on her knees. There is a cool breeze from the ocean, a murmur of faraway climates, other worlds. Migratory birds have been passing through, on their way north. They are like sad messengers to her,
each call a reminder that her own, home-loving birds have migrated to
another realm, perhaps that of extinction.

I have become sentimental, she writes, apropos of nothing, then continues.

*Something has changed between us. The tenderness was there, the first days;
that's all there's ever been, shared between us, this wonderful physical joy, and
tenderness.*

*Now he comes to me seeking release, and in my fear I cannot be tender. It
must have changed a few days after my return. This distancing, this coolness.
As if he were elsewhere.*

*He does not seem to desire me, as he once did. He desires desire itself, the
bare pleasure, the release. There is something terribly cold, unwittingly brutal
about that; it is making him a stranger. I gave him the Zulu sculpture and he
looked embarrassed, and told me I shouldn't have. Not the feigned modesty of
someone who is actually happy you've given him something: no. He was almost
annoyed.*

She hesitates, then writes: *He must have found the card, and it must
have something to do with the way he is acting.*

Why won't he say anything?

Christian cannot sleep. When he came back from Black River, Fran
was already asleep. She looked tired even in sleep; restless. He crawled
in next to her, to enfold her and hear her murmur of welcome and reassurance. But after a short while he decided to go back to his own
room. Now he tosses and turns, and the words of his conversation
with Sean tumble over and over in his mind with a clanking, jarring insistence; was it wrong to sleep with her, he wonders. Why does sex always complicate things with women? Why does the alchemy of their

emotions transform a man's desire and gestures into this larger, demanding thing which imprisons him in the end?

Irritated, he brushes aside the mosquito net and reaches for his flashlight. In the ghostly light the geckos scatter. He can hear the surf against the reef, the barrier of sound against his experience, just as the booming of an army's shells once defined the limits of his life. Nermina, Nermina. You are alive, he murmurs, testing the words, a question. *Ti si živa,* soft syllables full of hope. He has been thinking of Fran, blaming her emotions, but in reality it is still this incorruptible love for Nermina which borders his life.

He sits with his elbows on his knees and his hands dangling toward the floor, fingers intertwined. He stares into the blue light cast by the flashlight, the indistinct pile of books, papers, and clothes that litter his only chair. Not a chair for sitting, a pointless chair that may as well metamorphose into a desk or a bookshelf. He threw everything there when he was clearing up, after the burglary, and he hasn't had the heart to tidy things away properly. He knows there are unopened letters from his mother, and newsletters from the ICRC. He does not want to be reminded of that time. Like a failed marriage, a black hole in his life, voiding experience; those borders collapsed in upon themselves.

Then I should throw these things out, he thinks, sleepless at two in the morning, thoughts pounding. He goes to the chair, lifts it over to the side of the bed. Insects scatter, disturbed at nocturnal games, while Christian attacks the pile.

Fran is sleeping, dreams weighing her to her bed. She knows that at some point during the night Christian left her; now the anticipation of seeing him again has entered her dreams, and she smiles, murmurs, embraces the pillow, the sheet, the folds where his body would lie. She hears his voice, a soft murmuring, but she cannot distinguish the words. Be quiet, she says in her dream, you're talking so much I can't hear you.

So when she wakes and he is standing next to the bed, she stretches her arms out to welcome him. But he doesn't react, stands there petrified, a frozen man, rigid with the surreal glaze of dreams, the legs which won't run, the free fall which won't stop, the waking which won't come. Fran sits up, frowns.

What is it?

In answer he brings his hand forward. He shows her a picture, a cobbled square with a fountain, people sitting in cafés; in the background, a minaret, hills. Then says very quietly, so she almost misses his words, Nermina is alive.

Fran is back on the street, the day she stood in the sun, waiting for him, the pile of letters in her straw bag, burning with their secrets. How long ago was it—three weeks? A month or more? She sees him walking toward her, remembers her fear, her temptation, then the nervous expectation with which she placed the small pile of letters on his chair. Why did he ignore them for so long?

She feared her own gift for prophecy. And now time has caught up with itself and he is looking at her, grave astonishment carving his features. He wants comfort; he wants reassurance that he has not gone mad, or been swallowed by his dreams. Sit, sit, urges Fran, and she holds him gingerly. She hesitates to tell him she knew about the card— he might think she had read it, or worse, hidden it; only he can explain why he took so long to find it.

When he begins to sob, she holds him tighter, murmurs words of comfort, meaningless maternal refrains to tell him that he is not alone. Hides her own anguish in the words that seem to come from as far away as childhood—there, there.

Christian looks at her, takes in her small, neat form, her hair short and sleep-tousled, the wise lines that frame her smile and her eyes, and the sum of her parts adds up to something greater. This causes a surge of emotion or anticipation: a confusing, long-forgotten impulse.

You see, he says, for so long I gave up hope. I used to call the Red Cross in Sarajevo, nearly every day, and they had no news. I believed she must—that she couldn't have survived. Not long ago I found out her husband was alive. But there was still no news of her. Now Dubravka, she's heard—

He looks down. Fran searches around her for a tissue, finds nothing; Christian lifts the edge of the sheet from the bed, removes his glasses, buries his face in it.

She turns to him and says, You'll want to go and find her, I know. You must go and find her.

Christian nods, then shakes his head. He looks at Fran again, and now she is like a stranger.

He holds her but they do not make love. They pretend to sleep, yet they are both awake, listening to the calls of geckos and the surge of the breakers. They picture futures, possible scenarios, as if thoughts could determine lives, or forestall the unexpected.

Christian wonders how long Dubravka's postcard had lain undetected among the forgotten letters in the tumble of his room—and before that, how long it had been in the post office, uncollected. While Fran was in South Africa he was oblivious of anything but the damage on the island. The date on the postmark was illegible, it could have been sent weeks before.

Even now he knows he will not be free of guilt. *She's had a difficult time,* said the postcard.

He had not known, then, how to hold her. Nermina had suffered, because of him. A deep fear enters his sleeplessness: that she will not want to see him.

And Fran? She stirs in his arms. Perhaps she is asleep now: she shudders, dreaming. Fran, who restored him to life, to dreams, as nearly as anything, anyone—until this simple card—could have done.

Dreams come, ambivalent messengers. A child is reaching for him, but no matter how he strains to touch her, to hold her, she is always just beyond his grasp. Then Fran by his side, murmuring, I'll stay here. He reaches again for the child, and this time his hands close around her small form, but as he lifts her up she struggles and it is not a child in his hands, not at all, no, it is one of Fran's birds, frail and splendid. As he opens his hands it flies away.

Early morning. Fran has left the bed and is sitting on the veranda, a mug of coffee between her palms. She listens to familiar sounds, surveys her realm, its illusion of continuity, extinction a bird's flight away.

She wonders, with such evidence before her, if it is not time to return to the classroom, the library. If the field has not become too vast, too cruel, too much like life. She thinks of Professor Smits, his comfortable, unperturbed, unconscious existence. She thinks of Berkeley, layer upon layer of civilization occulting the raw difficulty of existence. There are other difficulties, to be sure. She wonders if there is a place for her somewhere.

Christian, she is certain, will return to Bosnia. For him this was merely an interlude, not his real life. A way station, she thinks, a resting place. My body the comfort of consolation.

With such evidence before her, wonders Fran, is she doomed to suffer from solitude, or is it a place she can tame after all? Of course the illusion of society, of continuity—pairing, mating, families—is another of Nature's clever tools. Ah yes, Mr. D, it's all about reproduction, ensuring the survival of the species.

She smiles to herself. A consolation, that: she feels less lonely already. Isn't loneliness, after all, a human construct, arising from that same illusion—its counterpart, its secret fear, its shadow? *If thou dost not go forth and multiply, thou shalt be one, and alone.*

Does knowing this really make it less painful? What private realm will she inhabit then, outside the illusion?

Christian awakes and remembers that something has changed. In a corner of the room, sunlight drapes the ordinary and familiar objects of life: Fran's clothing hanging from pegs on the wall, her pile of books, a basket of worn scratchy opera tapes, a small cane chair. He stares at the chair—the caning is beginning to come unwoven, and he has been promising himself he would fix it. Now there is something pulling him, saying, You don't need to fix it, now; and something else saying, What has changed? Of course you'll fix it.

He lies motionless for a long time, in the womblike security of the mosquito net. Scenes fill the space. There is Fran's scent on his skin, but all his urgency, all his emotion go toward the imagining of Nermina. It is late spring, or early summer; there is a pale sunlight. Nermina is wearing jeans and the T-shirt she had on the last time he saw her. She is walking along the banks of the Miljacka, and sometimes her arms are empty, and sometimes she is holding a child. How old? How old is a child who is one's own and whom one has never known? With whom one has not counted the days, and each marvel which marks each day? Boy or girl? He imagines Nermina, over and over, along the open stretch by the tall apartment blocks, the long open car-free stretch with its rich foliage of trees above the river, she would go there to walk with a child, a safe place, now, if she goes there she must have a child.

But now another figure is walking along the Miljacka with her, a tall gaunt man, an old man, war-aged; he is smiling, and he puts his arm around Nermina, and they look down at the child, who is holding a small bear, or a doll, or a piece of bread, and together they smile.

Together? No! Christian turns away from the sunlight, wraps his arms around his head as if to restrain his thoughts. But after a moment the picture returns, and now it is he who is in that sunlit stretch, only it is winter, now, and the sun has turned to fog, and he is alone. This is a memory: true, he has never been there with Nermina, but he was there once during the war, a fog-safe day when the snipers could not see their targets, and the city was open, briefly, the fog like the breath of a hundred thousand captives, Let us live.

She's had a difficult time.

Vlatković emerges from the fog, and he is smiling, inviting Christian for a drink, and with dread Christian knows this man has the definition. *Difficult.* What lay behind the word. How he pronounces it. In Serbian, *teško,* a soft word, almost lulling. A word you can whisper. Deceptive.

Vlatković is hovering above Christian, leaning close with his plum-breath, whispering, *teško.* And Christian receives a primitive certainty, the only certainty in all these imaginings: that Vlatković is responsible, and must be brought to justice.

There is a sound. Fran comes into the room, stands above him. It's late, she murmurs. Would you like some coffee?

Christian motions for her to sit by him. The mosquito net separates them. Fran looks at him: tenderness fills him, seems to fill the space within the net, billowing and airy.

I've come so far on the path of forgetting, thinks Christian, perhaps I should keep going. Perhaps it is too late to go back; Nermina is with Sead, again. Perhaps the child died, or was stolen or was never born alive; I could not bear to know that.

He looks at Fran through the netting. Her features are softened; he cannot see her clearly without his glasses. He thinks she might love him. He fears her love, because it will be strong, like her will.

And yet. It is like the place of forgetting, safe and lovely. He could stay there awhile, and then it would be too late. She would hold him, and he would begin to love her.

It does not seem such a bad future. He acknowledges his fear of the outside world, of the past, and the ease of Fran. She will make him forget his fear, and his anger. They can build.

Perhaps he does not see her clearly: her own difficult life. He does not see that soon her own childlessness will protest that he must know, that he must find his child.

For now, he reaches for her. She holds his hand, but resists when he tries to pull her closer. No, she says gently, I've got work to do, and so have you.

All day Fran seems to avoid him, disappearing to other parts of the island, cataloging storm damage, searching for clues. Christian clears debris, then makes plans for a new aviary. He is aware of distance, now, and on the veranda at sundown he asks her, with uncharacteristic bluntness: Fran, what is bothering you?

She leans back into the cushions of the wicker sofa, pushes her hair away from her forehead with her palm. Because she hesitates, he goes on, Don't think things have changed because of the news from Sarajevo. I know you believe this changes everything. But I've been thinking. You know, if Nermina is with her husband . . . it is better.

And the child?

And the child will be raised as their child. They need that child, it needs them.

Christian reaches over to Fran. She allows his touch but does not respond, does not look at him.

He is giving her a chance. The possibility she so often held to the light. And yet she sits there in a deep and stubborn chill, remembering Satish, and her certainty of loss, and she believes she has already lost Christian.

But it is more than that. There is the gesture toward Nermina, and the child. Their survival must be honored. She can understand Christian's argument, its human logic, but she also senses his fear. And that is why she will be the stronger one.

Fran has observed the seeming cruelty of certain birds, when the time has come for a fledgling to leave the nest. How the parent nudges the small, helpless thing over the edge, into the void. And it discovers its wings: it is able to fly.

She sees this cruelty as strength.

Again they sleep side by side; Fran turns away, implies that she does not want him to touch her. The next morning the silence and distance remain like a residue of their chaste sleep. After breakfast, Christian tells Fran with a barely restrained anger that he has an errand in town. Her face creases suddenly, briefly, the only betrayal of the struggle she is waging within herself.

Christian runs some errands in Curepipe, then goes to Bertrand's, seeking Dutch courage. He hesitates to confide in the older man, yet again, to tell him about Nermina, about Fran, but instead he says only, as if trying out the words for substance or hollowness, I might be leaving Mauritius soon.

You're not serious. I thought you were getting married?

Christian shakes his head. That's all over, Bertrand. I'm sorry. It was one big mistake. A cultural misunderstanding.

Mais non! protests Bertrand, spreading his arms as if to show proof, in his own life, of the potential for cultural understanding.

Christian shakes his head again, reaches out his glass for a refill. You were going to tell me about Satish and Razel.

Bertrand guffaws and says, You're too late for Razel. His chauffeur found him slumped over in the back of the car, dead as a dodo. Heart attack, something like that. Even the rich don't escape.

But if it's of any use to you, the story goes that it was Satish's father who organized the strike back in the 1940s . . . there was a strike at the sugar works and it got out of hand, Razel's father reacted violently, arresting people, beating them, until a few of the workers broke into his house and in a mad rage killed him and his wife. They say Satish's father was among them, maybe even the actual assassin. So you see . . . A bad business.

Bertrand shakes his head. Sometimes this island is just too damn small.

Christian takes a moment to register the news. Then looks at Bertrand sharply and says, There's a séga dancer called Jean-Baptiste who works for Razel, at one of his hotels. I'm trying to find him.

Bertrand raises his eyebrows. Can't help you there. There are dozens of séga dancers on this island, you know. What do you want with a séga dancer? Lessons?

Christian laughs in spite of himself, claps the older man on the back in an uncharacteristic gesture of affection. Then says, May I use your phone?

For a split second he pauses when he hears her voice. He has just returned the wedding suit and sent a check to her parents to reimburse them for some of their expenses. And a letter of apology, abjectly pleading instability: they must see it is in their daughter's best interests. To give himself courage he tells himself that if he is calling now, it is because he has a right to: his dues are paid.

She is professional in answering; he takes a deep breath, says her name.

A pause, then, What do you want?

I need your help—I need some information.

The line is silent. If hurt obstinacy emits silence. He continues, Your friend, Jean-Baptiste, the séga dancer that we saw that day, from the car—

I can't believe it. You call me and then you ask something like this. Besides, he's not my friend.

Where can I find him? Which hotel does he work at?

Why do you want him?

Please, Asmita, don't ask questions, just tell me where he works, or lives, or something.

I must be daft. Hold on.

There is a pause and he can hear her hand being placed over the receiver, muffled conversation. Then she comes on the line and says, Le Grand Lagon.

He thanks her, then pauses for a moment, not knowing what to say. She is silent, waiting; finally he asks, Are you well?

As well as can be expected.

Her bitterness surprises him. Hastily he says, Keep well, then. Shakes his head at his own awkwardness, and hangs up.

He turns to Bertrand, who has been watching him with the bemused expression he reserves for Christian's woman trouble.

How do I get to the Grand Lagon?

Christian feels in his pockets for the keys to the Land Rover. He waves to Bertrand, heads toward the shady street where he last parked.

He drives along the eastern coast, through idyllic, impoverished fishing villages poised above the lagoon, beneath wooded slopes and fields of cane. He is grateful for the twisting roads, the concentration they require. Children and dogs dart in front of him; bicycles weave, and Christian wonders idly if it is from drunkenness or merely a gentle rhythm of life. He prepares what he will say to Jean-Baptiste. He thinks of Vlatković, wonders what he learned there which might be of use. For Fran's sake. It's the least I can do, whether I stay or go.

He does not want to think about Nermina, or the child—not now, not yet.

The young man walks toward him, jauntily at first, then more slowly when he recognizes Christian. His handshake is wary, yet firm; he looks around as Christian invites him out to the bar by the pool and offers him a drink.

How have you been, mate? How are things out on your island? inquires Jean-Baptiste, but Christian merely looks at him for a moment, wondering how to begin. Then he says, I have a problem; maybe you can help me.

Jean-Baptiste leans back, pulls a cigarette from his shirt pocket, and searches for a lighter.

You told me once you knew Satish, who used to work out on the island, right? asks Christian.

Jean-Baptiste blinks, looks away as he fiddles with his lighter, trying to shelter the flame from the breeze. Then he says, I knew him. He was my friend.

Your friend?

He was. If you have time, I'll tell you.

I have time.

Two small boys playing in the shade of the *bois d'ébène,* of the acacia. They stage wars with bugs, crawling armies of martial carapace. One is Hindu, one is Creole; they are from different neighborhoods, and everything conspires against their future friendship, except the friendship itself, which started the day they met on Egret Island.

As they get older, they see less of each other but preserve a mutual respect and a secret pleasure in each other's company. Ji-Bé is laughter and lightness; Satish is ideas and intensity. But each one is astonished and a bit dismayed by the other's chosen future. Satish worries that Ji-Bé will be drawn into illegal dealings through his séga dancing at Razel's hotels; Ji-Bé is dismayed by Satish's boss—an American woman—and not a little envious of his pay. Still, they encourage each other and share dreams of independence: for Ji-Bé, his own séga troupe; for Satish, a chance to study at the university and become a full-fledged naturalist like Sean—the man, he insists for Ji-Bé's sake, who runs the program on the island.

It's still our island, he murmurs to Ji-Bé. The British cannon is still there, they've fixed up the old house. Our bugs are there; sometimes I expect to see you spring out from behind the pandanus bushes.

Until one day Yves de Froberville calls Ji-Bé into his office at the Grand Sud and explains that he has a delicate mission.

At first Ji-Bé thinks he must shake his head, protest: he cannot get involved in anything that will hurt his friend. But as he listens to de Froberville, watches the slight nervous tremor of his chin, the shaking of his hands as he offers him a cigarette, Ji-Bé decides, fatally, that it would be best to accept de Froberville's proposition: that way he will know, and he will be able to protect his friend—because if he doesn't agree, they'll certainly find someone else who will.

De Froberville has already recruited boys from the poor neighborhoods in Port Louis who will do anything they are told. They have drug habits, gambling debts: an endangered species is a rich man's luxury which they will be only too happy to destroy. Ji-Bé suspects that de Froberville thinks he is just another boy like them; all the easier, he thinks naïvely, to play a *double jeu*. And the pay offered is handsome.

When Ji-Bé tells Satish what he has been hired to do, Satish is horrified, looks for a moment like the wild child who could be angered into a fistfight and not know when to stop. Not to alarm him further, Ji-Bé does not tell Satish that Razel would not have too many scruples, given past history, if something were to happen to Satish.

Look, says Ji-Bé to Satish, I can try to warn you. I will meet you here every week, at this time, and let you know what I've found out. I can try to fool them, too, they're not so smart.

But if Razel isn't getting results, he's going to suspect—

With those *voyous*? *C'est normal*—they're always drunk, at the racetrack, that's why they don't do as they're told. Besides, I can lie to him, you can help me, make him think he's getting somewhere.

Ji-Bé winks at his friend; he believes he has the situation under control.

One evening at dusk they meet at the Croix du Sud for a drink. Ji-Bé warns Satish: Tonight or tomorrow, they're going over to leave a mongoose. That's all. You need to set a trap. Or make sure no one gets on the island. They're going to come over on a pirogue. It's part of their plan, to harass her until she gives up or until there are no species to protect, *ti konpran sa?*

And what about you, Ji-Bé, what can you do at this end?

I'm going to hang around, listen, invite them to the racetrack—

They drink more than they ought to. Satish remembers an errand in Mahébourg, a trivial thing Fran asked him to get, flashlight batteries or something like that. She was upset when he left, but he couldn't help that, couldn't tell her he was meeting Ji-Bé, or why. He could skip the errand, perhaps it wasn't worth the trouble, but then he thinks he doesn't want to disappoint her.

Perhaps if he had gone straight to the island, and not to Mahébourg, he would not have encountered the four drunken boys from Port Louis, whose mission was, contrary to Ji-Bé's warning, not to harass but to kill.

And me? What about me? Christian asks after a long pause. You were on the pirogue the night I collided with you—I recognized your laugh.

Razel saw what happened with Satish, and he knew that the woman had nearly left after that. He had good spies—he knew the birds were disappearing. Extinct—pff!

Jean-Baptiste clicks his fingers, a magician's gesture.

Spies?

Well, your girlfriend didn't mind telling de Froberville what she knew.

Christian shakes his head with disgust. The birds are one thing, he says angrily, but a man was killed, and you're all right with that, being a murderer? Trying to kill me too?

Hey no, mate, not murder! Causing an accident, a close call. Creating a situation—pff! To frighten you, that's all.

That's not how I see it.

There is a heavy silence while Jean-Baptiste absorbs his accuser's gaze. Then he turns to look at Christian and says, Satish was my friend. The only one I could trust. And look what happened. Do you think I care about a stranger like you after what happened?

He pauses, then says, almost angrily, With the money Razel had promised me to get rid of the birds, I could have started my own séga troupe, could even have gone abroad on tour. Do you know what that means here? We are poor people, you sometimes forget.

He waves his arm around the hotel, including the palm trees, the swimming pool, the rattan furnishings and bar and tropical plants, the expensive reconstituted paradise where one night might cost a year's salary. Then he pounds his fist on the table and looks angrily at Christian, who pulls back.

Maybe it will make you happy to know I never saw one rupee of that money. And now the bastard has died on us—and for what? No one got a thing out of it. He didn't get his island, I lost my best friend and never saw a single rupee.

His island?

Jean-Baptiste looks for a moment at Christian with a mixture of irritation and surprise, as if he cannot believe Christian has failed to grasp this vital point.

Monsieur Razel was afraid. All his life he was afraid, you've never seen anyone so nervous, always looking around to see who's there, to make sure there are no strangers, nobody he hadn't already bought off. Why do you think he wanted the island? He thought if he could be alone, with just a few bodyguards, then no one could get him, he'd be safe. He could relax. For his retirement, so to speak.

Jean-Baptiste pauses while Christian sits back and thinks about what he has just heard. Then Jean-Baptiste chuckles abruptly to himself, an engaging sound so unlike his shrill, hearty laugh that Christian looks at him and says, What now?

Jean-Baptiste leans closer and lowers his voice. They said he wanted to surround himself with young women, only he didn't want anyone else to see, you know? So if he were alone on that island, he could do what he wanted. Be his own government. Have a harem, ha, ha! And you know, he had a thing about your boss, he used to call her the unseducible birdwoman.

Fran? He didn't even know her. They never met.

Oh, but they must have, when she first came here he wanted to get to know her, maybe he thought he could charm her into leaving the island, who knows. But he said she was the only woman who ever completely escaped him.

Jean-Baptiste chuckles again softly and adds, He was an ugly old goat, but he usually got his way with women. He had that fine fiancée of yours working for him, didn't he.

Christian again shakes his head with disgust, but Jean-Baptiste ignores this and says hopefully, And what about your bird?

Pff, says Christian, looking hard at him. But not because of Monsieur Razel—if that gives you any satisfaction. Because of the cyclone.

Christian stares at Jean-Baptiste for a long time in silence. He could go to the police, have him arrested, seek some sort of justice. But is there justice? Can anything be undone, smoothed away by retribution? Nothing Christian does will bring Satish, or the bird, back; weary, he can summon no desire for revenge. He looks at Jean-Baptiste and says, You can go to the police with the names of the boys who've been attacking the island.

In any case, says Jean-Baptiste, almost inaudibly, they won't be going there anymore, they probably never got paid either.

Do it anyway. I'll say you weren't involved, if it comes to that.

Christian drives slowly back along the coast to Mahébourg. At one point he pulls over and switches off the ignition. He closes his eyes and thinks about what he has learned. Again he sees the roadblock, the tank, the poplars. Imagines not Nermina, this time, but Fran. How she might calmly, now, drive around the roadblock. How fate would wave her through. It was not her fault.

Back on the island, Christian holds Fran gently, even when she resists: I have news, he says, let me hold you.

She is in a kernel of existence, an embryonic beginning that is close to death. In this quiet simple place she is strong and unafraid. She is able to look back now, and accept.

Go, then, she said finally. Go and do whatever it is that's so bloody impor-
tant that you won't take me with you. Go.
Satish looked at her now with sadness. Do you need anything else, besides
the batteries?
No, no. I'll go tomorrow, on my own.
Fran—
It's okay. I'm sorry. Just go.

She sat on the sofa with her eyes closed and she did not see him go. She lay
there and thought of how she loved him, and that she was her own worst en-
emy, and that when he came back she would apologize and make everything
right again, and they would go on as they had before.

She sits on the sofa with her eyes closed and thinks of what Christian has told her.

Poor, misguided Satish, who only wanted to protect her, to protect her frail birds, and could not gauge the depth of sacrifice.

The island, at last, is free. To celebrate, Fran decides to cook a wonderful dinner. It soothes her to plan, to give herself to the manual task of creation: chopping, slicing. A sautéed chicken with tiny peppers from the island of Rodrigues: colors are bright, flavors are subtle. But for all that she has little appetite, suspects the flavors are wasted on her. She is preparing her resistance, shoring up defenses.

They talk lightly at first, with relief. Christian tells her what Razel had said about her; her laughter peals through the room, that good, untamed laughter, contagious and free. I don't give a shit, she says joyfully, not when people—correction, men—like him are concerned. But when did he ever meet me? I don't recall ever seeing him. What did he look like?

Christian shrugs. Sixty, small, expensive clothes, thin and pale, blue eyes like the lagoon on a cloudy day, bad teeth—

Suddenly she sees herself in the early weeks before Satish, sitting opposite the well-dressed older man. Her right of refusal; her intuitive recoil. Her sense of something wrong, even then. She looks at Christian and grows thoughtful; for a moment she allows Satish to pass between them again, a tremor of memory.

When they have cleared the plates away and sit with only their half-empty wineglasses, Fran says softly, not looking at Christian, You know you must leave.

Fran, I told you—

No, Christian. It's not only that. In the mail there was a letter: I'm losing funding. I won't be able to afford to keep you much longer.

Fran's face is solemn in lamplight; Christian's is pale and stunned. They compose a quiet scene, two lovers facing each other across a small table in the warm lamp-glow, with their grave expressions, and their hands extended on the table, not touching. As if they fear the outcome of this lovers' quarrel that is not a quarrel but a strange and sad negotiation. There are terms of surrender, there are provisions.

Look, Fran is saying. Of course I don't want you to leave. But if you stay I can't pay you. And you know where that would leave us. She pauses, then says, And there's something else. Something you ought to consider.

Christian looks at Fran. She is no longer his Fran but a strong and competent counselor, the kind of woman he often encountered among the aid workers: earnest, determined, and unhesitant.

I've heard, she says quietly, I've heard and I don't know if it's true, I hope it's not true but perhaps you can confirm this, that Muslim women who were, let's say, shamed during the war were often rejected by their husbands. I mean, you don't know where they took her, what happened, how can you be sure that Nermina's husband—

Christian is visibly startled by her words. How like a man, thinks Fran sadly, not to think of something like this. There is no such shame reserved for men, ever. Calmly, she continues, So in fact . . . if he is a traditional sort of man, they may be together in name only, if that.

And what must I do? Just show up, just like that, and hope he's rejected her?

There is anger in Christian's voice, and Fran sees her plan is working.

You don't show up. You find out first.

She can see the hurt in his eyes, almost an accusation as he says, Well, I can find out from here. I can call from Mahébourg. I'll find Dubravka, she'll know.

They sit on in silence, Fran looking away into an empty middle distance, Christian looking down at his hands, as if they belonged to someone else.

The lightness of him, of his presence in her life, air and feathers and flight. Their lovemaking like a pause in her evolution, an enchanted error, fruitless yet graced with a purpose of hope.

It seems so ordinary. Like the regular shopping run. Only this time there is a phone call that could change everything.

Christian goes alone to Bertrand's to use the phone, while Fran goes to the bank and the post office, as usual. Again she thinks of the postcard and wishes she could have severed time, done things differently. As it was she had been miraculously granted a few weeks of his presence—could it have been more? If she had hidden the postcard for good . . . no, she would have had her own feelings of guilt and deception to live with. Now she will live with her longing, whatever time's verdict may be.

At the post office there is a letter from the foundation whose support has been crucial. She skims it: upon review of her latest report the board has voted not to renew funding for the next fiscal year. So her sacrificial lie was a self-fulfilling prophecy.

She will not think of the irony of this now, another deep tremor in her life. Walls collapsing around her.

She waits by the Land Rover in the sun. A strange thought comes to her: a last, best hope. That Nermina will indeed be with her husband, and will ask to be forgotten. That her courage in forsaking love will be equal to Fran's: a curious self-effacing altruism. Perhaps, thinks Fran, I will be spared; perhaps I will be chosen after all.

Briefly, hope takes wing, a pale trajectory across the vast sky.

She looks down the street. A young man is walking toward her. The sunlight catches him, sharpens his smile. Sharpens her longing. Intensifies and concentrates time and inevitability; there is no infinity. All her future, like the past of a drowning man, is compacted into that space of sunlight, that time measured by Christian's steps, as he approaches. She must know. There are two scenarios, two futures, the sunlight is a prism, refracting her reason, causing her imagination to dazzle with hope.

She cannot read the gaze behind his sunglasses. This troubles her; now more than ever she needs to know what he might be thinking. But he smiles, a long smile, and raises his hand, grazes her arm with his fingertips, an intimate greeting. Then suddenly he is holding her, and for a moment her hope stays aloft. She can feel his solidity as a presence. His shirt smells of sunlight. Time expands. He says nothing, just holds her for a very long time. Then murmurs, so softly she almost does not hear him, I'm sorry.

Time contracts. His solidity now no more than a memory, no more tangible than the smell of sunlight.

A biblical sky, scattered with rising stars. Christian ferries Fran across the lagoon. Their forms are moon-pale against the blue light; the lagoon a clear depth. Their short journey holds peace, an image blenched of time, that you could hold like a painting in your memory. But that would be to make them symbols—man and woman on the journey through life. Someone else, however, is steering.

Christian looks behind him, into the swirling water. And in the trick-light of emotion he sees the tendrils yet again, long dark locks spilling, turning in the wake, Nermina's face upturned, lagoon maiden, water sylph, huntress of his dreams. I have survived, she seems to say, despite your loss.

The oil lamp casts the shadow of her curled fist across her note-book, her pen poised above a blank page. But she is not writing. She is listening to the sounds of nightfall: the ever-present surf, a dying wind in the trees, the conversation of birds—fodies, mynahs, bulbuls, warning of darkness, urging haste.

In the end, she writes, slowly and often pausing, *it made no difference about the postcard. There is no way I could have changed the evolution of events. Things have a finality about them, and you realize that is the way they were always meant to be.*

He was changed, these last few days. The sorrow I had always known as part of him was gone. Perhaps it was that sorrow I had come to love, after all. Like the mourner-bird. That vulnerability; his broken wing.

So I mended his broken wing. It could not be otherwise: it is my nature.

And yet. And yet. There was something about the way he suddenly lighted upon my life—it was, after all, against the natural order of things. Not unlike the cyclone, or the sort of thing, if you were religious, you would call an act of God.

Fran sits on in darkness on the veranda, listening to the hum of night insects, and of her thoughts. At last she hears the sound that she has been listening for with a painful anticipation: the raucous, metallic roar of the airplane as it lifts off from Plaisance, across the lagoon. The evening flight to Vienna, a few minutes late. And for a few seconds its roar fills the night, obscuring the height of the sky or the expanse of the ocean around her. For a few seconds that's all there is, this sound and what it means, as if it were reverberating with the restoration of her solitude. And then the island's silence returns: a silence so deep it resonates with absence, and loss.

Fran goes to bed, and surrenders her solitude to dreams. Transformed there: they tell her of a martyred city, where empty windows like the eyes of the untimely dead stare at the arrogance of the living, but where a man is about to be reunited with a woman and a small child.

And toward dawn her dreams announce the return of the mourner-bird, long exiled in fear of storms.

There is much to be done, but upon awakening Fran decides to lie in bed a moment longer: to be sure. Her body aches for Christian, but then she hears the cry and, a few moments later, the answer. And as the bird's song enters, deep and familiar, she thinks of lovers long separated, and thinks that this might be a song of reunion: not mournful, no, not mournful at all.

author's note

Egret Island is based on a real island off the coast of Mauritius. Île aux Aigrettes is indeed a nature preserve, established in 1965; rehabilitation work began in 1985 under the auspices of the Mauritius Wildlife Appeal Fund and is ongoing; a visitors' center was opened a few years ago.

Given the size of Mauritius, it is easy to get a good understanding of the progress made in conservation and restoration—and the work which remains to be done. The Mauritian kestrel was saved from extinction, populations of pink pigeons, echo parakeets, and Mauritian fodies are all on the increase. However, as everywhere, ecology on Mauritius is threatened by growth and human expansion; Mauritius has a booming tourist industry and a rapidly expanding population, and the fragile ecosystems of the lagoons are being damaged by over-fishing, dredging for sand, and the usual water sports.

The mourner-bird, as ornithologists will have discovered for themselves, does not exist. It is, rather, an imaginary composite of creatures which might have existed and been threatened with extinction by virtue of their own beauty.

Marco Polo's birthplace has been disputed; some say he was born in Venice—he was indeed a Venetian—but you can visit the house of his birth on Korčula, an island off the coast of Croatia. Korčula was, however, ruled at that time by the Venetians.

acknowledgments

This book came about through a combination of serendipity, imagination, and research but would not exist at all without my family. My thanks go to Mary Anna for first inviting me to Mauritius, and to Nat and Prittee for their ongoing and boundless hospitality, *un grand, grand merci*. More serendipitously, thanks to Joyce Gubelman for inviting me to hear David Quammen's lecture at the California Academy of Sciences.

Many thanks, for taking me on the first tour of the Île aux Aigrettes, to Malcolm and Roselle; and for the second tour, and putting up with all my amateurish questions, to Lucy Bhageerutty, Steve Ewing, Karen Varnham, and Rina Woolaver. To Kavita and Ravi for a fine day at Pamplemousses.

In Switzerland, my gratitude to the Château de Lavigny Writers'

Retreat for the welcoming space and support which helped to jump-start the novel, and to Dominique and Sylvie Praplan of the International Committee of the Red Cross.

In San Francisco, heartfelt thanks go to my agent, Irene Moore, for her generous faith in the manuscript, and in New York to my editor, Sally Kim, for her patience, insight, and enthusiasm.

Two invaluable resources for the background on island biogeography and the extinction of species have been David Quammen's *Song of the Dodo* and Gerald Durrell's classic *Golden Bats and Pink Pigeons*. Finally, although I never got to meet him because it was Halloween that day, I owe much gratitude to the naturalist Carl Jones, because without his exemplary work and sheer determination to rescue the Mauritian kestrel, my own book would surely never have taken flight.

Superb read. Enjoyed
every word. Suspenseful,
romantic, hopeful. AP.